WHERE THE STARS LEAD

PICT BY TIME
BOOK 2

MIA PRIDE

DRAGONBLADE PUBLISHING, INC.

ARE YOU SIGNED UP FOR DRAGONBLADE'S BLOG?

You'll get the latest news and information on exclusive giveaways, exclusive excerpts, coming releases, sales, free books, cover reveals and more.

Check out our complete list of authors, too!

No spam, no junk. That's a promise!

Sign Up Here

www.dragonbladepublishing.com

Dearest Reader;

Thank you for your support of a small press. At Dragonblade Publishing, we strive to bring you the highest quality Historical Romance from some of the best authors in the business. Without your support, there is no 'us', so we sincerely hope you adore these stories and find some new favorite authors along the way.

Happy Reading!

CEO, Dragonblade Publishing

CHAPTER ONE

W EARING HER BURGUNDY prescription glasses, Emilie sipped a glass of red wine while she leaned over her laptop, scrolling through Scottish genealogy archives until her eyes burned. It was her nightly routine and the one thing sustaining her as she lived within the 300-square-foot flat she rented in Edinburgh by herself. The top right corner of her screen contained a calendar and clock set to her best friend Caitriona's time, serving as Emilie's only link between her and Cait. She wasn't sure how accurate the clock was, but these days, Emilie stared at the time in ancient Scotland more than she looked at her own.

Bumping her knee on the glass top coffee table, Emilie mumbled a curse as wine sloshed out of her glass and dribbled down her oversized gray sweater. "That's going to stain," she sighed, but she kept scrolling through the names of people long dead, squinting at her screen as she tried to unlock genealogy clues. The site she used regularly had been very useful. So far, Emilie had found several branches of her tree that went back several centuries into Scotland, but most had died out by the 11th century.

Hunting down her ancestors had become more than a hobby—it was an obsession. She supposed being raised in an orphanage for three years before becoming adopted, only to lose her adoptive parents by seventeen, would lead many people to seek some biological link to other humans.

For Emilie, it ran so much deeper. Ever since Cait left the year 2023 to return to her husband, King Brodyn, in 685, Emilie had floundered like a fish out of water. Their archaeological dig had wrapped up after Caitriona disappeared, and nothing but mysterious modern bones had been found in the cave. Funding disappeared, and the team went on to other projects. But, Emilie couldn't move on. She had nothing to move on to. Caitriona was her family, and though almost 1,400 years separated them, remaining in Scotland was Emilie's best option to stay close in case Caitriona ever crossed over to their time again.

Several failed attempts to travel through the veil of time herself had left Emilie discouraged and lost. Still, Edinburgh was the best place for her, she'd decided. Full of Scottish culture and ancient history, it was still modern and bustling, the perfect combination for Emilie. Most of all, it was far away from the Moray caves that constantly rejected her entrance after sweeping her best friend away.

Here in this picturesque city, Emilie had found a flat right on the Royal Mile where Edinburgh Castle loomed just outside her window. The museum where Emilie guest spoke was within walking distance, and nightlife lent itself to several side gigs such as bartending or running tours. During her downtime, Emilie often visited the genealogical association in town, where extensive research had helped her get on track to find living relatives—but it wasn't only the living Emilie hoped to find.

As Emilie scanned the screen while she clicked on family lines, she found one that caught her interest. She groaned in frustration. She only had thirty minutes until she was due to meet a new group of people for a tour. Emilie's pulse rate pounded in her ears as she reviewed the new genealogy line that continued farther and farther back in time, already reaching the 9th century. The names became harder to pronounce, but she recognized several old Gaelic or Celtic names appearing on the screen, many associated with royalty.

Downing the last bit of wine in her glass, Emilie took a large bite out of her croissant, wiping the crumbs off her face with the back of her hand. She had lost all sense of decorum living in this small space alone. But her obsessive behavior paid off as a particular name popped up on her screen, making her nearly choke on her croissant.

"Oh, my God! I have to call Sam!" Emilie squealed and grabbed her phone, dialed, and put it on speaker. Samuel, Emilie and Cait's archaeology mentor, still passed back and forth through time and kept Emilie updated on Caitriona's life. It was hard; her heart ached to hear about their son, Lucas, who would one day be King of the Picts. She was pleased that Cait was happy, but she longed to speak with her friend and hear these updates herself, not through Samuel. She wanted to hold Lucas and be his fun, quirky Auntie Emilie. Instead, she was known as "hot-mess-Emilie" to her fellow historians at the museum. They weren't wrong.

As she waited for Samuel to answer the phone, she slipped into her tour guide costume, a long brown dress that resembled a peasant woman's attire from the Middle Ages, with flowing sleeves and ties lacing the front.

"Hello?" Samuel's familiar voice answered.

"Sam! I found them on my line! Way, way down on my line, but their names are there!" She began to braid her long blond hair and wrap it into a bun.

After a long pause on his end, Samuel finally spoke. "You found Lucas and Cait on your line?" He asked with hesitation in his voice.

"Yes! Lucas is a great-grandfather from dozens of generations ago. I haven't counted the generations, but he's there. Cait is my ancestor!" Emilie puffed for breath as she ran around her tiny flat, gathering her keys and slipping on her work boots.

"What's all that noise? You're fading in and out—it sounds like you're calling from a cave," Sam complained.

Emilie moved to her desk to begin printing a copy of her genealogy. "You're on speaker, and I'm getting ready for work.

I'm going to be late." She grabbed the pages as they shuffled into the tray, folding them, and shoving them into the bodice of her dress. After she completed tonight's tour, she would take the list to the Genealogy Centre to cross reference some information. "But I just found the genealogy and needed to tell you."

"That is pretty incredible," Samuel said with a light chuckle. "As every generation passes, your number of ancestors doubles, so it makes sense that you found a connection. Still, it's pretty amazing. It really shows how important our line of work is, to keep people from today connected to their past."

"I know, right?" Emilie picked up her phone and clicked it off speaker mode before she left her flat, stepping out into the chilled Edinburgh evening. Elation flooded her as she shut the door. A man stood on one corner playing bagpipes, and cheers from patrons watching a rugby match wafted on the air from the pub across the street. A double-decker bus drove past just before Emilie crossed the street and stepped onto the cobblestone walkway. She loved the sights and sounds of her Scottish home even if she didn't always find her job as convenient as she wished. Even now, she could see the scheduled tour group waiting for her just outside Greyfriars Kirkyard, a small group of huddled tourists, and she sighed.

"It's time for my side gig. I gotta go. Are you going to see Caitriona soon?"

"Actually, finals just ended, and we have winter break at the university, so I was planning to check in on her. Time passes differently between our eras. It feels like Lucas ages several weeks every time I visit."

"Can you tell her what I've discovered when you see her? I wish I could visit. Stupid cave won't let me through."

Samuel sighed on the other end of the line. "I'm sorry, Emilie. I know how difficult this has been for you. I worry about you refusing to go back to California."

"There is nothing to go back to. I have no family. Cait was my roommate and best friend. Without her, I may as well stay here. Besides, I love Edinburgh."

"Have you seen much aside from your laptop screen?" Samuel said with a touch of humor, but Emilie understood his genuine concern for her.

"Of course! There's so much history!"

"Yes, but you spent your entire school career working toward your archaeology career."

"And, I will go back to that someday, I swear. I'm just a little... lost right now," she mumbled. "Sorry, but I need to get going, Sam." Her emotions ran much deeper than she was willing to say. Loneliness weighed down her heart, and a longing to see Cait again consumed her. However, she decided to keep those feeling to herself, lest Samuel pressure her to join another dig. She just wasn't ready.

"I'm always here for you, Em. I will tell Cait your exciting news when I see her again. She's had many visitors lately as Brodyn looks for potential marriage alliances with other tribes. It's been stressful for Cait to have so many potential enemies in their village. She can use some good news."

"Ok, Sam. Chat soon!" She wanted to continue the conversation and ask more questions, but her life awaited in the form of excited tourists hoping to explore the underbelly of Edinburgh and discover its many dark secrets. Indeed, it held many.

Stepping up to the crowd, Emilie smiled and got herself into character, doing her best Scottish accent. "Welcome to the Underground Vault tour! Tonight, ye will learn many secrets about Edinburgh, especially those just beneath our feet."

The crowd nodded and smiled, and Emilie understood their excitement. She'd been in the vaults dozens of times, but the sense that she'd somehow gone back in time never went away within those limestone walls, dripping with dank water from the streets above.

As Emilie guided the tour through the streets, she pointed out key monuments and buildings of note before bringing the group of seven down one of Edinburgh's many closes, which once were surrounded by gates that enclosed the city every night but were currently more like dark alleyways. She explained how, once the gates were closed, nobody was allowed inside or outside the city, and the criminals and those without homes disappeared into the city's dark underbelly, much like this group soon would.

Standing before an inconspicuous door set inside an old, cobbled building, Emilie swished her brown skirts and turned to face the antsy tourists. "Behind this door is a whole new—or rather—very old world. Nobody has access to the vaults unless they have a key." Reaching into her pocket, Emilie gasped and searched herself with a frown. The tourists all watched in dismay as she searched for the key.

"Just kidding!" she said as she pulled out the key. "Sorry, I know that was mean. But there will be more than one unexpected event tonight, so I was just preparing ye."

The group laughed with relief and waited with bated breath as she slid the key into the lock, and the old wooden door creaked open. Pulling out a flashlight, Emilie stepped inside and shivered as she always did. Not only was it musty and wet like a cave down here, but the chill went bone-deep. Some said it was simply the cold from the limestone walls, but others believed the many spirits haunting these walls added to its chill. Emilie wasn't sure which answer was correct, but she'd heard enough stories to believe ghosts haunted this area. Edinburgh was a giant hotspot for paranormal activity. Until moving here, Emilie didn't understand why so many books, movies, and legends spoke about magic in Scotland. Now, she felt the magic daily.

"Watch yer step. It's verra dark and wet in here. We will walk past the many vaults but only enter a few."

"Why were these built?" one man asked as he snapped photos of the area.

"The vaults, as ye will notice, all have an arch shape because they are actually the arches that support the South Bridge that was completed in 1788. Ye may not have even realized ye stood on a bridge while ye walked because it looks like part of the street, but if ye look over the short wall, ye can look down and see that ye are literally on a bridge as people walk beneath ye. The arches created vaults that were used by local taverns and shop owners to store goods, but it didnae take long for people to discover that the limestone walls didnae keep the moisture out, and the food stores soon spoiled. The vaults became uninhabitable, as ye can see, with all the moisture from the street dripping down. Dinnae worry, it's only water these days, but back then, it could be any manner of liquid. I will let yer imagination decide."

The crowd cringed and chuckled, following Emilie through the main walkway, gawking as they passed several gated-off vaults. Her lantern cast ominous shadows as she walked, their shuffling steps echoing off the walls.

"Why can't we enter all of these," one woman asked, pointing at the locked vaults.

"Good question," Emilie said, stopping in front of one that drew a large crowd for a good reason. "These days, the vaults are privately owned. The tour company owns a couple, and those are the ones I can show ye. Once the shop owners removed their items from these vaults, their purpose became much more sinister. Criminals began to hide down here, as did the homeless since it was illegal to sleep on the streets. There was no ventilation, light, or sanitation, and people crammed inside here, up to a dozen per vault. Now, look around this small space." Emilie brought the tour guests inside the vault with her. "With just eight of us in here, it's pretty cramped. Imagine sharing this space, without indoor plumbing, with other people. It was full of disease, and many people suffered greatly before dying down here."

Stopping in front of one gated vault, Emilie told the group to look through the bars. Gasps echoed off the walls, and a few people stepped back. "It looks like a devil-worshipping cult lives here!" one older lady said, backing up and shaking her head.

"It does appear that way, and these are occult items, but it was for a good purpose, not evil. Rumors of one particularly nasty spirit down here spread. Many said it was aggressive. A group of pagans bought a vault to store their items in while they tried to remove the spirit. Would ye like to see this vault?"

Everyone nodded, and Emilie led the way, hating the chill that spread through her body every time she stepped into this place. A circle of stones rested in the middle of the vault, and Emilie turned to face everyone before leading them inside. "This is the original vault the pagans occupied. The evil spirit was said to exist inside here, but it was supposedly too strong for them to cast out. The legend says that one night, it got so aggressive that it attacked the leader. He was alone, so his only option was to try a trapping spell by gathering stones and placing them in a circle, as ye see here at yer feet." She gestured.

"Is that the original circle?" one man asked, gaping at the stones.

Emilie nodded. "Aye. They claimed to have been able to trap him within this circle. Stones are notorious for holding onto energy, both good and bad. That's why areas made of stone, such as caves, castles, and these vaults, tend to become haunted, especially when the place witnessed so much human misery. That energy stays within the stone.

"After the leader created the trap, issues with the evil spirit supposedly ceased, so the ceremony was deemed successful. Everyone was warned never to step inside these stones, lest ye will be faced with a terrible presence. Once their work was done, the pagans cult left but asked that their belongings be stored within the vault we saw earlier as a reminder to all who enter that these caves are not to be trifled with. But even so, in fact, a few people have witnessed a banshee in these vaults. Does anyone know what a banshee is?"

One lady raised her hand. "It's like an old woman who appears to people. She screams as a warning to them that death is near. Either they or someone they know is going to die soon. Then it disappears."

"Exactly!" Emilie said. "The vault where she supposedly

appeared is just beneath a pub that was later named 'The Banshee' to solidify its claim to fame.

"Between 1835 and 1875—no one is exactly sure—officials eventually filled the vaults and pushed everyone out to clean up the city. Over the decades, the vaults were forgotten. It wasn't until two drunk university students accidentally put a hole through their rented flat's wall that they discovered another room on the other side. When they told their landlord, they were worried he'd kick them out, but instead, the landlord knocked down the entire wall, and soon all the homes and businesses attached to them were able to claim their vault if they wished. That's why many of these are privately owned."

As Emilie guided the group back toward street level, she answered their questions and did her best not to feel affected, but the vaults always made her feel uneasy and off-kilter. Luckily, she never had to remain alone for more than a few minutes as she walked through to lock up.

She thanked the group for their time and questions, pleased when everyone applauded and handed her wads of cash for tips. After recommending local pubs and restaurants near the Grassmarket area, Emilie waved to the group and sighed as she re-entered the vaults.

Another chill gripped her, and she shivered as puffs of breath escaped her parted lips while she held the shaky flashlight.

"God, I hate it down here," she murmured. Remembering the genealogy list stuffed down her bodice, Emilie perked up. She would lock up and head to a pub to peruse it and have a drink, she decided. The trip to the Genealogy Centre would have to wait one more day since the tour ran slightly longer than usual, anyway. At least it gave her something to look forward to tomorrow.

Reaching the vault with the stone circle, Emilie cursed under her breath when she dropped the keys onto the floor. They clattered against the stone, and the sound echoed against the vaulted ceiling, bouncing back and forth, almost like whispers.

When she bent over to grab them, echoing footsteps down the long, dark corridor made Emilie pause.

Nobody else should be in here unless someone from her tour wandered off, yet she'd seen all seven people in the tour walk away at the end of her presentation.

"Hello?" she said, standing up straight and shining the flashlight around the area. Nobody was there. "I hate this place," she said again, fumbling to grab the gate so she could shut it and lock it.

She felt a rush of air tickle her neck and the hairs on her nape stood on end. Looking over her shoulder, she saw an old woman with wild gray hair and dark eyes staring silently at her. Emilie shrieked and stepped backward into the vault.

The woman's torn white robes and shriveled skin made her look ancient. Perhaps homeless people still found their way into these vaults, Emilie thought. Remembering the cash tips she clutched in her hand, she wondered if the woman required food or lodging.

She held out the cash for the woman. "Do... do you need something? The tours are over for the night, but I can—"

The old woman slowly opened her mouth, widened her blackened eyes, and bellowed a shrill, head-rattling scream that made Emilie scream in response. Stumbling backward to escape the woman, she tripped on something and twisted her body, only to realize she plummeted straight toward the center of the forbidden stone circle. "No!"

Her body landed with a thud, and she heard something crack inside her wrist as it hit the side of a sharp rock, but she could not escape gravity's inevitable grip. Her forehead hit another rock, and Emilie grunted as pain lanced her skull and lights flashed behind her eyes for only a second before everything went black.

CHAPTER TWO

S EARING PAIN THROBBED in Emilie's temples as she slowly opened her eyes. A faint light filtered through, making Emilie moan as her eyes adjusted. When she tried to roll over, another shot of pain slashed at her wrist, making her wince.

"Hello?" she croaked through a dry throat, closing her eyes and pressing her palm against the side of her head as the sound of her own voice overwhelmed her senses. The air smelled briny and not at all dank or stuffy as it usually did, and she wondered what could cause musty vaults to smell like the sea. She tried to sit up using her uninjured wrist as support, but her vision blurred and her stomach roiled. Carefully, Emilie laid flat again and took a few steadying breaths. She was alone and likely concussed.

The last thing Emilie remembered was seeing that old woman and hearing her scream before falling into the stone circle. "Oh, no..." How long had she been stuck down here? If it was morning, maybe another tour guide would arrive soon to open up the vaults. While she had a key to lock up the inside vaults, only her boss had the key to lock up from the outside. Shifting through her pockets, Emilie found her phone, and relief washed over her. She could call her supervisor and get help.

Lying flat on her back, Emilie stared at the stone ceiling, squinting into her phone's bright screen, cringing against the sharp, throbbing pain behind her eyes. "No bars. Crap!" She should have known her phone wouldn't work down here. She'd never had to use it, but she'd heard plenty of tourists griping when they tried to video-call a friend from inside the vaults only to find themselves out of range. She'd always inwardly chuckled at those people, who were entirely incapable of just being in the moment and detaching themselves from modern conveniences. Emilie even complained to her boss once about using her flashlight, preferring a gas lantern, but he'd insisted the flashlight was more reliable.

"Hello... lady... are you still here?" Her efforts to speak to the screeching old woman were in vain as nobody answered her calls for help. Groaning, Emilie steeled herself, knowing every movement was going to hurt, but she had to get out of this creepy place, and she might even need to go to the hospital if she had a broken wrist, skull fracture, or concussion.

Blood rushed to her head when she sat up, and she paused, waiting for the dizziness to subside. Running a hand over the large lump on her forehead, Emilie sighed with relief when no blood coated her fingers, though she felt the remanence of dried blood covering a sizeable goose egg that would definitely be bruised for the next week.

When Emilie looked around, her brow furrowed as her heart rate kicked up. Where was she, and why was light filtering in? There was no natural light inside the vaults. When she noticed that she no longer sat inside the stone circle, Emilie looked over her shoulder and shrieked when she saw a single thistle growing out of a freshly disturbed mound of dirt.

"No, no, no..." Her senses heightened as her years of archaeological training kicked in. Why was she sitting beside what appeared to be a fresh grave, and why was a thistle growing from the rocky soil? It reminded Emilie of the thistle that Caitriona had found atop the gravesite in the cave. Cait and Emilie had believed the bones belonged to King Brodyn of the Picts, but once the remains were dug up and examined in a lab, they contained modern dental work and a metal plate in one of the legs. Was this the same grave or a different one? How could it possibly be the same grave when it had been located in a cave in Moray, yet she was beneath the South Bridge in Edinburgh, over 170 miles away? Was it some Scottish tradition to plant thistles atop graves? It had to be. Otherwise, Emilie would be faced with a different reality that she wasn't quite ready to accept.

Looking at the stone walls, Emilie waited for her eyes to focus again, and she knew immediately where she was. Familiar Pictish symbols littered the walls, and the entire chamber was dark except for the small amount of filtering light coming from the cave's central alcove.

Emilie knew this space inside and out as she'd studied it and its pictographs for months after Caitriona disappeared into its depths and never returned. How had she gotten here? She could think of three options, but only one made logical sense. Either someone had found her and driven 170 miles overnight just to abandon her to her fate, or she was hallucinating from a head injury, or she had somehow fallen through time. As insane as the last option sounded, the first one was absolutely ridiculous, and Emilie immediately ruled it out.

Though she couldn't rule out that she may be hallucinating, and though most people believed time travel was impossible, she knew firsthand it existed. Cait had fallen through this same cave. But time travel wasn't the only issue. It was translocation. Emilie hadn't been in this cave when she fell, so why was she here?

Another possibility crept into Emilie's mind, sending icy tendrils of fear and shock through every nerve ending. Was she dead? If she wasn't hallucinating, then perhaps she had succumbed to her head injury, and her spirit had gone to the place she longed to be: the year 686, where her best friend Caitriona ruled as the Queen of the Picts alongside her husband, King Brodyn.

Could souls time travel?

Slowly, she rolled onto her knees and carefully stood up, looking at the grave site near her feet. Bending over to touch the thistles' stem, she yelped when a thorn pricked her finger and made her bleed. *Can one feel pain in a hallucination or while dead?*

Emilie didn't know, but she started to rule those options out.

From her conversations with Samuel, Emilie knew that Taylor, Caitriona's psycho ex-fiancé, went through the cave to kill Brodyn but ended up dying when Samuel shot him. Anya, the mysterious older woman Emilie had heard about, buried Taylor in the cave and planted a thistle to mark the gravesite, something she often did. Was Emilie standing beside Taylor's grave site?

A chill ran down Emilie's spine, and she stepped away, knowing exactly how to navigate her way out of the cave even if she couldn't explain how she'd gotten there in the first place. But when she left the cave, her previous knowledge failed her. Unlike the coastline of 2023, here—now—much of the coastline still existed. The cave wasn't in danger of flooding at high tide as it had been when her archeology team excavated it. Without melting glaciers and sea levels rising, there was a greater expanse of coast to walk along, and the cliff rising above the cave's entrance was now covered in bright purple thistle plants as far as she could see. Emilie's stomach knotted up, and her nausea intensified.

The sea breeze whipped her brown skirts around her ankles as Emilie carefully maneuvered the rocky shoreline heading west toward Burghead. She knew which way to travel, but she wasn't certain what she would find. As she walked and observed the landscape, Emilie became convinced that she had been propelled back into time, but in what time she'd landed, she couldn't say. These shores had seen plenty of change as tribes fought for power. Were the Picts still controlling this land, or was it English now? Or, had she gone so far back in time that she would encounter Vikings?

The uncertainty of what and who she would find made her body quake and her knees wobble. But with no sign of a village or modern lights, she knew her only option was to head toward Burghead and pray she would find Caitriona and not an aggressive tribe of people.

Soon, the sun descended below the ocean's horizon, and the

pink-streaked sky quickly faded to black as Emilie walked along the coast. Stopping, she looked up and caught her breath when brilliant stars sparkled overhead, larger and more prominent than ever before. No lights stifled their gleaming brilliance, but that only made finding her way more challenging, with only the half-moon's haze to light her way. Deciding to use her phone's flashlight, Emilie stopped in her tracks, looked up at the sky, and cursed into the darkness. Somewhere between the cave and this strip of shoreline, Emilie had dropped her phone. Her hands had been so numb from the cold, the world so black, and she so focused on finding her way, she'd not noticed when or where it fell through her frozen fingers. She made a mental note to return for it in the morning, for an artifact like that could cause much fear and confusion if found by locals. The last thing she needed was to be accused of being a witch.

Locating the ever-faithful North Star winking down at her, Emilie determined she was heading in the correct direction, not that she had any other option with a cliff to her left and the vast ocean to her right. Straight would carry her westward, and she would allow the stars to guide her.

Her cheap leather slippers did nothing to protect Emilie's feet from the sharp rocks. Every step was a testament to her ability to compartmentalize pain, something her adoptive mother, Susan, used to praise her for—before she passed from cancer. As her disease had progressed, she'd told Emilie she wished she could shove the pain aside, too. As advantageous as her ability was, what Susan didn't realize was that it was also a curse borne from the need for survival from being raised in an orphanage before being tossed about in foster care. Eventually, she was adopted by a lovely couple who truly loved her, but soon, Emilie lost them both as well. From foster home to foster home, Emilie never had someone to call *Mom* after Susan died.

Sucking in a deep breath, she gritted her teeth against the pain in her head, wrist, and feet as she trudged forward against the increasing wind and frigid darkness. The waves lapped against the shore, offering a soothing white noise that Emilie focused on until she saw something looming in the distance. It looked like nothing more than a silhouette, but it was not simply a cliff or mountain. It had to be Burghead, or whatever Burghead was called at whatever time this was.

"Now what?" Emilie whispered, staring at the sky. If Caitriona or King Brodyn were not there, Emilie would be in extreme danger. Women were nothing but property in these early Christian years. They were traded, married off, used as broodmares, and worse. A shiver ran up her spine. She couldn't just walk up the hill to the gates and ask for Queen Caitriona.

"Why am I even here?" she asked, looking around for a place to hunker down for the night. Perhaps a plan would come to her by dawn. She was cold, hungry, and injured, but she was alive and intended to stay that way. She hadn't fallen through time just to end up with her head on a pike.

"Halt! Who are ye, and why are ye on our lands?"

A man's deep voice startled Emilie, and she shrieked, clutching her chest as her heart jumped into her throat. His words were strange yet understandable. Was this the Pictish language? It sounded like a combination of Gaelic, Latin, and P-Celtic languages; fortunately for Emilie, she knew those languages well due to her specific education. Still, the combination made for an intriguing sound, and though she understood the language, she wasn't sure how to respond appropriately.

"Speak, or I will assume ye are a foe. Ye dinnae want that, lass."

Squinting up at the man on a horse, Emilie saw that he wore a tunic and trousers that were not modern. His black hair hung lank around his face, making his features even harder to see in the dark.

"Who... is your..." Emilie paused and tried to decide what word they might use for "king". She decided to stick with Latin, for many tribes understood the language or shared its root sounds. "*Rex? Qui est rex tuu?*" she asked slowly, hoping he understood that she needed his king's name.

"King?" the man responded, and Emilie nodded. "Why do ye ask? Who sent ye?"

"Caitriona? Brodyn?" Emilie watched the guard's eyes widen with understanding, and she waited with bated breath, praying she wasn't too early or too late in time to find them here.

"Queen Caitriona and King Brodyn are hosting King Arwyn and cannae be bothered. Who are ye to them?" His eyes narrowed, and Emilie took a step back when his horse shifted impatiently.

She decided to stick with Latin since he understood it well enough. "I am Queen Caitriona's sister," she said, which was mostly true. They'd always been as close as sisters, and she felt it held greater importance than saying she was her best friend. "I've traveled very far. I'm injured, and I need help."

The man looked her up and down, regarding her clothing. As far as her education had taught her, her dress was a bit more detailed than the tunics women wore in Pictish times, but at least she hadn't shown up in skinny jeans and a tank top.

"Ye arenae from here."

"No. I'm from where Queen Caitriona is from," she said carefully, unsure what these people knew about Cait. At least Emilie was in the right place and time to find Cait, but she had to convince this towering beast of a man to take her there.

"Ye are a Scot? From Dal Riata?" He asked. Was this a trick question? Is that where they believed Cait came from? It was more realistic than saying she was from a land that had yet to be discovered and that this was all dust in her time.

"Yes. Please, bring me to Caitriona. She will tell you. I'm hurt. I need food and rest." Emilie wasn't above begging at this point, and despite her ability to push the pain aside, she was only human, and her entire body throbbed.

Without a word, the man jumped down from his horse and began to rummage through a satchel tied to his horse's saddle. Her mouth dropped open when she realized he was even larger than he had appeared on horseback. When he pulled out a length of rope, Emilie yelped and stepped back, tripping over a rock and landing on her backside, the one part of her body that hadn't hurt—until now.

"No!" She yelled as he yanked her up and grabbed her wrist. "Ouch! You're hurting me! My wrist is injured!"

Whether the man understood or not, he continued to bind her wrists without looking her in the eye. When his large hands wrapped around her waist, she tried to flee, and fear gripped her. "Let me go!" She kicked him in the shin, but the man didn't flinch as he flung her onto his horse and mounted behind her. She knew being a woman in these times was dangerous, but it was incredible that the first man she met already had her bound. Nausea roiled in her belly again. How could she have studied these people her entire life and still find herself in immediate danger, bound and held hostage by a man who resembled Shrek with Professor Snape's hair?

"I'll take ye to the king and queen." He urged his horse forward as his hands slid around her waist. "Ye are too thin. Ye should eat more."

Emilie wanted to claw the man's eyes out, but she couldn't without the use of her hands. Why did men think it necessary to tell a woman to lose or gain weight? She could tell him that he smelled and needed to shave, but since she was at his mercy, she pursed her lips and decided that getting to Caitriona in one piece was better than offending an ancient warrior.

The horse trotted up the hill as she struggled to stay upright, and the village walls loomed ahead, looking like the old fortified hillforts Emilie had studied for years. Seeing one in person made her stomach flip with excitement, even if she was bound with rope atop an ogre's horse. Soon, she would see Caitriona, and everything would be just fine.

DESPITE THE MUSIC and laughter filling the longhouse, Goodwin stared straight ahead at a wall, drinking his ale and avoiding conversation. He generally enjoyed frivolity, but these kings from tribes all over the land continued to come, and none of them were good enough for Murielle. Goodwin found nothing to celebrate while his childhood friend was being pawned off.

Meanwhile, Queen Caitriona bounced her wee son Lucas upon her lap with a broad smile while King Brodyn discussed a marriage alliance between his sister and Arwyn. Aye, he understood why it was necessary and always knew this day would come, but now that it had, a sick feeling consumed his stomach. He did not trust this King Arwyn ap Rhys of Gwynedd.

"Ye look as if someone kicked yer horse's arse," Ronan said with a chuckle as he shoved Goodwin's shoulder.

"I wish someone would kick Arwyn's arse," Goodwin grumbled before sipping more ale.

Ronan, one of his best friends and fellow warriors, looked over his shoulder to regard King Arwyn speaking with Murielle and Brodyn in the corner. "Ye say ye arnae in love with the king's sister, but yer face says otherwise."

"Why does everyone assume I am in love with Murielle? Can a man not care for a woman without loving her?"

"Nay."

"Nay?"

"Nay," Ronan said again. "Name one woman ye've cared about that ye didnae love."

"My mother. Hated the woman. She was evil, I vow, but I still cared about her."

Ronan snorted and shook his head. "So, ye care no more for Murielle than ye did yer evil mother?"

"I grew up with her and Brodyn. I ken Murielle better than most. She is an unusual woman with a fierce spirit. She always hoped for a love match, though she always kenned that was impossible. I had hoped that King Brodyn would change his mind once he fell in love with Caitriona. Cannae he see how difficult this is for his sister?"

Murielle's laughter rang out through the hall, and Goodwin turned and narrowed his eyes at her before looking at King Arwyn, who leaned against the wall and appeared to capture her attention with some witty story.

"Aye. She seems miserable," Ronan said wryly. Goodwin wanted to punch Ronan in his smug face, but what good would that do? Besides, he knew Ronan would only punch him back, and though Goodwin enjoyed a friendly fracas now and again, he was in no mood for friends or fighting.

"I need some air." Without looking at Ronan, Goodwin placed his empty mug on a table and headed out of the door, glad to feel the cool night air on his heated skin. His sword hung from his belt, swinging at his side as he walked toward the stables to visit Boudicca, his trusted mare. A gust of wind whipped his brown hair around his face, but he was too frustrated to care. There was no point in explaining why Murielle's arranged marriage bothered him as it did. Despite what others believed, Goodwin was not in love with her. Aye, she was beautiful, independent, intelligent, and humorous, but Goodwin had grown up beside her, knowing she was always meant to marry a king. But no king that came to call inspired his trust, and that twisted his insides to knots.

Arwyn ap Rhys, in particular, had a dark energy he hid behind handsome features. Goodwin had seen this all too often in his life and he knew that if Murielle didn't accept his offer, there could be trouble. Why couldn't Brodyn see the same thing?

Reaching the stables, Goodwin pushed his hair out of his face and walked toward Boudicca's stall, grabbing an apple from a barrel. "I guess it's just ye and me," Goodwin whispered to his mare, running his callused palm across her brown and white speckled back. "Talorc is dead, Brodyn is married with a bairn, and Murielle will be married soon. I suppose loneliness is a warrior's lot, isnae it?"

Goodwin had enjoyed years of frivolously taking lovers, but

as he approached turning twenty-seven years old, had fought in several battles, and watched all of his friends either die or start a family, he was ready for more in this life. But, it would have to be found within these walls. He couldn't leave Brodyn. After almost losing Brodyn last year during a battle with Northumbria, Goodwin had contemplated his own life achievements. Not only was Goodwin his most loyal companion, but he was also his best fighter. Aye, he was renowned for his prowess in combat, but wasn't there more to a man than his ability to swing a sword?

As Boudicca ate the apple from his palm, Goodwin heard hooves rapidly approaching the stables and he straightened his back. Extra guards had been assigned to watch the land outside the gates since rival kings had been calling on Murielle but hearing one approach meant something was amiss.

Stepping away from Boudicca, Goodwin walked outside the stables just as Lawrence halted his horse. A woman sat in his saddle with her arms bound and her golden hair whipped into a frenzy about her flushed face. Narrowing his eyes, Goodwin stepped closer to regard her. She wore a tunic unlike anything he'd seen, though it wasn't overly odd like the clothing Queen Caitriona had arrived in, with strange fasteners she called buttons. But its laced, fitted bodice was unlike the ones he'd seen anywhere else. He also couldn't help but notice that beneath those laces, her breasts strained and heaved. He forced his gaze back to Lawrence. Obviously, this woman was scared and didn't need him gawking at her.

"Who is this, and why is she here? Are there others?" he asked.

"Nay, she was alone." Lawrence dismounted and roughly pulled the lass down with him. When she hissed in pain as her feet hit the ground, Goodwin stepped forward to help her stand. Her yellow-green eyes regarded him before she looked away, saying nothing.

"She is hurt," Goodwin murmured as he noticed the large bump on her head. At first, he had thought it was a shadow, but up close, he realized this woman had suffered an injury. "Untie her hands, Lawrence."

"She says she is Queen Caitriona's sister. I cannae untie her. She knew all of their names. She could be trouble."

Goodwin looked at her and tilted his head to observe her. "Are ye from Dal Riata, lass?" This was a trick question, for very few people knew where Queen Caitriona was really from, and it wasn't Dal Riata as everyone else believed.

She shook her head and frowned, daring to glance his way.

"Do ye speak?"

Lawrence scoffed. "Aye, she speaks, but oddly. She was speaking Latin. Who speaks Latin unless they be Angles that still use the Roman tongue?"

Goodwin regarded her for a moment, but still, she remained silent, appearing anxious and overwhelmed. He pitied the lass. Time traveler or just a lost soul, she seemed vulnerable and desperate for help.

"Why do ye speak Latin?" he asked in that language. He knew his speech wasn't perfect, but their language was a mix of languages, so he did his best to communicate.

"I figured he'd understand it," she replied. "I don't speak Pictish. I need to see Cait."

This woman claimed to be Caitriona's sister and called her by her familiar name, "Cait," which only Brodyn used. "What is yer name, lass?"

"Emilie Wilshire."

"Not Murray? Wouldnae ye have the same surname as Queen Caitriona if ye were sisters?"

"Please bring me to her. She will explain. I'm hurt." Emilie lifted her bound hands. "My wrist may be broken."

Goodwin found that he understood her words well and that her accent was similar to Caitriona's. Something was atypical about this woman, but he sensed the truth. "Ye arenae from here, are ye?"

She shook her head, and Goodwin sighed, pulling a knife

from his boot. She stepped back with a gasp, and he put out a hand. "It's for yer binds." Gently, he grabbed her hands and slid his knife through the rope.

When her hands were free, she rubbed her injured wrist and winced. Goodwin saw a bruise on it and knew she had told the truth about the injury. "Come with me. We have visitors from Gwynedd here, so there are many people in the hall, but I will take ye to Queen Caitriona and let her decide what to do."

"Thank you," Emilie said, moving away from Lawrence and closer to Goodwin, which made him smile. Lawrence wasn't a bad man. He was only doing his job but as a warrior, he did lack gentleness at times. But Goodwin prided himself on his ability to read people. He knew Emilie was special, perhaps even from the future like Caitriona, but he couldn't say as much in front of the man without sounding insane.

When they began to walk, Emilie stumbled again, and Goodwin stopped. "Yer feet are injured, as well?"

"Everything hurts," she said. "I didn't expect to end up here, and these shoes..." she looked down, and so did Goodwin. He frowned at the flimsy leather slippers she wore. They did not appear to be made for anything other than existing.

Goodwin opened his mouth to ask permission to carry her, but he sensed this strong-willed woman would refuse his help despite her obvious pain, so instead, he bent down and scooped her up behind her knees.

With a squeal, Emilie wrapped her arms around his neck to stabilize herself. "You don't need to carry me," she hissed and struggled.

"I think I do. As ye said, ye are injured. Ye weigh verra little, so 'tis not an issue."

"Your friend said I was too thin, also. Why do you men think it's okay to comment on a woman's appearance? I didn't tell him he needed to bathe."

Goodwin laughed loudly and unexpectedly, liking the fire in her eyes when she got defiant. "Aye, that he does. Lawrence isnae one of our more refined warriors, but I vow we are not all such brutes."

"Obviously not. Thank you for cutting the ropes and for... helping me." She flushed and turned her face away, and Goodwin smiled again. She was a bonnie lass. Even more than bonnie. She was the most beautiful woman he had ever seen, even if her forehead had a huge knot.

As they neared the longhouse, voices, laughter, and music buzzed in the air, and candlelight flickered, illuminating the entrance.

"Cait is in there?"

"Aye, with King Brodyn and their son."

Emilie gasped, and her eyes widened with delight. "Lucas is there?"

Goodwin stopped in his tracks, suddenly wary. "Ye ken Lucas?"

"No, I have never met him, but I know all about him from Samuel, and—" When Goodwin's brow dropped, Emilie pursed her lips, clearly wondering if she'd said too much.

"Ye ken Samuel?" he asked.

She nodded. "He knows Cait and me very well. Do you know Samuel?" she asked, now frowning back at him.

He shifted her in his arms as he nodded. "I do. And I am one of the few people here who ken where he and Cait are truly from."

Emilie bit her bottom lip, and Goodwin's eyes narrowed on her mouth, more intrigued by the moment. "Then you know where I am from. But I don't know how I ended up here."

Goodwin swallowed, feeling his stomach sink. She might have been the bonniest lass he ever laid eyes on, but she wasn't from here and more likely wouldn't be staying. He didn't understand why that thought disturbed him. He knew nothing about this woman. She could already be married with children at home or perhaps had no interest in him at all. It was best that he reminded himself of this now and every time he saw her, for she would be gone soon enough.

Stepping into the longhouse, Goodwin maneuvered through the crowd as Emilie clung to him. As villagers noticed the strange woman in his arms, the voices slowly died as all eyes landed on them.

"Oh, my God! Emilie?" Queen Caitriona's face grew white as she handed Lucas to Brodyn, who sat beside her, and ran over to Goodwin. "What... how... why?" Caitriona looked Emilie up and down and frowned. "Are you okay? Are you hurt?" She spoke rapidly with her odd accent, but she spoke the Pictish language, and Emilie seemed to understand it.

"Cait!" Emilie struggled to get out of Goodwin's arms, so he carefully placed her on her feet, sorry to lose what little connection they had as she turned her entire attention over to Caitriona. The women embraced, and Goodwin saw tears slide down their cheeks. "I don't know! I was at work, and then... something really weird happened, and I ended up... here," Emilie leaned in and whispered to Cait as everyone stared at the scene, "I hurt my wrist and hit my head. This isn't a delusion, is it?"

"Definitely not," Queen Caitriona said. "We need to get you over to Anya's."

"Emilie?" A man called out.

Hearing her name, Emilie looked over her shoulder and squealed when she saw Samuel walking away from his conversation with Murielle. Goodwin didn't miss the confusion and disappointment in Murielle's eyes when Samuel walked away from her to greet Emilie.

"Sam!" Emilie lunged at him, and the three time-travelers huddled together as Brodyn approached to meet Emilie.

No longer needed, Goodwin backed away and left the longhouse, leaving Emilie to reunite with her friends. He had no place in their mysterious world. Nor had he a place in Brodyn's anymore.

It was best that he remained scarce and avoided Emilie until she left, for already, he was drawn to her in a way he couldn't explain, nor did he wish to try.

CHAPTER THREE

"**W**HAT YE WITNESSED was a banshee," the old woman named Anya told her while she cleaned up Emilie's wounds and bound her wrist with thin strips of linen. "'Tis a dark omen of death, lass."

After Brodyn and Samuel helped Emilie reach Anya's home, Caitriona trailing them with Lucas in her arms, Emilie explained everything that happened up until this point, and Cait refused to leave her side. As frightening as it was to be in the year 686, with Cait by her side, Emilie felt more at home than she had in a long time.

Holding Lucas in her lap, Emilie bounced the six-month-old on her knees and made silly faces to make him laugh while Anya finished bandaging her. "Yes, we've heard about a banshee showing up in the vaults before, but I didn't think it was a real thing," Emilie replied belatedly.

Anya narrowed her eyes at Emilie and shook her head. "There are many things in this world that we cannae understand, but they are most certainly real. Did ye ever think to go back in time? Nay, but here ye are."

"This is true," Emilie said, worrying at her lower lip. "But, does this mean I'm going to die?" She looked around the room at the worried faces, but only Anya seemed to know the answers, even if they weren't what Emilie wanted to hear.

"Ye or someone close to ye is in mortal danger," Anya warned. "Is anyone in yer family ill?"

"I have no family. The only people who matter to me are in this room."

The people around her exchanged glances and worried frowns. A banshee was a legend to her, but to them, it appeared, it was as good as a fact.

"Well, that doesnae bode well," Brodyn grumbled. "I've heard much about ye, Emilie, and I am pleased to have ye here with us, but now we must do what's needed to keep us all safe until we can isolate the threat."

Emilie carefully observed this man who was both King of the Picts and her best friend's husband. It was surreal to stand in his presence when only months ago, she and Cait were digging for his bones. He was larger than life, standing taller than the average modern man. By ancient measures, Brodyn was a giant with a commanding presence. It was no shock to Emilie that his legend, even if inaccurate, lived on for nearly 1,400 years. And yet, he seemed soft, doting, and caring for those he loved despite being a revered warrior on the battlefield. She was awestricken and would need time to wrap her brain around the unfolding events, yet it was hard to focus on anything other than the banshee and who her warning pertained to.

"What if *I* am the threat?" Emilie asked with a frown. "Perhaps I shouldn't be here, Cait. I don't want to put any of you in danger."

"Nonsense, Em. You were brought here for a reason." Cait took the baby from her with a toss of her head and propped him onto her hip.

"Aye," Anya interjected. "This land, it kens what it's doing when it pulls people through the stones. I dinnae ken why the banshee showed itself to ye, but it isnae a coincidence that ye ended up in this place right after. Whatever the answer is, ye shall find it here."

"Are we doomed? Can we change the fate that the banshee warned about?" Cait asked, looking at Anya and Sam.

"I have learned that fate cannot be changed," Samuel added.

"I have spent endless lives stuck in the time loop that brought you to Brodyn, and no matter what happens, the result is always the same. However, this doesn't mean anyone is fated to die. It means Emilie was fated to end up here to help herself or someone else. Why else would she arrive if not to save one of us? If she was the one destined to die, she could have done that in 2023. No, she was brought here because one of us is in danger." Sam walked over to Emilie and smiled down at her while she sat on a bench. "You *do* have a family. Have you already forgotten why you called me yesterday?"

"Oh, yeah!" Emilie perked as she remembered the paper folded up in her bodice. "I printed this out because I meant to research it more. I never expected I would get to show you in person." She reached for the paper and saw Caitriona's amused look when she pulled it out and unfolded it. "Don't judge me."

"I would never," her best friend said with a chuckle.

"Look at this." Emilie handed her the genealogy report and beamed. "I am a direct descendent of you and Lucas!"

"What?" Caitriona looked at the paper with wide eyes. "That's crazy that you're able to find this out!"

Brodyn looked over Cait's shoulder and cocked his head. "What is this parchment?"

"This is a list of my ancestors dating back to your time. I found it online—um, in a place of research... I mean. Anyhow, I printed it out."

Brodyn dropped his brow and shook his head. "Your time holds many mysteries to me. But, if ye are truly our descendent, that means yer in danger if we are."

"That's right!" Cait gasped. "Em! That must be why you were sent here. One of us is in danger, and if we die, you never exist!"

"Nobody is going to die," Brodyn said sternly. "I won't allow it. We will put guards on all of ye until we discover whatever threat brought a banshee to Emilie. In the meantime, we are surrounded by the enemy while Arwyn is here."

"But, he is here to secure peace through marriage. He

wouldn't dare try anything..." Caitriona said hesitantly.

"We need Murielle and Goodwin here for this conversation."

Samuel stepped forward and touched Emilie's shoulder. "I will go find them and return. You, Caitriona, and Lucas need to stay put."

Emilie suddenly felt like everything was falling apart. As much as she wanted to see Cait and meet Lucas, she hadn't expected to end up here, and now that she was, panic set in. "I... I don't belong here."

Anya chuckled. "That's what Caitriona said when she arrived, and now look at her."

"That's different. She actually did belong here! She saved the world by marrying Brodyn!"

"Not the world, Em! Just all of Scotland. No biggie," Cait said with a wink.

"You joke, but this is scary! I saw a banshee! Someone is going to die!"

"It was a warning, lass. We will do all we can to stop it. Ye were sent here to warn us. I dinnae believe ye would be here if this wasnae preventable," Anya said as she examined the bump on Emilie's head. "Ye do belong here, even if temporarily. Once this is over, ye can decide to go, but for now, ye are injured and mayhap concussed. Ye arnae going anywhere for now. Try to enjoy it if ye can."

The door opened as Samuel returned with Murielle and Goodwin, and Emilie swallowed, seeing the warrior who carried her enter the room, sweaty and shirtless. *Still massive. And now, half naked.* Her stomach fluttered.

"Ye asked to see me, my king? I apologize for my appearance. I was restless and needed some time on the training field." His eyes locked on hers for a moment before he turned his gaze to Brodyn. Emilie's heart rate kicked up a notch, and suddenly, she felt like she was drowning as she struggled to breathe. Never had she seen a man with such muscles on his chest. It wasn't like men who went to the gym daily. This man had the physique of a trained warrior, and it showed.

"Goodwin, Murielle. Come closer," Brodyn said as he continued to explain everything that had just been discussed. "Until we identify a threat, I need guards on Emilie, Lucas, Murielle, and Caitriona."

Murielle, the beautiful blond-haired, blue-eyed sister of Brodyn that Emilie had heard all about from Caitriona and Samuel, stood beside Goodwin with shock on her face. Emilie couldn't help noticing how the woman clung to Goodwin's muscular bicep.

"We have Arwyn's men all over the village. Any one of them could be a threat," Goodwin said, using his free arm to wipe sweat from his forehead. His muscles bunched and contracted as he moved, and with Emilie sitting on the bench in front of him, she was eye-level with his chest, doing her best not to stare or flush more than she knew she was. What was with the men of this era and their bare chests?

"Aye. We want peace with him, but perhaps we need to put off finding ye a husband for now, Murielle. As it is, they have overstayed their welcome, and I fear they are now lingering to use up our food stores to weaken us."

"Perhaps he just likes me," Murielle said defensively. "Is that so hard to believe?"

"Nay, but I never promised ye to him. I said I would consider him as a suitor. We have several to consider. The question is, do ye like him, Sister?" Brodyn responded.

"Och, nay! I like none of them, if ye are finally asking! I never wanted this, but I ken it's my place to marry a king for our benefit, so I shall do as I am commanded."

"Ye ken I dinnae take pleasure in pawning my sister off," Brodyn groused. "Until they are gone, and we believe the threat has passed, we will postpone marriage talks and keep ye all under guard. I will deal with Arwyn."

"I can guard Murielle," Goodwin said. "I will assign Ronan to Queen Caitriona and Lucas. Mayhap Lawrence can guard

Emilie."

Emilie frowned but remained silent. Why did disappointment churn in her belly when Goodwin offered to guard Murielle instead, and pawn her off on that brute, Lawrence?

"Nay, Goodwin," Brodyn said. "Our house is full due to the Arwyn's many men and servants he brought along. There is no place for Emilie. Murielle has a room already and will be easier to guard. I need ye to guard Emilie at yer home and keep her in yer sights at all times."

Goodwin's eyes snapped in her direction, and she felt coldness radiating off of him. What had made him change so swiftly toward her? His kindness and easy smile now felt wholly imagined.

Still, she couldn't help but notice that his eyes were yellowish-brown, reminding her of a piece of amber gifted to her as a child by Susan. Seeing that same amber color staring back at her in Goodwin's eyes made her heart leap despite his grimace. It was one of few items Emilie cherished in this lifetime. Not only was it the last gift her mother gave Emilie before she succumbed to her illness, but it sparked Emilie's life-long fascination with ancient objects and had inspired her to become an archaeologist.

Was he upset that he couldn't guard the beautiful Murielle, or did he truly dislike Emilie for some reason? She didn't know, nor did she understand why she cared. He had made her feel safe in his arms as he carried her so tenderly, but she was a fool to believe he did it for any other reason than duty and honor.

"Ye want her to stay with me?" Goodwin asked with confusion lacing his tone and distorting his features.

"Aye, she will be safer there, away from the others. It's just until we sort this, Goodwin." As the loyal warrior he was, Goodwin nodded his acceptance and stared straight through Emilie as everyone discussed her without speaking directly to her.

"I can handle Lawrence," Murielle said with a smirk. "He guarded me once before."

"Aye, and ye made the man miserable," Brodyn groused at

his sister with narrowed eyes. She shrugged proudly, and Emilie felt a spark of admiration for her. Cait had told her that Murielle was a strong, independent woman and would do well in modern times with her fierceness. In this time, however, she was lucky to have a doting brother who allowed it.

"Fine, make Lawrence miserable. He deserves it for binding my friend's wrists," Caitriona said, smiling at Emilie and reminding her that she had an ally here amongst this chaos.

"We will make the arrangements." Brodyn looked at Emilie as he took Caitriona's hand in his. "Ye are verra precious to Caitriona, and she is verra precious to me. Goodwin will take good care of ye."

Emilie looked up at Goodwin warily and felt something shift between them when he raised a brow and gave her the smallest of smiles. "Are ye ready to come home with me, then?" He reached out a hand, and she hesitated, looking over her shoulder at Caitriona.

"You are more than safe with Goodwin, Em. He's a good man, and he understands our delicate situation."

Nodding, Emilie took a deep breath and accepted Goodwin's hand, allowing him to support her weight when her entire body screamed in pain. She had started the day in modern-day Edinburgh inside her lonely flat and would end the day in ancient Pictish lands inside this shirtless warrior's home. She wasn't sure who was in danger or what the threat was, but at least she wasn't alone for the time being.

GOODWIN OPENED THE door to his modest home, keenly aware that the woman beside him was used to a world full of wonders that he couldn't even imagine. To her, his home would feel like a dungeon. As an unmarried man, Goodwin required nothing more than a bed and basic furniture. He ate at the longhouse, bathed in the stream, and often traveled with the army. Aside from the need to sleep, he was rarely home.

Clearing his throat, Goodwin escorted Emilie into his dark house and began to build a fire, gathering logs from a pile in the corner. "This is it. I ken it isnae much." He struck his flint stones together to create a spark and threw in dried moss until the fire sparked to life. Gently blowing, he fed it kindling until the logs smoldered. Standing up, he noticed Emilie staring at him strangely, then remembered that he still wore no tunic.

"Och, my apologies." Walking over to his small storage chest, he removed a fresh tunic and covered himself to make her more comfortable.

"Don't apologize. I'm sorry you got stuck with me." She stepped up to the fire and rubbed her hands together. It was his turn to observe her now as the firelight lit up her feminine profile, illuminating her high cheekbones and slim nose. "I will do my best not to burden you."

"'Tis no burden to do as my king commands," Goodwin said, and she frowned, apparently realizing that she was only there because he was ordered to guard her.

"Right," she replied, looking around the small space before smiling. "This place may be larger than my flat in Edinburgh."

"Flat?"

"A small living space, similar to this. One room with a kitchen, a bed, and a bathroom. Oh, that's a room to in which to bathe and… use the chamber pot," she said.

"Ye bathe and shite in the same room?" Goodwin asked with a furrowed brow, and Emilie laughed.

"It's better than it sounds, I assure you. We don't actually use chamber pots."

Everything she said was confusing but intriguing, but he resisted the urge to ask more questions. She was still tired, injured, and required rest. Somehow, her explanation that his home was larger than hers made Goodwin feel slightly more at ease.

"Well, I have no bathtub in here, I am afraid. If ye wish to bathe in the morning, ye may go to Queen Caitriona's home."

"Where do you bathe?" she asked, cocking her head with mild interest.

"The loch or the stream outside the gates. It allows me time to find privacy and clear my mind away from training."

"That sounds lovely. I'd enjoy that."

"Ye would prefer to bathe in the freezing loch than in the queen's herb-scented, hot water bath?" A gleam in her eye told Goodwin that this woman enjoyed adventures, and he appreciated that sense of spirit, for he felt free when he was one with nature.

"Don't get me wrong. I will be using her bath tomorrow. My muscles are very sore from the horse ride. We aren't used to that in our time, but yes, surrounding myself in nature while I bathe sounds wonderful. The feeling of the cold water against my naked skin while surrounded by trees and animals is a perfect reminder that I am alive... for the moment." Her eyes shifted away from his and back to the fire, and though thinking about her naked in the loch prompted images in his mind that she'd likely smack him for if she knew, he had to remember that she was here because her life was potentially in danger.

Stepping forward, Goodwin put a hand on her shoulder, feeling his pulse quicken when her lashes fluttered, and her hazel eyes met his. "I vow to guard ye with my life."

"Right, because you were ordered to," she said, with a sigh.

"I need no order from my king to protect ye, lass," he assured her.

"But, you wanted to guard Murielle, which I understand."

"Do ye? What exactly do ye understand about it?"

She shrugged and looked away from him again. "She is extraordinarily beautiful, and she is your best friend's sister. I assume you grew up with her and harbor some feelings for the woman. I'm nobody to you. So, I understand why you would rather guard her."

More and more, Goodwin found it frustrating that everyone assumed he was in love with Murielle simply because he knew her well and she was bonnie. "She is like a sister to me and nothing more." Goodwin didn't know why he felt the need to tell her that, but he couldn't tell her he preferred to guard Murielle because he had no interest in growing attached to a woman who would be gone soon enough. He wasn't one to grow attached to women, but he already sensed that Emilie was different, and not just because she came from another time.

"Oh," Emilie replied, showing no emotion. Good. It was better that way. Emilie was the queen's best companion and Brodyn's family, even if very distantly. She was above Goodwin in every way.

"Ye will sleep in my bed as long as ye are here. I shall take the floor."

"Oh, no. I couldn't do—"

"Ye will take the bed. There is no arguing it." Walking away, Goodwin rummaged through his chest once more to find a suitable tunic for her to sleep in, for her clothing was caked in dry mud. "Here. Ye may wear this to bed." He tossed her the tunic, and she caught it, wincing when she used her bad wrist.

"Och, I'm sorry," he said, coming closer. "I shouldnae have done that."

She waved his concern away. "I have a perfectly good hand to catch with. It's my fault I used the wrong one."

Goodwin shook his head. "It's my job to take care of ye. I shouldnae have forgotten about yer wrist." He looked down at her foreign tunic and noticed the strings holding it closed were double-knotted.

"Will ye require help?" he asked, praying she said no.

Looking down, she grumbled and cursed under her breath. "I shouldn't have done that. I didn't expect to fall through time, land on stones, and injure my wrist when I got dressed for work today." She gave a nervous chuckle. "I believe I can handle this myself, though."

Goodwin nodded and turned his back. "I will be laying just over there. I willnae look, I vow. Unless ye prefer I leave the house."

"No, no. Turning around is just fine, thank you." While she struggled with her bodice's ties, Goodwin gathered his furs and a wool blanket to make himself a sleeping spot on the floor opposite the room. He removed his tunic, laid down, and rolled away to face the wall. Having her in his home was unexpected and unnerving, but more unnerving was the physical effect she had on him. The quickening of his pulse and fluttering in his gut were not the usual sensations he felt even when in close proximity to a beautiful woman, but Emilie was by far the most beautiful woman ever to enter his home. Even with a knot on her head, she managed to steal his breath every time he looked at her.

She created the other, more commonly expected effect, as well, and Goodwin groaned under his breath as he listened to her own moans of frustration, trying to remove her tunic with an injured wrist. Her sounds reminded him of lovemaking, and it had been too long since he slaked his lust. In fact, since the battle when Brodyn almost died, Goodwin had been looking for more and soon realized he wouldn't find it with any of the women from this village.

"Uh, Goodwin?"

"Aye?" he asked, continuing to stare at the wall.

"I think I need help after all."

Goodwin stilled and hesitated. Undressing her would be a pleasure, but it would be a torturous one. "May I turn around?"

"Yes. I somehow have made it worse," she said with a frustrated huff.

Turning around, Goodwin saw the jumbled mess of ties hanging from her bodice and crinkled his nose. "Aye, that ye did." Getting to his feet, he walked over and stood before her. The hearth fire popped and crackled, casting shadows about the room, supplying only a dim light to aid his cause.

Before taking the strings in hand, Goodwin looked at Emilie, awaiting permission. When she nodded, Goodwin grabbed them and squinted. "Turn more toward the fire," he murmured as he bent closer to her bodice to inspect the jumbled strings. Her breasts rose and fell rhythmically with her breathing, and he sensed she was just as unnerved by his closeness as he was by hers, only he couldn't sense if she was attracted to him or afraid of him. He hoped it wasn't the latter, but the former could prove disastrous. Never had he hoped a bonnie lass found him unagreeable until now. For all Goodwin knew, he paled in comparison to the men she knew from her time.

Determined to focus on the knot and not her cleavage, Goodwin honed his concentration, doing his best, but the knot wouldn't budge. "I'm going to have to cut them, lass." He looked up at her, and again, she nodded her consent. Turning toward the small table near his bed, Goodwin grabbed his knife and gently sliced through the strings, causing her bodice to loosen and expose more of her bountiful bosom. By God, Goodwin had never been this close to a partially unclothed woman without having plans to remove his own clothing, as well.

Her chest rose and fell faster now, and Goodwin looked up at her only to see her eyes focused on his bared chest. Biting back a smirk, Goodwin was pleased to know she liked what she saw, even if nothing would come from this attraction.

"There, ye are free from yer binds," he said before turning away.

"But…" Emilie reached out and touched his arm, and he saw the bound wrist, reminding him that she couldn't finish the job. "I… I can't—"

"I know," he grumbled, making her frown.

"I'm sorry. Tonight, will be the only night I stay here. I will stay elsewhere tomorrow night, so I am not a burden."

The only way she burdened him was by being far too bonnie. "Ye arnae a burden, Emilie. 'Tis unnatural for me to unclothe a woman for any other purpose than—"

"Sex?" she added, tilting her head.

"I dinnae ken what that means."

"Making love?" she added, and his hands stilled when he looked at her.

"Ye are a bold woman to speak so openly of such things." It sounded like a scolding, but he meant it as a compliment. The images this woman provoked simply by existing in his presence were enough to drive him mad with desire.

Emilie shrugged, and her bodice gaped slightly more, revealing an odd lacy piece of fabric beneath it. "Where I come from, it's perfectly normal to discuss. It's not the shameful thing it once was. But I didn't mean to make you uncomfortable."

"Removing a beautiful woman's clothing while she stands near my bed will do more than make me uncomfortable." Goodwin cleared his throat. "Now, cannae ye slip it down yer hips without using yer wrist?"

"No, it has to be pulled overhead." Emilie lifted her arms, and Goodwin nodded.

Reminding himself that he had seen dozens of naked women in his lifetime, Goodwin bent down to gather her skirt in his hand and tugged it over her hips. His knuckles grazed another bit of fabric, and he paused, wondering why a thin strip of cloth wrapped around her hips.

"Oh, that's my underwear," she breathed, shifting nervously when his fingers touched her hip.

"Underwear?" he repeated softly, confused by so much of what she said.

"We wear garments beneath our clothing."

He still didn't understand but continued his mission and pulled the dress up and over her breasts, closing his eyes so he didn't violate her privacy. The less he saw of Emilie, the better.

Emilie laughed when she saw his eyes squeezed shut. "Relax, I am not naked. I still have my undergarments on. You don't need to walk around like a blind man."

"I think I need to do just that," Goodwin said warily as he kept his eyes shut and turned away. "Anything else I can do for ye?"

"No, thank you for your help, Goodwin."

That was the first time he heard her speak his name from her tempting lips, and he quite liked the sound of it. "As I said before, 'tis my duty to aid ye in any way. Good night, Emilie."

"Good night," she repeated, and he sighed when he heard her climb into his bed.

Laying on the floor, Goodwin rolled over and stared at the wall, willing his lusty thoughts away and hoping he didn't dream of the lass, for he wished to forget her all together.

CHAPTER FOUR

S TARING UP AT the thatched roof in Goodwin's home, Emilie struggled to turn off her wandering thoughts. She lay in a Pictish warrior's bed in an ancient fortification that no longer existed in her time. She felt safe in his presence, and it helped that Caitriona trusted him with Emilie. Her thoughts should be on the threat that sent her here, but right now, all she could think about was Goodwin. He had called her beautiful. The thought still warmed her, and she rolled over to see his back facing the wall.

Wearing his tunic and nothing else, Emilie shifted on his straw mattress. The pile of furs beneath her were comfortable and warm, and she stared into the dying fire until her eyes grew heavy. When next they opened, Emilie shot upright in a panic and climbed out of bed, disoriented in the blackness. Her hip bumped something, and Emilie screeched as she felt around in the dark, trying to remember where she was.

"Emilie." Hands gripped her waist, and she screamed before recognizing the voice and remembering where she was.

"I'm sorry," she whispered, unable to see anything now that the fire had died. She shivered and huddled closer to his warmth, needing comfort. "I woke up and forgot where I was. I'm afraid of the dark," she admitted with embarrassment.

"Yer safe," he whispered, rubbing his large hand over her back to calm her.

"I thought I was in my flat and knocked over your table. I'm sorry," she murmured against his chest, feeling his hard muscles against her cheek as his heart thumped against her ear. Somehow she found it soothing to be in his arms.

"Nothing to apologize for. Stay here while I make the fire."

She nodded, realizing he couldn't see her, so she stood still as she heard him shuffle around his home, throwing wood into the hearth. Sparks lit up the room just before the logs caught fire, and Emilie saw Goodwin bending over to blow on the flames until they spread higher.

"There ye go." Goodwin stood up and turned to face her, his face growing serious when he saw her.

Dropping her brow, Emilie wasn't sure why he suddenly looked so intense when he had been nurturing just moments before. His gaze roamed her body, and she looked down, realizing the problem. Once Emilie had climbed into bed, she had removed her bra and underwear, slipping into the tunic he offered her. But never had she expected it to be so thin. With the firelight illuminating the fabric, her entire silhouette was on display, including her erect nipples.

Emilie's eyes widened, and she tried to cover herself, cursing under her breath. "I…" Words escaped her as she stood frozen before Goodwin, whose chest gleamed in the firelight as it rapidly rose and fell.

"Are ye trying to test my mettle, lass?" he asked as he groaned and ran a hand through his loose, brown shoulder-length hair. His short beard framed his chiseled jaw, and Emilie just stared, slowly shaking her head.

"Nay? It feels verra much like ye are trying to test me."

Growing defensive, Emilie quickly grabbed a blanket from the bed and wrapped it around her shoulders, ensuring her nipples were covered. "How could I be testing you when I couldn't even remember where I was when I woke up?"

"Or, mayhap 'tis all a game to you." Goodwin raised a brow at her, and she scowled back.

"Wow. You think a lot of yourself, don't you?"

"Ye'd not be the first lass to come into my home, disrobe, and display herself in an attempt to bed me."

Emilie scoffed at his arrogance. "Believe it or not, I don't need to play games to get a man in bed with me, and I don't seduce men I barely know! If you find yourself attracted to me, that is your problem, not mine."

"Ye are standing in the middle of my home wearing nothing but a sheer tunic that shows yer every curve! Wouldnae it be insulting if I wasnae aroused?" Goodwin retorted before taking a steadying breath and turning away from Emilie.

"I'm wearing what you gave me to wear! Now you're blaming me for it? How typical! I see men are the same no matter when or where they are from!"

Clenching his jaw, Goodwin turned back toward her and stepped closer, a cold look on his face. "If I were like other men, lass, I'd have already had my way with ye whether ye wanted it or nay. I am nothing like other men. Nothing." He turned away again and paced his floor.

Guilt niggled at Emilie. This man had let her into his home and borrow his clothes and had been nothing but a gentleman to her. It bothered her that he accused her of seducing him, but she had to remind herself that she was not like the women of his time, and he was caught off guard by her near nakedness, which she admitted caught her off guard, as well.

"Goodwin, I'm sorry. We are both tired, and you were forced to bring me here and guard me. I'm sure you have better things to do with your time than look after Caitriona's friend. You've been kind to me. I just don't like being made to feel guilty for having breasts. I did nothing wrong. I woke up scared and forgot where I was or what I was wearing."

Sighing, he turned to her with softened features. "Nay, lass. I should apologize to ye. I accused ye of being like the other women who throw themselves at me, which I'm usually fine with." He gave her a crooked grin. "Ye are a beautiful woman in my bed and also happen to be under my guard. But ye are correct, 'tis arrogant of me to assume ye would seduce me.

Perhaps neither of us are like the others, aye?"

"Yeah, I guess so, or else we'd already be naked together in the bed." Emilie pursed her lips after she said that, closing her eyes and holding her breath. What was wrong with her? She couldn't stop thinking about him naked, and she'd only known him a few hours. Maybe she wasn't so very unlike the other lassies, after all. She'd never play games to get him into bed, but she certainly wasn't immune to dreaming about it. Being alone in this small space with a man as attractive as Goodwin was not working for her libido.

Goodwin stared at her with an unreadable expression that made her stomach flutter and tighten. She wasn't doing well fitting in here with her modern manners. "Anyway, I'm going back to bed. Thank you for helping me and for restarting the fire. I promise not to be a problem anymore."

Emilie hastened back to the bed and rolled over to face the wall, too mortified to look in his direction. It had been way too long since she had a boyfriend, and her career made her travel so often that sex was almost nonexistent. She had to remind herself that this wasn't about Goodwin or how attractive she found him. This was simply her human nature rearing its ugly hormones.

"Good night, Emilie," she heard him say before he shuffled back to his makeshift bed.

Closing her eyes, Emilie vowed to keep her mouth shut and distance herself as much as possible from the man despite his command to follow her. That would be a problem, but she would just pretend he wasn't there. How hard could that be?

A KNOCK ON the door had Goodwin scrambling to his feet, glad for the distraction. He obtained no sleep after his confrontation with Emilie. The woman vexed yet intrigued him simultaneously, and his innate attraction to her didn't help. Her comment about them lying naked together in bed, if they were like other people, made him very much wish they were like other people. But, she was a time traveler whose life was in danger, and he was the guard assigned to her by his king and her best friend, the queen. His duty and loyalty were more important than his lust for the woman.

When he opened the door, Queen Caitriona greeted him with her usual warm smile and Lucas on one hip. In her other hand, she held a pile of folded linens. "May I come in?" she asked, peeking into the room to see if Emilie was awake.

"Cait!" Emilie must have been pretending to sleep because she had been silent until this moment. Now, she bounded out of bed with the energy of a woman who'd been up for hours after a good night of sleep. This time, he noticed, she'd remembered to wrap a wool blanket around her body.

"Hi! I know it's early, but you have no clothes to wear, so I figured I'd bring you some. I know what it's like to end up here without proper clothing."

Goodwin cleared his throat and stepped aside, also relieved that Emilie would have appropriate clothing to hide her enticing curves. It would make his assignment much easier if he didn't have to stare at her nipples.

"You're the best. Though I do miss my taco sweater right about now." Caitriona burst out laughing, and Goodwin pretended not to hear since he didn't understand what a taco or sweater was.

"I'm into fitness! Fitness taco into my mouth!" Cait and Emilie said at the same time, bursting into more laughter.

"God, I'm so glad you're here, Em, even under these circumstances."

"Me, too. And, I got to meet Lucas!" Emilie put out her arms, swiped the bairn from Caitriona's arms, and immediately made the wee lad giggle with her silly sounds and faces. Goodwin watched from the corner, unable to hide his amused smile. He liked that she had a lighter, playful side, though why he cared, he couldn't understand.

"No offense, babe, but you need a bath," Caitriona said to Emilie, who smiled widely and nodded.

"I'm dying for one!"

"Good, come back to the house with me, and I will get you all set up."

"What's the plan?" Goodwin interrupted as he strapped his sword to his side and slid his knife into his boot. "Is Arwyn preparing to leave?"

Caitriona wrinkled her nose. "You will need to speak with Brodyn while Cait bathes. Arwyn isn't happy about being sent away. We told him we'd consider his suit, but apparently, the man hoped to leave with a bride."

"The man is going nowhere with Murielle until she's ready," Goodwin groused, his temper flaring. He disliked these pompous kings who showed up expecting Murielle to fall at their feet. This was an alliance, but Murielle still had to accept the man, or Brodyn wouldn't accept the match.

"That is what Brodyn said, but Arwyn accused him of being weak and allowing his women too much power. I have a feeling we have only made things worse with the man."

"It's a shame King Caedan passed away before negotiations were set for their marriage. His nephew is not trustworthy."

"Which is why Brodyn hopes to ally with him," Cait said. "'Keep your friends close and your enemies closer'. We can discuss this more at our home. Why don't you step out so Cait can get dressed?"

Nodding, Goodwin obliged, glad to be away from Emilie for a moment, even though he still remained in front of the house, watching Arwyn's men mill about the village as if they lived here. Goodwin forced his features to remain neutral, but he wouldn't be at ease until they were off the land, and Emilie and the royal family would hopefully be safe. What happened after that, Goodwin didn't know. Would Emilie leave immediately after Arwyn departed? Part of him hoped she would so he could get back to his usual training routine, but another part hoped she stayed longer, so he got to know her better. To what end? He asked himself. Why was he interested in learning more about her if she would be gone soon?

When the women stepped out of his home, Goodwin looked at Emilie and almost remarked that it was nice to see her with clothes on, but he knew such a statement would raise Queen Caitriona's brows. However, Emilie did look lovely in a long, flowing, blue tunic that hugged her curves in an enticing way. Emilie appeared to be avoiding eye contact with him, which he found helpful, and he decided he would do the same.

"Let us go." Walking with the women on either side of him and Lucas in Emilie's arms, Goodwin looked around the village, appearing at ease but always on edge. One of them was in mortal danger, and Goodwin wouldn't allow anyone to approach until he knew they were safe from harm. With his hand on his sword's hilt, he guided them through the village and up the hill to the royal dwelling. When he entered, Anya and Murielle were inside laughing as they baked bread, and Murielle was covered in flour.

"Who let Murielle near a kiln?" Goodwin said as he stepped inside.

"If I'm to be a wife, I should learn to bake bread at the very least, aye?" she asked, laughing at the mess around her.

"Ye will surely have servants for that," Goodwin said, stepping closer to wipe flour from her cheek. When he turned around, he saw Emilie's eyes look away quickly, and he wondered if she was jealous of his relationship with Murielle. Though maybe that was just wishful thinking on his part.

"I dinnae wish to depend on a man or servants. I like to be self-sufficient," Murielle said as she tried to knead the dough despite it sticking to her hands.

"You were right, Cait," Emilie said. "Murielle would do well in our time."

Murielle looked over her shoulder and beamed at Emilie. "Thank ye. I hear ye have more say over yer life in yer time. I long to be like my sister here and do things myself."

Goodwin watched the women interact and appreciated that they all got along well.

"Anya, I'm taking Emilie upstairs to bathe," Caitriona said.

When the women started toward the stairs, Goodwin followed.

"Where do ye think yer going?" Murielle asked with a raised brow.

Irritation boiled beneath Goodwin's skin. Did these women not understand they were in danger? "Until Arwyn and his men are off our land, I am not letting Emilie out of my sight. Where is Ronan? Is he not supposed to guard ye?"

"He has been," Murielle huffed. "But I demanded that he leave me alone. I'm fine within these walls."

"This is why I requested to guard ye! Because yer a bull-headed lass that nobody else can control! I kenned ye would chase yer guards off! Ye arenae safe! Dinnae ye understand that?"

Emilie paused and looked at Goodwin with a frown, but he didn't care if she thought he was overreacting. He had a task to do, and he wouldn't hesitate to run any man through who came near his charge.

"Murielle, Goodwin is right," Emilie said to his surprise. "I am here for a reason. All we know is that one of us is in danger. It sounds like Arwyn is angry that he was asked to leave. Until he does, I beg you to keep Ronan nearby. Remember, I'm a blood relative to Lucas. That means you and I are also blood relatives, and you may well be the one in danger."

Also, to Goodwin's surprise, Murielle nodded her head in acceptance. "Fine, I will let Ronan back into the house, but ye cannae be in the chamber while Emilie bathes!" she said with exasperation.

"I plan to guard the door. No man will come near her." Done being told how to do his job, Goodwin followed Caitriona and Emilie up the stairs until they reached Murielle's room.

"I have the bath ready for you in here. Take your time, and

meet me downstairs once you're finished," Cait said.

"Thank you!" Emilie's eyes lit up when she looked inside the room and saw steam rising from the wooden tub. Lavender floated in the air, and the hearth fire flickered beside the tub.

"I will remain in front of the door. Arwyn's men are all over the place, and I dinnae trust them."

She nodded. "Thank you, Goodwin. Hopefully, they will leave soon, so you won't be burdened by my presence anymore."

Before he could say anything else, she shut the door, leaving him to stare down the corridor while he waited, wishing she didn't see herself as a burden.

Through the thin wooden door, Goodwin heard Emilie singing an odd song about splashing in the tub, and an unavoidable smile crept across his lips. She was certainly full of spirit for a lass who plummeted through time and banged up her head, which already looked much better by this morning. A purple bruise remained, but the bump had disappeared, making Emilie only more beautiful today than yesterday, though he wasn't sure how that was possible.

Shouts floated down the corridor, and Goodwin grabbed the hilt of his sword, tuning out Emilie's singing and going on alert. As the shouting intensified, Goodwin took a step away from the door before stopping himself. He couldn't leave Emilie unattended, especially if a fight broke out among Brodyn and Arwyn's men.

"I came all this way for a bride, and I am nae leaving without one!"

"King Arwyn, King Brodyn didnae say ye couldnae marry his sister. He asked that ye give him time to make arrangements and discuss the match with Murielle."

An angry growl rumbled through the air just before Arwyn shouted again. "Ye think me a fool? I ken how many suitors she has turned away! King Brodyn gives his women too many opinions! Make the lass marry me, or not only will this feud continue, but ye will also have a war on yer hands."

Goodwin listened intently, his blood boiling as he listened to this arrogant man shout at Lawrence. Cracking his knuckles, Goodwin narrowed his eyes as the voices grew closer.

"I will relay yer message to the king," Lawrence said, following behind Arwyn as he came into view, storming down the corridor, red-faced and spewing venom.

"I willnae be played like a flute. Ye asked me to travel here to discuss a marriage alliance, and I am here! I willnae leave without my bride!"

Brodyn appeared at the other end of the corridor, looming in the shadows with his hand on his sword's hilt. Goodwin looked at his king, awaiting command.

"Arwyn, ye willnae come onto my land, into my village, inside my home, and tell me how to manage my family! We werenae enemies. King Caedan, yer uncle, was a good man willing to make peace with or without a bride."

"I am not my pathetic uncle!" Arwyn looked at Goodwin and scowled before turning back to Brodyn. "Is he guarding yer sister?"

Brodyn remained silent, staring menacingly back at Arwyn. Lawrence gripped his hilt as he stood behind Arwyn, ready to fight if given the command, but Goodwin knew Brodyn well enough to know he wouldn't command another man to kill a king. If needed, Brodyn would handle Arwyn. Goodwin also knew a war would break out immediately between Arwyn's men and Brodyn's if anything happened.

"Step aside, or I will break down this door."

"Ye have no authority over me," Goodwin replied calmly. "Ye willnae enter this room and keep yer life."

"Ye threaten me, do ye?" Arwyn looked at Brodyn and smirked. "Yer man has threatened a king. What will ye do about it?"

As Arwyn stepped closer, Goodwin looked straight into the man's brown eyes, unshaken by his pompous behavior and threats. Ronan appeared behind Brodyn, but soon more footsteps rumbled up the stairs, and men from both kingdoms flooded the corridor, swords at the ready.

"Goodwin, bar the door!" Brodyn shouted, and Goodwin immediately stepped back, opened the door, and shut it behind him, placing the bar across the inside just as roars flooded the corridor.

Emilie stood in the corner of the room dripping wet with a small linen wrapped around her body as she shivered, and her lank hair dripped down her shoulders. "Wh-what is happening out there?"

"King Arwyn isnae happy about being sent away. He seeks Murielle."

Emilie's eyes widened, and she stepped closer. "Is she in danger?"

"I can assure ye that Brodyn hid Murielle, Lucas, and Caitriona away. But ye are in danger if they break down this door." Finding her borrowed blue tunic bunched up on the floor, Goodwin bent over and tossed it to Emilie, who caught it with one hand while gripping her towel with the other. He saw the faint blue bruise on her injured wrist and winced. "Are ye able to dress yerself?"

She nodded.

Goodwin turned away and faced the door, listening as the scuffle outside the chamber escalated. He itched to run out there and join the fight, to protect his king and fellow warriors. But, he knew he had to stay here and guard Emilie at all cost. Brodyn and the other warriors could manage Arwyn and his men without him, though it chafed to not fight beside his king.

When the door began to splinter as men slammed against it, Goodwin turned to Emilie and grabbed her, pulling her to him. Thankfully, she was fully dressed, but she clung to him with fear. Looking at the floorboards, Goodwin guided Emilie toward Murielle's bed. "Climb under the bed."

"What?" Confusion laced her features as she clung to his arms, her body quaking with cold or fear, he wasn't certain.

"There is a tunnel beneath this chamber that will lead us outside the village. 'Tis why the bed is built higher than most—to accommodate the hatch. Go, go!" The splintering sounds vibrated off the walls, and Emilie shrieked as she scrambled to climb beneath the bed as Goodwin followed behind her. Feeling around, he found the loose boards and lifted them to find a dank and dusty hole.

Sliding down, Goodwin grunted as he landed on his feet and reached up for Emilie, who stared wild-eyed at him as she lay on her stomach beneath the bed.

"I've got ye, lass. Let's go."

"But... spiders. I'm petrified of spiders!"

He scowled at her, trying to control his temper. "Ye ought to be scared of the men on the other side of that door because if they get to ye first, yer Banshee's warning will come to fruition."

Sucking in a deep breath, Emilie put out her hands and allowed Goodwin to pull her down. She gasped when she fell on top of him with a thud, her skirts tangled around her legs. Just as he heard footsteps enter the chamber, Goodwin pushed Emilie aside and clambered onto his feet, sliding the hidden board back into place. They were plunged into damp, dank darkness.

Panting, Goodwin placed his hands on his thighs and caught his breath. "They willnae find us down here, but we need to push our way through," he whispered.

"I can't see anything!" she softly cried, clutching his tunic. Taking her hand, Goodwin guided her through the darkness, using his free hand to feel the sides of the tunnel.

Some creature squeaked near their feet, and Emilie yelped but continued to follow Goodwin through the darkness.

"I thought ye dug in dirt and caves with Queen Caitriona. How are ye afraid of wee critters?" he asked as he gripped her hand.

"I am not afraid of rats, but I don't like feeling them clawing at my legs," she hissed. "As for spiders, I can't help it. I don't allow it to control me, but do I prefer not to walk through dark, crowded, underground areas. Yeah, plus I'm afraid of the dark, remember? So, this is my nightmare," she whispered. "Aren't you afraid of anything?"

He paused and thought about her question as they walked. "Aye, I am."

"Well, what is it?"

"Failure. Disappointing my king. Dying alone."

That last confession made Emilie stop in her tracks, and Goodwin came to a halt to prevent dragging her. "Everyone fears dying alone," Emilie said, squeezing his hand. He appreciated her support and reassurance that his fears were valid, unlike her fear of the dark and spiders, but he didn't have time for sentiment. They needed to get out of here, and once they did, he needed to find them shelter. He knew where he was going, but it was a long, dirty journey.

After several silent moments of walking, Emilie asked, "How much longer is this?"

"It leads out of the village, lass. It's long, but we are almost out."

"Should I ask how you know about this secret tunnel beneath Murielle's bed?" He heard the curiosity in her voice, but more than that, he heard what he may have mistaken as jealousy. He pursed his lips together, not sure if he was pleased or not. Whatever connection they had, it was fleeting, and she would be gone within days, he reminded himself.

"I take it your silence means it's none of my business," she murmured. Goodwin stayed silent until he felt the tunnel turning west toward the sea. He had a good reason for knowing about the tunnel, but he didn't feel like explaining himself while cobwebs clung to his face.

"We are almost out," he said. "Just around this turn." Just as he spoke the words, light shone through an exit, and Emilie sighed with relief, allowing Goodwin to sprint them forward into the fresh air.

She coughed the second she stepped outside of the tunnel,

surrounded by woodland on one side and the loch on the other. "Thank God," she wheezed and shrieked, frantically swiping at webs across her body as she spun in circles.

Goodwin stepped up to her and stilled her flailing body. "Relax. We are safe." Carefully, he pulled away a clump of webs caught in her drying blond hair before dragging his thumb across her cheek to remove a smudge of dirt.

Emilie's hazel eyes locked on his and her mouth parted while she panted for breath. He could tell she wished to say something but that she hesitated. Even covered in dirt and webs, she was singularly the bonniest woman he'd ever laid eyes on, and the urge to pull her close and kiss her sweet lips nearly won out against his better judgment, but he resisted.

Her eyes searched his features as she looked up to his height, still clinging to his hand. "You should never fear failure, Goodwin. You are the most capable man I've ever met. You saved me."

Emilie nibbled on her lower lip as she gazed at his mouth, slowly leaning in. He knew what she wanted, and he wanted it more than he had ever wanted anything in his life—more than he wanted the fresh air he breathed. But just before she closed the distance between them, Goodwin took a step back, knowing she was overcome with emotion. If ever he had a chance to kiss her sweet lips, it wouldn't be because she felt she owed him a boon for saving her life.

"I was only doing my duty," Goodwin said, looking up at the angry gray clouds accumulating above them. "Follow me. We need to get to shelter. A storm is coming."

CHAPTER FIVE

GOODWIN CUT A swift path through the woods, clearly knowing his way around the terrain. Silently, Emilie followed, doing her best to fight back the sense of embarrassment and rejection that hung in the air. What had she been thinking when she almost kissed Goodwin?

She hadn't been thinking at all. It was pure instinct, she told herself. He was handsome, strong, intelligent, and had saved her life. Emilie had been overcome with emotion after running from Arwyn and his men, but Goodwin's reminder that he simply did his duty helped to snap her out of the moment.

Now, she allowed him to lead her deeper into the woods, feeling large drops of rain pelt down from the sky, bouncing off leaves overhead before landing on her head. Soon, she was drenched, and Emilie sighed, wondering if she would ever be clean and dry again. At least the rain washed away the dirt and webs from the tunnel.

Soon, a small wooden hut came into view with the loch just yards away from the entrance, and Emilie perked up, praying they would have shelter soon. "Is that where we are heading?"

"Aye." Goodwin pushed through brambles and dodged low-hanging branches as he held her hand and carefully guided her toward the cabin. Her unbound wrist throbbed, and she wished she had had time to rewrap it after her bath, but the pain was lessened from the day before, and she no longer believed it was broken. Still, a purplish-blue bruise marked the injury, and she winced if she turned her wrist.

Reaching the cabin, Goodwin pushed the door open and dragged Emilie inside, which was not much warmer than outside. He hurried about the room, knowing where everything was located, which made Emilie even more confused.

"You've been here before." She shivered and did her best to wring the water out of her water-laden skirt, but the dirt floor turned to mud at her feet.

"Aye," he responded as he threw logs into the hearth. Soon, a fire sparked to life, and Emilie was grateful for his fire-building skills. She stood near the fire to warm her hands, wondering what she was to do now. She was cold, wet, and stranded.

"How did you know where to find this place?"

Goodwin glanced at her sideways before walking over to a chest in the corner. "It was built as a shelter in case of attack. 'Tis my duty to ken where it is should I need to deliver someone away from the village."

"You mean Murielle."

"Aye."

Emilie cleared her throat and watched as Goodwin pulled clothing from the chest. "You are in love with her, aren't you?"

"Nay." Goodwin stood up and tossed a white pile of fabric at her. "Put this clean tunic on."

Emilie looked at it and frowned. "Why, so you can accuse me of 'testing your mettle' when it turns out to be sheer?"

Goodwin eyed her with clear annoyance, and she sighed, turning away to change out of her soaked tunic. His moods changed with the wind. "Look, if you're angry at me for thinking about kissing you, I assure you I won't try again," she said, slipping the long white tunic over her head. "I understand now."

"What do ye understand?"

She turned around, finding his back turned to her while he also changed into dry clothing, but he had yet to pull up the trousers. His muscular backside flexed, and Emilie gulped, quickly turning back around. Good grief, they didn't make men like that anymore. At least in her era.

"I understand your situation," she said, trying to sound unaffected.

"What situation is that, lass?"

"You're in love with Murielle. That's why you won't kiss me."

Strong arms gripped her shoulders and spun her around, making her gasp in shock when she found herself looking up at Goodwin's narrowed amber eyes. "Ye think I must be in love with another woman if I dinnae kiss ye? Mayhap I dinnae wish to kiss ye. Is that so hard to believe?"

Emilie frowned and crinkled her brow. "Of course not."

"Are ye so confident in yerself that ye assume every man wants ye?"

"What? N-no…" Emilie shrugged out of his grip and turned away from him, angry at him for being so crass and angry at herself for being so affected by his every movement and word.

He spun her around again, and she smacked his bared chest. "Stop that! You've made your point!"

"What point have I made, Emilie Wilshire, from the year 2023?" His wet hair hung around his shoulders as water droplets ran down his chest, but she tried to focus only on his face.

"That you're not attracted to me and don't want to kiss me. And that's fine because I don't want to kiss you either. I don't even know what I was thinking." She huffed and pushed against his chest to keep her distance, but he remained as unmovable as stone.

"Ye were thinking we'd burn hotter than the flames of hell if we dared to cross that line." Goodwin stepped closer, and Emilie stood her ground, unwavering.

"Maybe I was," she dared to respond, placing her hands on his chest, feeling his heartbeat beneath her palm. "But I was wrong."

"Ye are wrong," he whispered, leaning closer.

"About what?" His lips hovered above hers, so close that they shared the same air. Emilie's body suddenly warmed despite the chill in the small wooden room.

"About everything. I am not in love with Murielle, I am attracted to ye, and I do want to kiss ye more than I want my next breath."

His eyes searched hers, and she felt the tension in his muscles as he fought for restraint.

"Then, what's stopping you?" Emilie asked, reaching up to run her index finger along his lower lip, watching his eyelids lower as he struggled to keep his composure.

"I cannae even remember anymore."

"Well, when you do, you know where to find me." Emilie turned on her heels and started to walk away, pleased when she felt him tug her back toward him again.

"Damn ye, lass. If I kiss ye, I dinnae ken if it will ever be enough! Is that what ye want to hear?"

Emilie swallowed and closed her eyes, tingling all across her body as his words caressed her flesh and rain pounded on the thatched roof overhead. She wanted more than just a kiss, but she sensed Goodwin's inner struggle and respected his need to keep his duty separate from his personal desires. Nodding, Emilie stepped away.

"Emilie." Hearing her name whispered from his lips, she turned to face him yet again, wondering how long they would do this dance before they gave up or gave in.

His lips crashed down on hers, and she immediately clung to him, wrapping her arms around his neck as they battled for control like ships lost at sea without anchors. Like the storm battering the world outside these walls, a storm brewed inside Emilie when Goodwin slipped his tongue into her mouth and groaned, gripping her hips possessively. Beneath the thin tunic, she wore nothing else, and his hands rested dangerously close to her backside. Emilie ran her fingers through his wet hair before sliding her palms down his back, heart racing as his palms slid down to grip her bottom and press her against his erection.

As they both struggled for dominance, hands wandered and

tongues tangled, making Emilie's heart beat like a drum against her ribs. He stole her breath and warmed her entire body with his desperate need rising to a dangerous level, but Emilie's matched his. She wanted him enough to forget any logic. It didn't matter that she was in danger or would be leaving soon. It didn't matter that they had only known each other for a day. That one day had felt like an eternity as they'd shared small spaces, experienced danger, and fought this insane animalistic attraction. Emilie had heard of chemical connections to people, but she'd never experienced such an intense desire for someone so quickly. That's all this was, she told herself—two people with physical needs and nothing more. No regrets, no attachments.

When his hands slid beneath her tunic and up her bared stomach, Goodwin detached his lips from hers with a groan. "Yer skin is so soft," he mumbled against her mouth as he glided up to her breasts, gently cupping them with a moan.

Her nipples pebbled, and her body quaked. Emilie's mouth stifled his next groan as she reached down to pull his trouser string, fumbling to push them down his hips with an urgency she couldn't remember ever feeling.

"God, I want ye, Emilie. Ye drive me mad." Lifting her beneath her rear, Goodwin carried her toward the bed and dropped her onto the mattress, staring at her with an intensity that rocked her soul as he removed his boots and trousers, standing before her naked. His impressive erection stood proud, and Emilie's core tingled with need. It had been so long since she slept with any man, but the consuming lust she felt was so much more than simply a pent-up libido. This man pulled forth desire Emilie had never before experienced, and she ached for more.

"I want you, too," she whispered, removing the tunic and baring herself to his eager gaze. The hearth fire raged, warming the room and casting a glow that highlighted every sculpted muscle of his hardened body. "You are, by far, the hottest man I've ever known."

"Is that a good thing?" he asked, obviously not understanding her word choice.

"Oh, it's good," she said with a raised brow as he stepped closer, hovering above her as he scanned her length with approval. She did the same, knowing that once they connected, she would never be the same. That was the effect he had on her— raw, intense, instinctive attraction.

"Yer body is made for breeding," he said as he leaned over her, softly kissing her lips. Emilie paused and furrowed her brows.

"Excuse me? In my time, that's not really a compliment."

He arched a brow as he climbed onto the bed, hovering above her, and settled between her legs. "Where I come from 'tis the greatest of compliments." He cupped her breasts again and leaned down to suck one nipple into his mouth, making her squirm and arch as the pleasant sensation shot through her body. "Full, ripe breasts," he whispered as he moved to the other breast, flicking her nipple with his tongue.

"Narrowed waist and with curvy hips to drive a man wild," he continued, moving his hands down her belly to grip her side. Sliding his palms beneath her, he cupped her backside and squeezed, leaning in to whisper against her lips, "And an arse sculpted by the gods, meant to drive me out of my mind."

"Well, when you put it like that..." Emilie felt like she had been thrown into a fire, her body burned so hot for this man. His words, so raw, so passionate, made her heart beat so quickly that she struggled to breathe.

"And this..." Goodwin slid a finger between her legs, and Emilie instinctively responded by arching her hips and widening her legs for him, closing her eyes as he caressed her until she cried out. "That is the sweetest part of ye, I imagine."

When she opened her eyes, Emilie saw Goodwin's amber gaze glittering with mischief, and she sucked in a breath as he lowered his head, running his tongue along her sensitive flesh.

Emilie gripped the coarse wool blankets on the bed and cried out, feeling as if she had entered into her greatest fantasy, but this was real. Goodwin was solid, flesh and bone. His long hair hung about his face, and his masculine scent of wood and smoke consumed her, making her want every part of him.

"Goodwin! I need... you... more..." she sighed through parted lips just as he lifted his head and straddled her with his proud manhood positioned between her legs.

"Ye want me, lass?"

"God, yes!"

"I vow, ye cannae possibly want me more than I want ye." And before she could respond, he thrust into her, gripping her hips as he pulled her down onto him with a need that Emilie matched, breath for breath.

Lifting her hips, Emilie met his frantic rhythm, her hips moving in tandem with his, their bodies becoming one. He gripped her breasts and leaned in to kiss her, their tongues meeting and breath mingling as they panted, grappling at the edge of ecstasy.

"Just like that!" Emilie cried, thrashing her head to the side. "Yes... Oh!" Pleasure built with every thrust, and Goodwin kept pace, sweat forming on his brow. He watched her with rapture as she tensed and shuddered, waves of pleasure flooding her body as she gripped his backside and pushed against him, screaming out as she drowned in the depths of euphoria and adrenaline.

Goodwin roared with his final thrust, grunting as he collapsed atop her and rolled her to the side, cradling her in his arms. "By all the saints," he gasped, pushing sweaty hair away from his forehead.

"Now, can we stop pretending we aren't attracted to one another?" Emilie said with a chuckle as she rested her head against his chest, their legs tangled together.

"Can we stop pretending this is only attraction?" he asked, tilting her head up to search her gaze.

Emilie licked her lips and felt the fluttering in her stomach as her heart throbbed. "Isn't it?" she asked.

"Nay, and ye ken it."

"Whatever we feel for one another, Goodwin, we both know this is all we can give one another," Emilie said, sadness erasing the thrill she had just experienced. She felt a strong connection to Goodwin, yes, but to what end? She would soon be gone, and there was nothing more for them than this physical connection that she would never forget as long as she lived. She'd never forget *Goodwin* as long as she lived, she realized. Aside from the mind-blowing physical relationship they just shared, he was funny, kind, loyal, everything she ever wanted in a man... but he also lived over 1,300 years in the past. How could Emilie possibly expect more from this?

Goodwin propped himself up with on an elbow and looked down at her. "I ken ye cannae stay, Emilie. Ye have a life of yer own in a place I cannae follow. But cannae ye admit to yerself that we have something between us that is greater than the physical?"

"I just don't see the point of going there, Goodwin. Let's not complicate matters."

"Most women would say 'tis a bit late for that," Goodwin said defensively.

"I'm not most women," Emilie said, sitting up and swinging her legs over the bed, turning her back on Goodwin. "I understand the difference between love and lust."

"Oh, do ye now?" Goodwin said with anger in his tone. "I didnae realize ye were a loose woman. I apologize for thinking ye were capable of more emotion."

Emilie spun on her heels and charged toward him, pointing a finger in his face. "Don't you dare insult me like that! I haven't been with a man in over a year! Can you say the same for yourself?" Goodwin cocked a brow at her, and she scoffed. "With a woman, of course. Don't be an ass."

"Nay, I cannae say it's been that long."

"Then how dare you call me loose because I acted on a physical attraction that you also felt and also acted on! You really are just like every other man! It doesn't matter what time you're from, you're all the same."

Bending over, Emilie scooped the bunched-up white tunic off

the bed. Her blue tunic was sopping wet and now covered in mud from the ground. Growling, she picked that up and draped it over a chair to dry then picked up the white undertunic and shook it. It was damp but at least it wasn't muddy. She looked down at it instead of at this man who'd stolen her heart. "I'm sorry if you wanted more from me than I can give you, Goodwin."

Standing from the bed, he walked over to her and stared down at her with disgust on his face. "Och, dinnae ye worry about that lass. I got exactly what I wanted from ye."

Goodwin may as well have ripped her still-beating heart out of her chest. Closing her eyes, Emilie fought back the tears, cursing herself for allowing him to get under her skin. Of course, she cared about him, but wasn't this like one of those movies where people think they are in love after experiencing trauma together, like *The Bodyguard*? She'd only known him for a day! There was no way these intense feelings for him were real, even if the pain in her heart was.

Despite her best efforts, Emilie felt a tear slide down her flushed cheek, and she swallowed her pain, wiping it away. Regret laced Goodwin's features when she opened her eyes, but there was no need for his regret. She didn't regret laying with him. It had been the single most powerful moment of her entire life. Sex like that could easily make a woman believe she was in love, but once the rush was over, surely Emilie would realize it was all a whirlwind. A modern woman and an ancient man couldn't possibly have a good relationship. Sure, Brodyn and Cait were happy, but that was different. They were soulmates who'd found one another time and again in every lifetime. They were literally made for one another. Goodwin and Emilie? Not so much.

"Emilie..." Goodwin put out a hand to wipe her tears, but she smacked it away.

"Don't. You said what you needed to say, and so did I."

"I didn't—" she turned her head and walked away, but he grabbed her back.

"Stop pulling me back to you! You're not sorry about what you said. You're sorry that what you said hurt me. I'll get over it." Slipping the white tunic over her head, Emilie covered herself and wrapped her arms across her body, feeling lost and vulnerable in this small space. The rain still pattered outside, but it had slowed down, and Emilie needed fresh air.

"Where are ye going?" Goodwin shouted as he pulled on his trousers.

"Outside!"

Goodwin grabbed her hand and pulled her back. "Ye cannae. 'Tis raining."

"You know, it does rain in 2023. I won't melt."

"It's dangerous!"

Emilie turned around and poked a finger into his bare chest. "We are in the middle of nowhere, and I doubt there is anything more dangerous out there than in here because if I share space with you for one more minute, I can't be held responsible for my actions!"

Barefoot and scantily dressed, Emilie stomped off toward the loch and down the slippery slope. She figured there was no point in trying to remain dry or clean in this wretched place. At least she could get away from the man who tore her in a dozen directions. How she wished his words didn't cut so deeply, for they served to prove that her feelings for him were real despite her best efforts. But hopefully, with a little space and time to think, she could snap back to reality and come to terms with what had happened.

When Emilie stopped at the loch's shore, cold mud slid between her toes, and she panted, trying to collect herself. Her body shook, and she wasn't sure if it was from the cold or nerves, but Goodwin's words shook her, ruining any connection they shared.

Thunder clapped in the distance just as the ground began to vibrate and shake beneath her feet. Emilie frowned, looking around the terrain. What was happening? Did Scotland have earthquakes?

"Emilie!" Goodwin shouted her name just before pulling her down to the muddy ground, slapping a hand over her mouth as a party of horses and armed men rode past them. "'Tis Arwyn and his men," he whispered into her ears. "It appears they have left Pinnata Castra."

"Good, then we can go back," she whispered, staring down into a mud puddle as he lay atop her back.

"Aye but wait for them to pass. They are not known to be gentle with women."

"And this is the man Brodyn wished to marry Murielle to?"

"Nay, not really, but he wished to listen to the man and see if peace was achievable. Clearly, it isnae. I dinnae ken why they would be riding through here, though, when there is an easier path to take."

A cry drifted on the wind, and Emilie stiffened. It was the sound of an infant, and bile caught in her throat as she shoved Goodwin off her. "Do you hear that?" Emilie clamored to her feet, slipping in the mud before righting herself. "That's Lucas's cry! They have Lucas!"

"Ye cannae ken that," Goodwin said slowly, getting to his feet.

"Who else would it be? They stole the Pictish heir! They will kill him! Oh, my God!" Emilie spun around to look at Goodwin. "This is it! This is why I'm here! They are going to kill Lucas if I don't stop them!"

"Listen, Emilie… we dinnae ken any of this. We need to head back and see what happened after the fight in the corridor. If they took Lucas, Brodyn will have a score of men on their arses right now."

Emilie jerked out of his grip and looked at him, knowing what she had to do. "You can go back, but I'm going after them!" She took off running, waving her hands as she raced full speed toward the traveling group of men, shouting for their attention.

"Emilie!" She heard Goodwin shouting, but she needed to be seen and captured by Arwyn. It was the only way to get to Lucas.

"Hey! Over here!" she shouted as the last horse passed.

"Halt!" The man shouted. "'Tis a lass!"

Arwyn's army stopped, but Emilie kept running toward them, her mind blank of any consequences. She needed to save Lucas, and nothing else mattered.

Goodwin followed behind her, and she turned to glare at him. "Go away! You're going to get yourself killed!"

"I'd rather die than let them take you!"

"They have Lucas!"

"We will get him back, but not alone! We need help! They willnae just kill him. They will want an exchange!"

"I release you from your duty to me! I want to be captured! I need to be with Lucas to keep him safe!"

Arwyn turned his horse and slid off its back, then approached her with a smirk on his face and his sword in one hand. "Who are ye, lass? Why do ye wish to gain our attention?" His gaze shifted to Goodwin, and Arwyn narrowed his eyes. "Ah. If it isnae Brodyn's best warrior. I should run ye through right now. 'Twould send the message to Brodyn that we are willing to kill for our cause."

"I am Queen Caitriona's sister and Lucas's aunt! Give the baby to me!" She knew what she asked was impossible. Emilie was aware that she had sealed her fate. Arwyn would take her captive along with Lucas, but she felt no fear. Adrenaline kept her standing tall. This was her cause, and she knew it now beyond a shadow of a doubt. She only prayed the man had any honor and wouldn't kill an unarmed man. Or a woman and an infant. "Let Goodwin go. He is unarmed."

Arwyn gripped his sword's hilt in his hand with a white-knuckled grip, glaring at Goodwin before stepping closer to Emilie.

"What is yer relation to this man?" he asked slowly, and Emilie understood the motive. He wished to hurt Goodwin without killing him.

"He is my lover," she said without a quiver in her voice. It was the truth, after all.

"Ah." Arwyn rubbed his short dark beard and regarded Emilie. "I can see a bonnie woman beneath the filth." Quickly he grabbed her arm and pulled her to him. She gasped from the sudden move but wasn't surprised that he did it.

"Emilie!" Goodwin charged forward, stopping when Arwyn placed his blade against his chest, aimed at his heart. "Let her go!"

"Nay. I think not. One more step, and I shall take yer woman before I take yer life. Would ye care to watch me plow her?"

Goodwin narrowed his gaze and spat at Arwyn. "Emilie..." The desperation in his voice made Emilie feel sick to her stomach, but she had made her decision, and there was no going back.

"Goodwin, stop! Just go!" she cried.

"I willnae!" he roared, seemingly unaffected by the blade tip digging into his flesh as a small drop of blood ran down his bared chest.

Emilie switched to Latin, hoping this Briton king didn't understand her words. "You are no good to any of us dead. Don't be a fool. Go tell Brodyn that he has Lucas and me. That's the only way we will make it back."

"Why did ye sacrifice yerself?" he asked with pleading eyes.

"I needed to be with Lucas," she insisted. "Now I will be. Just as you must protect Brodyn and Murielle, I must protect Lucas."

"What have ye said to him?" Arwyn snarled, gripping her arm painfully.

"I told him to stand down!"

"Smart lass." Arwyn lowered his blade. "As much as I wish to end ye now, ye are no good to me dead. Go back to yer king. Tell him I have his heir and his wife's sister. Terms will be communicated soon."

Turning, Arwyn sheathed his sword and dragged Emilie over to his horse. She heard Goodwin shouting and cursing as Arwyn tossed her onto his horse, and she cast a look back at him, hoping he understood that she had to do this. Even more than Goodwin's need to protect Emilie, she needed to protect Lucas. Not just because she would cease to exist if he died, but because he was an innocent child caught up in the wars of men. Caitriona's child needed Auntie Emilie, and there was no way she was running away.

Arwyn wrapped his arm around her waist and urged his horse into a gallop, jostling Emilie as wind and rain slapped her in the face, carrying her away from Goodwin and toward a fate she couldn't even imagine.

CHAPTER SIX

R UNNING FULL SPEED up the hill to Brodyn's home, Goodwin burst through the door, making Murielle and Queen Caitriona jump with fright. Tears ran down their faces. Meanwhile, Brodyn shouted commands at Ronan and Lawrence, preparing an army to raid Gwynedd and get his son back.

"I will kill him! He is mine!" Brodyn roared.

"Not if I kill him first, my king."

Brodyn spun around to look at Goodwin. "Thank God ye and Emilie got out of here before Arwyn and his men broke down Murielle's door. They took Lucas!"

"I ken they did. Now they also have Emilie."

Caitriona gasped and jumped out of her seat. "What? How?"

"I thought ye were safe in that cabin in the woods," Murielle said, turning white.

"We were. But, Emilie saw Arwyn's men as they rode by the loch. She heard the infant's cry, and she took off after them. Somehow, she knew it was Lucas."

"Ye let them take Emilie?" Brodyn demanded as his wife clung to his side and sobbed into his tunic.

"Nay, my king. I tried to stop her, but the lass allowed them to take her. She verra intentionally got herself captured so she could stay by Lucas. She believes she was sent here for this purpose. I ran here as fast as I could but had to take the long trail back."

Caitriona wailed, "We need to get them back!"

"We will, love." Brodyn did his best to calm his inconsolable wife, without success. She shook, gasping for breath.

"Murielle, please take Cait upstairs. She needs rest," Brodyn said to his sister.

"What I need is my son and best friend back!" she shot back.

"Emilie told Arwyn she is yer sister." Goodwin ran a hand through his hair. "I failed! I had one task, and I failed!" He began to pace. He wanted to run, to go after Arwyn, and get Emilie and Lucas back safely, but he had no choice but to wait for Brodyn's command. It was maddening. Every fiber in his body urged him to go rescue them.

"Nay, Goodwin," Cait said as she shook her head and wiped away tears. "Emilie does what Emilie does, with or without anyone else's permission. She sacrificed herself to be closer to Lucas. There was no changing her mind. I don't need to have been there to know this."

"Nay, there wasnae persuading her. Arwyn could have killed me, but he left me alive to warn ye that he will be ransoming them and sending terms." Goodwin left out his gut-gripping fear that Arwyn meant to harm Lucas even if he did receive a ransom. The man was unhinged and sought revenge for what he believed was a direct cut to his pride. Would he stoop to killing an innocent child in the name of vengeance? He didn't doubt it.

"I willnae be awaiting his terms. We leave now. Ye saw which way they traveled?"

"Aye," Goodwin said to Brodyn. "They traveled through the forest and past the loch to the south, near the cabin. I cannae shake the feeling that this was planned. Could they have kenned about the escape tunnel in Murielle's chamber and where it led? The odds of them traveling past the cabin, where no trail exists, feels contrived."

"If this is true, we have a traitor in our midst, but I cannae entertain such a notion without proof. My efforts must remain on getting Lucas and Emilie back," Brodyn said as he paced. "After the fight in the corridor, I commanded Arwyn to pack up and leave. I still dinnae ken how he got ahold of Lucas in the chaos. I had men guarding him and his nursemaid. We need to head out now! Ronin, gather the men at the stables. We will follow their trail. 'Tis a long journey south to his lands. We must catch them before they enter their gates, or we will have a greater battle on our hands."

Ronin nodded and ran out of the house, leaving the door swinging behind him. Slanting rain entered the home, and the wind howled a lamenting tune. The cursed storm wasn't going to relent, but neither would Goodwin. He and Lawrence followed Ronin, shouting as they ran through the village to round up the troops. "Grab yer swords and mount a horse. We have no time for supplies or rations!" Goodwin yelled as he headed toward the stables.

Villagers gathered around, huddling beneath awnings to watch as the king's men assembled. When Brodyn reached his side, Goodwin grabbed Boudicca's reins and saddled her for the journey. "There is more I should tell ye, my king," Goodwin said as he led his horse out of her stall. "Emilie was wearing naught but a man's tunic when she was taken. I fear for her safety and her virtue."

Brodyn readied his horse, Tatha, and listened without looking at Goodwin. "Is there a reason the lass was only wearing yer tunic?"

"Aye." Goodwin didn't wish to share his intimate details with Brodyn, but he knew his friend would come to his own conclusion. "We need to get to them both as quickly as possible. I would have followed, but only I kenned which direction they traveled."

Brodyn nodded and turned to look at him. "Then we will travel through the night to make up for the lost time. They will have to stop eventually. When they do, we shall slaughter them all. No prisoners."

Goodwin nodded and began to mount Boudicca when he felt Brodyn's hand on his shoulder. "Ye ken ye cannae fall in love with Emilie. She won't be here after this situation is resolved."

"I have never loved a woman and dinnae plan on loving one now."

"Not even Murielle?"

Goodwin looked at Brodyn and scowled. "I am not in love with Murielle! I was her guard for many years and nothing more! Whatever ye have contrived in yer mind is yer own doing. As ye are a brother to me, she is my sister."

Brodyn nodded. "Verra well. I shall never ask again. 'Tis surprising is all. I always awaited the day ye declared yerself." He mounted his horse and trotted toward the gates with Goodwin at his side and scores of men in his wake as women cried and huddled together, praying their men returned.

"And if I had? She must marry a king. Why else have kings been visiting so often?"

"If ye had, I'd have arranged yer marriage within a sennight. Ye think I wouldnae wish my sister to marry my best friend? Not only would she remain within the village, but she'd be with a man I trusted beyond measure. 'Tis why I've prolonged this decision for so long. I thought seeing men come to court her would finally break yer silence."

Goodwin regarded his friend, honored that he'd have him marry his sister, yet surprised he thought Goodwin wished for the same. "She is beautiful, and everyone kens it. But to me, she was always just Murielle, my best friend's stubborn sister, whom yer father commanded I guard."

"So, what of Emilie?"

"What of her? As ye said, she is leaving soon. We had but a moment."

Brodyn nodded and remained silent as the gates opened, and he urged his horse forward, to race down the hill at full speed while his men followed.

Goodwin and Brodyn veered away from the main trail and pushed through the forest. It required the horses to move at a slower pace but also cut several miles off their journey. Having better knowledge of the local land than Arwyn would benefit them greatly. But for now, all they could do was ride and focus on the task.

When the men finally stopped hours later to rest and water the horses, Brodyn dismounted Tatha and looked at his men. "Ye have time to piss and eat, then we continue."

Goodwin itched to continue immediately. Every moment was precious. Dusk approached, and soon darkness would prevail, but they needed to keep riding as long as possible. But it would do no good to run his mare into exhaustion and possibly lameness. Besides, Arwyn and his men would need to rest their mounts as well. He perused the landscape, looking for signs of their passing. Through the dappled shadows of the trees, he spotted a ray of sunlight reflecting off what appeared to be golden hair. Goodwin squinted and moved forward with his hand on his sword's hilt. As he drew closer to the poorly hidden spy behind the towering oak tree, he had no doubt who it was.

"Murielle?" Goodwin barked, his temper flaring. "Ye followed us? Ye careless, impetuous lass!"

But then Queen Caitriona's horse stepped from behind another tree. The queen speared him with an imperious gaze, holding her head high. "Careful, Goodwin. If she is impetuous, what does that make me?"

"Cait!" Brodyn stormed forward so quickly, Caitriona's horse shied, but she kept her seat and her control. The king grabbed at the beast's reins. "Ye shouldnae be here!"

"And why not? I have every right to be here! My son and best friend are in danger, and I couldn't just stay behind and pace while you do all the work!"

"And now, ye and Murielle are in danger! Did ye learn anything about Anya's warning? Until the threat is distinguished, ye were to remain guarded! Now, all four of ye are in danger!" Brodyn roared.

"Dinnae shout at yer wife, Brodyn!" Murielle scolded, hopping off her horse to battle her brother. "We are guarded. I think we are safe enough here among yer finest men, aye?" She raised a brow, challenging him as always, and Goodwin watched as Brodyn's face turned red with rage.

"Ye could have asked me rather than sneaking after us!"

"Ye would have said no!" she shot back.

"Aye, I would have, because this is the height of folly!"

"Husband," Caitriona said calmly. "We will not be in your way, I promise. And if you find Arwyn's party, we will remain hidden. You didn't notice us until now. We can be quite elusive. But you know very well I cannot stay behind while Lucas and Emilie are in danger. I would go insane. Already, I am insane with fear. Allow me to help rescue those who matter most to me. Give me that."

Goodwin bit back a smile as he watched how easily Queen Caitriona soothed the beast within Brodyn. His fists unclenched, his jaw slackened, and his eyes softened. Is that what love did to a man? If so, Goodwin was better off alone without outside influences impeding his life.

But as he thought of the effects of a woman's love, Emilie's face floated through his mind, and his heart raced as images of her laying beneath him, clawing at his back while she arched and moaned, her perfect breasts bouncing with every thrust, made Goodwin swallow. He closed his eyes, fighting off what he knew was more than just lust.

"Did ye hear me, Goodwin?"

Shaking his head, Goodwin looked at Brodyn. "Did ye say something?"

"Aye, I asked ye to stay in the back of the train with my unruly wife and sister."

Murielle shot him a smug grin before sticking her tongue out, and he narrowed his eyes in response. The wee wench always got her way, and Goodwin was always left to clean up her mess.

"As ye wish," Goodwin said to his king as the men mounted up again, prepared to continue their search.

"This is an exercise in endurance," Brodyn shouted to his men… and the two women. "Arwyn will ken we are coming for him. He left Goodwin alive to relay the message, but he always kenned I wouldnae remain home and await his word. Therefore, I suspect he willnae be resting until his horses cannae go any farther. So now we see who has more perseverance and strength of will—The Picts, or the Britons. Who will it be?"

"The Picts!" his men roared, raising swords as they bolstered their morale.

"Hell hath no fury like a mother scorned," Caitriona shouted, and the men cheered at her, making Brodyn shine with pride for his wife despite his best efforts to remain stern.

Goodwin looked at Murielle and scowled as he rode between her and Cait. "Ye better behave and listen to commands, or I vow I will leave ye to the wolves."

"I would have those wolves following in my wake by night's end," she said without irony, and Goodwin knew it to be true.

"I suppose ye have the world at yer command, dinnae ye?" Goodwin said wryly as they continued their journey. Caitriona listened but remained silent; likely too many thoughts raced through her mind for her to participate in idle conversation. Inwardly, Goodwin struggled to remain calm, as well. Horrible thoughts scrolled through his mind, but he knew that remaining stoic was not only part of his training. It was necessary to keep Queen Caitriona from going into hysterics.

"Everyone but ye," Murielle said with a raised brow. "I never could win ye over."

"Yet everyone still believes I'm in love with ye."

Murielle scoffed and waved it away. "People will believe whatever they wish. It makes a good story for the king's sister and best friend to be in love, I suppose."

"Aye, but none of them ken how truly awful ye are," he said with a proud grin, which to his surprise, made Caitriona chuckle before worry creased her tense features once more. A mother's love was endless, and Lucas was fortunate to have a mother willing to risk everything to get him back. "Even Emilie believed I was in love with ye."

"Perhaps it was when I touched yer arm at the longhouse after she arrived. Ye cradled her in yer arms, but it felt like much more than a guard caring for his charge. I suppose I wished to test her, to see if she noticed or cared."

Goodwin gave Murielle a side glance before looking straight on again, not wanting to reveal too much to her. "I dinnae think she cared."

"Yet she mentioned me to ye. That's all I need to ken."

"What does that mean?" Goodwin asked, shrugging his shoulders.

"If Emilie asked about Murielle, then she's interested," Queen Caitriona interjected. "She has enough going on in her life. It must have mattered to her if it remained on the surface of her mind."

"The lass has only kenned me for two days. Ye women lead too much with yer heart, always trying to find a romance story where one doesnae exist."

"Two days in someone's constant presence is enough to create feelings, Goodwin," Murielle said. "Especially under duress. Ye bond much quicker when it's life or death. Ask Caitriona."

"Ugh!" Cait said but nodded. "It's true. I was in love with Brodyn within two days of meeting him."

Goodwin silently listened, wondering if it was true. Did Emilie have feelings for him that she refused to acknowledge? Did he have feelings that he refused to admit to himself? After insulting her in a most horrifying way, he doubted Emilie would want anything to do with him, and he couldn't blame her. He'd meant to be hurtful, but he regretted the words immediately upon speaking them.

After their intense physical connection, Goodwin thought things were shifting between them until she said otherwise. He had lashed out defensively, and now he regretted it more than anything else in his lifetime.

Night crept up on the travel party, making it impossible to

follow tracks or signs of Arwyn. Their best hope was to continue south through the trees and look for the glow of campfires in the area, but Arwyn wasn't foolish enough to set up a camp unless forced to.

The horses slowed as they grew hungry and tired, and Brodyn signaled for the party to stop. "We cannae push these beasts any further without harming them. There is a stream just down this hill," Brodyn pointed into the distance, but Goodwin saw only dark branches illuminated by the moon's dim glow. "Water the horses and yerselves. Then, we need a new strategy."

Goodwin hopped off his horse before helping the women down. "We can split up. Some of us will stay back at camp while some continue on foot, searching the area. We will see track marks better with our feet on the ground."

"Agreed," Brodyn said with a nod. "Those who stay at camp will rest with the horses for a few hours. If we return without Lucas and Emilie, the rested half will head out. By dawn, we continue ahead if we havenae located them."

Goodwin nodded and helped divide the camp into two groups, ensuring the women stayed behind to rest despite their resistance.

Brodyn and Goodwin would lead both groups. Neither man would get any rest until Lucas and Emilie were found. With a score of men prepared to search the forest, Goodwin unsheathed his sword and gripped it tightly at his side. There was no way to know where Arwyn was or what he was thinking, but if Lucas and Emilie weren't in perfect condition when Goodwin found them, he wouldn't hesitate to gut the King of Britons.

"Someone make this bairn shut up!" Arwyn roared when the travel party was forced to stop for the night. He'd pushed their horses to their brink, but one broke a leg and had to be slaughtered, and the others were too exhausted and dehydrated to continue. His men didn't appear in better condition as one slid from his saddle and injured his head on a rock.

Emilie rocked Lucas in her arms and glared at Arwyn. "You stole him from his mother! He's hungry and scared!"

"Then feed the brat!" Arwyn snapped, pacing in the clearing.

"With what, exactly? He is a bairn! He needs his mother!"

"He will get his mother back as soon as I have the wife I was promised!"

Emilie cradled Lucas to her chest and spun in a circle, looking at the surrounding forest. Aside from dim moonlight filtering through the trees, darkness prevailed as animals scurried and leaves rustled in the wind. If only she could find her way out of here, but only wilderness surrounded them in either direction. She shivered in her tunic but dared not complain and draw attention to her sheer clothing. Lucas created a decent barrier for now as she cradled him against her chest.

"My king," one man said as he walked over. "We need food and a fire. The men cannae continue at this pace without nourishment and warmth."

"We cannae build a fire! It will give us away."

"Nobody is around us for miles in any direction, my king. I can go into the forest and hunt, but we require fire to cook the food. None of us have food stores, for we didnae expect to flee from Pinnata Castra with an infant."

Arwyn glared at his man and stepped closer with his hand on his hilt. "Are ye questioning my leadership, Carrick?"

"Nay, my king. But the truth remains that we need to eat, or we are doomed. The journey back to Gwynedd is too far to make at this pace without resources."

Arwyn growled and cursed under his breath. "Fine. Build a fire. Find some food, and shut this bairn up, or I shall do so myself!"

Emilie took a deep breath and looked at Lucas, whose face turned red as he screamed and flailed beneath his blanket. Panic set in. What was she to do? The answer was clear. She had to do absolutely anything to get Lucas back to Caitriona by morning, or the child would not survive without nourishment and warmth.

"King Arwyn," Emilie said, bouncing Lucas in her arms. "The child needs to be changed. Might you escort me to the stream down the hill so I can clean him off before he gets a rash? It may stop his crying."

"Ye had better not be tricking me, lass!"

"You can smell his backside yourself if you wish."

Arwyn curled his lip with disgust. "Let's get on with it."

Taking Emilie by the arm, he led her to the stream. "Ye want to get this obnoxious brat back to his mother, aye?"

Emilie's skin crawled when he touched her. He wasn't old or even ugly, but his soul was dark, and evil radiated off his being.

Her mind raced with ideas, but only one continued to make sense, even if it made her stomach churn to consider. "Of course, I do. I will do anything."

"Anything?" he asked, raising a brow at her.

Her mind wandered to Goodwin, remembering the intimate moments they shared, how natural it felt to be in his presence, how instinctively they came together like two parts of a whole. If only he hadn't used her for her body. Their connection had felt so real, but she supposed a man like him radiated passion with every woman he bedded. Emilie was simply the last notch on his bedpost. Anger and hurt flared in her gut, though she couldn't understand why she cared so much, especially now.

Still, she had enjoyed their lovemaking and knew she had to return to her own time. So, why did Goodwin, a man she hardly knew, occupy her thoughts and, as much as she regretted to admit it, her heart?

"Yes. Anything." Lucas began to wail again, and Arwyn cringed, grinding his teeth.

"I ought to drown that wee beast here and now!"

"You don't like bairns? As a king, don't you need to have an heir?"

"I like bairns enough when I can send them away."

She wanted to remind him that he stole this child from his mother, and any wailing Lucas did was directly Arwyn's fault, but she saw no benefit in this. Instead, Emilie removed Lucas's swaddle to access his soaked linens. The poor child had been sitting in his own filth for hours, and she bit back all the foul words she wished to throw at Arwyn. "It's all right, Lucas. Auntie will take care of you," she whispered, wading into the stream. Still, all she wore was the thin linen tunic Goodwin gave her and nothing more. She had run off without her shoes when she heard Lucas's cry, and her feet still pained her from the day before. But the cool water washed away the mud creeping up her legs and soothed the sores on her feet.

Kneeling into the water, Emilie dunked Lucas's lower body in the running stream, allowing it to clean him. He shook and cried from the cold, but there was no other choice. How else could she clean him up without any supplies? Once his rear was clean, Emilie walked over to Arwyn and held Lucas before him. "Take him for a moment."

"What? Nay!"

"I need to wrap him up again!" She handed Lucas to the hesitant king, who scowled and looked away as Lucas dangled awkwardly in his hands. Yanking at her tunic's sleeve, she heard the fabric rend as she pulled, hoping it was enough to use as a diaper. The sleeve was still mostly dry and her only option.

As Lucas kicked his chubby legs in the air, Emilie wrapped the fabric around him and tied it into a knot before taking him away from Arwyn and re-swaddling him. Arwyn looked at her with interest, and she hoped his mind was wandering where she wanted it to.

While they traveled, Emilie had been thinking of ways to appease Arwyn and safely return Lucas to Cait. Several ideas of escape had also run through her head, all falling flat when she realized there was no way she could outrun his men, especially with injured feet and while carrying a screaming child. However, one plan had occurred to her that could work, but it required Arwyn to make the first move. It was a plan she never thought she'd consider, but Lucas's life depended on it.

"Ye are good with bairns."

"I treat them like humans," she responded wryly.

He shrugged away her ridiculous notion that babies deserved respect and scrolled her body with interest. "Until now, I havenae truly seen ye. Ye are a bonnie woman." He rubbed his short beard and nodded his head. "Aye, I believe ye will do."

"Do? Do for what?"

"Ye and yer sister are from Dal Riata, nieces to the king there, aye?"

She nodded, having no idea what he meant, but she assumed Caitriona had told everyone she was a Scot from Dal Riata when she arrived.

"Ye are just as royal as yer sister."

"I suppose so…" Emilie acted as if she didn't know what he was thinking, but in fact, this was precisely what she hoped for.

"If yer Scots sister can become Queen of the Picts, ye can become Queen of the Britons. What say ye? I need a wife from another tribe to secure peace. Ye will secure peace with both the Scots and Picts."

"Peace cannot be achieved as long as you hold the Pictish heir hostage," Emilie reminded him.

"As I said—once I have the bride I traveled here for, I have no need for the bairn. I meant to ransom ye both, but now I believe I have a better plan."

"Oh?" Emilie raised a brow and held her breath, awaiting the words she expected to hear.

"Ye are just as bonnie as the king's sister. Aye, I do believe ye would make me a fine bride. I see ye would do well with the bairns, and Brodyn and I can put this all behind us."

Lucas's crying slowed as he began to doze off, which only worried Emilie. He weakened by the moment, losing his will to fight. Time was a luxury she didn't have.

"If I agree to marry you, you will help me get Lucas back to my sister tonight?"

"You make demands to a king?" Arwyn asked, running his knuckles down her cheek as he stepped closer. "Ye are a bold woman. I like that trait. But do tread cautiously. Wife or nay, I take no orders from yer sex."

Typical medieval asshole, she thought but kept her features still. "Marrying me will do you no good if anything happens to this child. Brodyn and Caitriona will never accept peace. Only war will follow. You said you would return Lucas if you had your royal wife. I'll agree to marry you, but you must first return Lucas."

Arwyn laughed and looked up at the sky. She did the same, seeing the stars twinkling high above. The North Star glowed brightly, a beacon reminding her how to return to Burghead. If she could find a way out of here, perhaps she could guide herself back to the village. Barefoot or not, half-naked or not, she had to try.

"Ye think I will deliver him before I marry ye? Och, nay… ye marry me here and now before my men, then we shall discuss his return."

Emilie licked her lips nervously, wondering what it was about these kings who married women without even knowing them. Brodyn rushed Caitriona to the alter, and now Arwyn did the same. If only he knew she was a tour guide from the year 2023. Any royal blood in her veins was diluted by several generations. She'd never known her parents, but most assuredly, they were not royalty.

"Fine. Let's get married," Emilie said, forcing a seductive smile. There was no harm in pretending to be intrigued. Wouldn't most women from this time want to become queen? Emilie could marry Arwyn, have him deliver Lucas back, then she could safely return to her time. She wasn't sure how Arwyn would behave when she disappeared, but that was something to deal with later. Once he was back on his own lands, he would never be allowed through Pinnata Castra's gates again, and Lucas, Cait, and Murielle would be safe from harm. Then, Emilie could leave, even if part of her preferred to stay.

Her short time with Goodwin flashed through her mind, images of them laughing, kissing, making love. She wondered where he was right now and if he was looking for them beneath these same stars. Knowing Goodwin, he was on the hunt right now, which made Emilie feel slightly better. One way or another, she would escape this man before ever reaching his lands where she would be trapped. But for now, she had no choice but to marry this foul human to save Lucas.

Smiling at her, Arwyn led her back to their camp, where he gathered his men around, holding her to his side. "Men, this beautiful woman is the royal niece of the Scots king, Domnall, and the sister to the Pictish Queen, Caitriona. She has agreed to marry me on this night to solidify peace with The Picts. In exchange, we will return Lucas to his mother."

The men nodded and stood around, shifting their feet as if they really didn't care what happened to the innocent child one way or another. Emilie listened, wondering how Arwyn could be obtuse enough to believe Brodyn would forgive his son's kidnapping and agree to peace, but she wasn't going to point out his ridiculous lack of human understanding.

"Ye will all stand as our witnesses as we handfast here and now. Carrick!" he shouted at the man who appeared to be his best warrior. "Cut a strip of linen off yer tunic! We need the binds for the ceremony."

"Aye, my king." Carrick pulled out a knife from his boot and, without hesitation, removed his tunic, baring a barreled chest covered in a thick pelt of dark fur. The man was undoubtedly half beast and didn't require his tunic to stay warm out here. Cutting a strip of linen from the bottom of his long tunic, Carrick passed it to his king, who gripped the dingy fabric in his hand. This had to be the grossest handfasting ceremony ever, but it only added to Emilie's determination to get as far away from these men as possible, as soon as possible.

Arwyn roughly gripped Emilie's injured wrist with his dirty, callused palm and draped the torn linen across them, making her hiss in pain. "Ye're ready to become a queen?" he asked with a raised brow and salacious grin. Emilie swallowed her bile and prayed this man wouldn't expect her to consummate the marriage immediately.

"I am ready." She shifted Lucas with her free hand and propped him onto her hip, reminding herself she did this for him.

"I, Arwyn ap Rhys, King of the Britons, take ye Emilie..." Arwyn paused and looked at her, making her roll her eyes with annoyance.

"Wilshire," she murmured.

"Emilie Wilshire to be my wife and Queen of the Britons." He wrapped the linen around their clasped wrists once.

Taking a deep breath, Emilie closed her eyes and said her vows. "I, Emilie Wilshire, take Arwyn ap Rhys, King of the Britons, to be my husband." Arwyn wrapped the linen around their wrists a second time.

"We are now bound together as husband and wife, and ye will be obedient."

Emilie never agreed to such nonsense, but she expected nothing less from a king during this time. There were still men in 2023 who expected obedience from a wife. Instead, she remained silent and allowed him to boast to his men that he came for the fairest lass in Pictland as his wife and found her. She also decided not to comment that he came for Murielle and was rejected. It would do no good to insult her new husband, but Emilie was determined to have the quickest divorce in history as soon as Lucas was safe.

Without warning, Arwyn pulled her to him and pressed his lips to hers, slithering his tongue into her mouth like a snake, and she pulled back in disgust but kept her features straight.

"Behold yer queen!" he shouted to his men, who clapped and cheered for their king. Lucas awoke and began to wail, making Arwyn scowl again.

"Shut that bairn up!" he roared. Married two minutes and already he shouted at her. This wasn't going to be a happy union.

"Good news for you, then. We can deliver Lucas back to his parents now that you have your queen."

Arwyn scoffed and snickered. "We will. Eventually." He began to walk away, but Emilie grabbed his sleeve, daring to pull him back.

"You promised."

"I promised I would return the brat. I never promised when. I will ransom him when we return to Gwynedd. If his parents want him back, they shall pay a price. It cost me much to leave my lands and travel here for a wife, yet they threw me out and made me a fool! Now, who's the fool?"

Anger and panic threatened to overpower her outward calmness, and Emilie clenched her fists. "He will die before making it back to your village! He needs nourishment that I cannot offer!"

"Then he will die, and I will still ransom him. His parents will pay to receive his body back."

Emilie wished to spew all manner of vile insults in his face, but she knew better and bit her lip. Lucas's survival solely rested in her hands now, and she had to play the obedient wife if she hoped to escape before they traveled further south.

Looking up at the stars again, Emilie easily found the North Star shining brighter than the rest, winking at her like a conspirator plotting her escape. She may not know where she was, but Pinnata Castra was on the north coast. If she could break away and follow the North Star, it would at least lead her in the correct direction.

"I'm going to get us out of here, Lucas," she whispered into the baby's ear as he squirmed and cried. "No matter what."

CHAPTER SEVEN

A S THE NIGHT wore on, Lucas grew quiet and lethargic, a detail that greatly pleased Arwyn but worried Emilie until her stomach ached, and panic gripped her. Men snored all around, littering the forest floor with their belongings.

Arwyn kept busy most of the night, planning with his men and helping them hunt, but finding a moment to run off was impossible. Emilie was surrounded. Finding a spot on the forest floor, Emilie used Arwyn's cloak to lay on, bundling Lucas close to her. By the time Arwyn had come to lay beside her, Lucas was asleep, and Emilie did her best to appear unconscious despite his attempts to wake her. If he couldn't wake her, he couldn't bed her.

Fortunately, Arwyn rolled the other way and soon fell asleep, his rhythmic snores working in Emilie's favor. After staring at the back of her eyelids for hours, Emilie dared to crack one open and lift her head. Lucas shifted beside her as she looked around the campsite. The fire still burned but would die out soon. She needed what little light it offered if she was to escape the camp without notice.

Perhaps Arwyn didn't expect her to run since they were in the middle of nowhere, or maybe he thought her too interested in being a queen, but he knew nothing about her, which furthered her cause. She wasn't like women from this time. She didn't require a husband, nor was she obedient. Her only goal was to get out of here and back to Caitriona.

Gently, Emilie picked up Lucas and cradled his swaddled body close to hers, relieved to feel tiny breaths escaping his sweet, puckered lips. He rooted in his sleep, and Emilie dearly wished she had milk to offer him. How long could a small child of only six months live without milk? She wasn't sure, but time was running out.

Taking a step, Emilie cringed when a twig snapped beneath her bare foot. She sucked in a breath and held it as she looked down at Arwyn, slowly exhaling when he didn't move. If Emilie could make it down the hill and to the stream, she could follow that north and be long gone before sunrise.

Taking another step, then another, Emilie gasped when Arwyn reached out and grabbed her ankle. "Where are ye going?"

"L-Lucas needs to be changed again, and I have to… urinate," Emilie stuttered. "If I don't change him, he will get a rash."

"Why do I care if the brat has a rash?" he hissed, still half asleep.

"He will cry more if he is in pain," she calmly reasoned, wishing she could kick Arwyn in the head for his callous behavior toward Lucas.

Arwyn released her ankle and rolled back over. "Go. Relieve yerself and change the bairn, but ye had better return soon or I'm coming after ye."

Silently, Emilie nodded, though she didn't know what "soon" actually meant, for minutes didn't yet exist at this point in history. Taking a relieved breath, she freely walked toward the water with Lucas. Her heart rate sped up faster than a revved engine, and she struggled to control her breath as anxiety kicked in. She had five minutes to get as far away as possible. If Arwyn found her and dragged her back, there was no telling what he would do to both of them. Lucas's life and her very existence hinged on the next five minutes. Her feet throbbed with every step, and she winced, hissing when small pebbles rubbed against her raw soles. Reaching the stream's shoreline, Emilie took one more fortifying breath and bolted. Adrenaline ran through her veins, numbing her pain as she focused only on crossing the stream and running along its length so she wouldn't leave track marks. She knew they would find her if she left a trail, seasoned hunters that they were.

Water splashed up her legs as she ran, holding Lucas close to her body. The North Star twinkled brightly overhead, the only thing guiding Emilie through the darkness. Moments passed in eerie silence as she fled past large boulders and trees that grew out of the water, praying she didn't trip on a root and send Lucas flying through the air.

When shouting voices stirred the night air, Emilie looked behind her with terror in her heart. Nobody was on her tail, but they would be soon. Cutting across the stream, Emilie felt mud sliding beneath her feet and slowing her steps, but she continued to push through. She knew that finding shelter meant leaving the wide-open stream and heading into the forest, which would create a trail. She only hoped she had made it far enough down the stream that Arwyn and his men looked closer to camp.

Emilie lifted Lucas overhead as she pushed through shrubs, gulping for breath, feeling her tunic rip as she ran. Hopefully, the lush layer of leaves coating the forest floor would cover her tracks better than the muddy shoreline had. Finding an area with towering oak trees, Emilie hid behind a thick trunk that was wider than she was, bending over to catch her breath. Lucas opened his eyes and began to wail, making Emilie panic as she looked around for any sign of Arwyn.

When someone grabbed her from behind and slapped a hand across her mouth, Emilie yelped and let out a muffled scream. With adrenaline running through her veins as she fought for her and Lucas's life, Emilie threw an elbow back and landed a gut blow to her assailant. She heard the man groan, but he didn't relent his grip.

"Em, it's me. Stay still." Emilie stiffened but didn't move, recognizing the voice. *Goodwin!*

When he removed his hand, she turned to see Goodwin staring down at her with concern in his blue eyes. Her heart pounded anew, not with the stress of her run through the forest but with relief and something she didn't dare name even now. "Goodwin?"

"Are ye and Lucas all right? I cannae believe I found ye."

Emotion lodged in her throat, and tears slid down her cheeks as relief washed over her body. "Oh, thank God!" She slid her free hand around his waist and buried her face into his chest as a deluge of tears broke free. "I was so scared," she sobbed and shook as he clung to her. "Lucas... he needs his mother. He's not strong enough... I'm so worried about him!"

"Let's go." Goodwin took her hand and guided her through the brush with the ease of a trained hunter. "Arwyn will be looking for ye."

"You have no idea," she whispered as she followed his lead. So overcome with relief was Emilie that Goodwin's parting words to her no longer stung. She was only grateful it was Goodwin who found her and not Arwyn. He looked back at her and creased his brow at her cryptic words but didn't ask questions.

"We've been out searching for ye in groups, but I haven't stopped. Nor has Brodyn. He will be beside himself by now."

"I did everything I could to keep him safe, but... but I'm not his mother. I can't feed him," she cried. "He's so weak."

Goodwin stopped and turned to look at her. The dirt streaks mixed with sweat on his skin and his red-rimmed eyes spoke of a man who had been through hell to find them, and she wanted to cling to him and never let him go. Never had she felt so safe in a man's presence. Only Samuel had ever made Emilie feel entirely safe, but their connection was that of a professor and mentor. With Goodwin, her heart raced, and her stomach fluttered even when she was in peril.

"Emilie, ye saved Lucas. We wandered these woods for hours without finding Arwyn's men. I was about to give up hope when I heard an infant's cry. If ye hadnae risked yer life to go with Lucas, he'd still be in Arwyn's clutches and wouldnae survive the journey south. Ye single-handedly saved him. Yer a hero."

She shook her head and swiped away the tears blurring her vision. "I'm no such thing. Anyone would do the same."

"That's where yer wrong, lass."

"You do know that if he dies, I die too, right? Doesn't that make my motive to save him selfish?" she asked, knowing that she would have done everything exactly the same even if Lucas wasn't her ancestor.

"Nay. I ken ye better than that."

Goodwin began to drag them through the woods again, but Emilie stumbled and hissed in pain. "Are ye injured?"

"My feet," she whispered, trying to suck up the pain.

Goodwin looked down at her torn tunic sleeve and bare feet, scowling. "Did he violate ye? Tell me right now. I will gut the man!"

"No, he didn't touch me. I had to cut my tunic sleeve off to make a new nappy for Lucas. But my feet are torn up."

Frowning, Goodwin scooped Emilie into his arms and resumed pushing through the trees while she clung to Lucas. Usually, Emilie would protest against the help, wanting to be strong and independent, but now that her feet dangled as he walked, her pain subsided. Also, she just really enjoyed being in Goodwin's arms, even if evil men were after them.

"Our camp is a half mile in this direction," Goodwin said. "Caitriona is there. Lucas will be fed verra soon."

"Cait came with you? It's a good thing you found me. I was heading toward the village, and Lucas needs her."

"She and Murielle followed us. Brodyn was furious, but there was nothing to be done by the time we discovered them."

Time passed as they silently pushed forward without signs of danger, and Emilie prayed she had seen the last of Arwyn. Should she tell Goodwin that she was technically the Queen of the Britons, or could she somehow avoid that topic? After all, it was the only way to convince Arwyn to return Lucas, and she wouldn't be here long enough to see him again.

It had been well over a day since she last slept, and being in Goodwin's arms made her drowsy, but she resisted sleep's pull, afraid of dropping Lucas. Fortunately, half a mile of travel went quickly, and soon their camp came into sight.

"Em?" Cait ran over to Emilie and took Lucas in her arms as she began to sob. "Oh, God! Thank you, thank you… you saved my baby!" Caitriona bundled Lucas to her bosom before looking up at Emilie with relief in her reddened eyes. "What you did was so stupid, Em! You could have been killed! But you saved Lucas, and I can never repay you."

Gently, Goodwin placed Emilie down, allowing her to grip his sleeve to keep her balance. "I did more stupid things than just run after him," Emilie said. "But I would do it all over again. He's worth any sacrifice. He's also starving. You should feed him right away. Oh, my missing tunic sleeve is wrapped around his little butt, probably covered in poop."

Goodwin looked at her oddly, probably wondering what poop was, but she decided that didn't need explaining. Meanwhile, Murielle hugged Emilie with an unexpected strength for her small frame.

"I'm verra glad ye are all right, Emilie. Arwyn didnae hurt ye, did he? Ye appear pained."

Emilie pointed to her feet. "I ran off barefoot when I saw Arwyn's party riding away with Lucas. There was no time to change. I just went after him."

Murielle pursed her lips and looked from Goodwin to Emilie. "Ye were outside wearing only this tunic?" Murielle looked shrewdly at Goodwin. "Were ye at the cabin?"

"Aye, but that isnae the important thing right now," Goodwin said, deflecting Murielle's line of questioning. "Lucas is safe, but Brodyn and half the men are still out there. We separated to cover more distance. I need a few men to head out and gather the others. Let them ken that Lucas and Emilie are back at camp. The sooner they return and we all head home, the better for everyone." Walking over to Boudicca, Goodwin rummaged through a large leather satchel and pulled out his cloak.

Walking over to Emilie again, he placed it on her shoulders, and she eagerly nuzzled into its warmth. The wool smelled like him, and she cursed her fluttered heart for reacting to his scent. "Thank you," she murmured, avoiding Murielle's suspicious gaze.

Ronan gathered three other men, who jumped onto horses and forged into the woods to retrieve their king with haste.

"Ye said ye did more than one stupid thing," Murielle said, standing beside Emilie as Goodwin handed her an oatcake. Emilie took a bite, not realizing just how hungry she was until it touched her lips, but she fought the urge to shovel it into her mouth like a Neanderthal.

"I had to do what was needed to keep Lucas safe," Emilie said between bites.

"Care to elaborate?" Goodwin asked, raising his brow.

She shook her head and took another bite. "Not really. Not now." She'd have to tell them eventually, but in the end, the marriage didn't matter nor would it ever be recorded in the pages of history. She'd be home soon, and Arwyn would be dust. "I'm just glad we made it back. I want to go home." At that moment, when Emilie thought of home, she realized it wasn't her Edinburgh flat she imagined. And it wasn't just Pinnata Castra that she envisioned, either. Home looked like Goodwin's modest space, sharing his bed, tangled up in the sheets with him at night. What a ridiculous thought. The last words he said to her before this ordeal was that he only wanted sex from her. Though she couldn't possibly be angry with him after he saved her life, remembering his words still stung but also kept her grounded in reality. No matter what her mind envisioned as home, Goodwin would never be the man she shared it with.

"Well, 'tis good to have ye back, Emilie," Murielle said with a smile, taking her hand and squeezing it before walking away.

Alone with Goodwin, Emilie wasn't sure what more to say, and she didn't want to rehash her marriage details, so instead, she yawned and stretched. "I should lay down while the others gather

Brodyn and his men. I haven't slept since before... before we..."

Goodwin looked at her then, his piercing amber eyes landing on hers with an intensity that stole her breath and made goosebumps prickle on her skin. It was a good thing his cloak fully engulfed her from the neck down, or he'd see her reaction to his merest gaze.

"Emilie, I wish to apologize for what I said to ye. Had I not said that, ye wouldnae have run off, and ye would never have been in danger. I've been beside myself."

"Well, then it all happened for a reason because I was in the right place at the right time."

"Only a lass as brave as ye would say that the right place to be was where the enemy rode by."

"Bravery has nothing to do with it. When a child is in danger, any decent human will risk themselves to save it."

"Still, I am sorry for what I said."

"Never be sorry for saying what you truly mean," Emilie said with a forced smile. There was no need to make him feel worse about it. He was clearly tired, distressed, and remorseful.

"I didnae mean it. Ye cannae think so. Not after what we shared," he said, stepping closer.

"Goodwin. We shared a few very, very good moments." Emilie grinned. They were the best moments she'd had in a very long time, but she wouldn't embarrass herself by saying so. "But it's what people who are attracted to one another do. I cannot be mad at you for only wanting a physical relationship with me. After all, what more could we possibly share?"

Goodwin shook his head. "It was more to me than that," he said, looking away from her as Murielle watched them from across the way.

"Murielle seems to know what happened between us."

He shook his head again. "She may guess, but she cannae ken for certain. 'Tis not her concern anyway."

"She thinks it is." Emilie looked at Murielle, who swiftly looked away and continued chatting with a guard near the fire.

"She is protective of me and naught else. Ye were curious how I kenned about the tunnel beneath her bed. I was her guard most of her life. It was my duty to ken how to keep her safe if danger arrived at our gates."

"Goodwin," Emilie placed a hand on his forearm and smiled. "It's none of my business. I'm just grateful you did know about that tunnel. Thank you for saving Lucas and me and thank you for carrying me across the forest for half a mile."

"Ye weigh nothing, lass."

"Now I know you're a lady's man," she said with a wink. "You know just what to say to make a woman smile. I'm going to lay down. My feet are killing me, and I may fall asleep standing up if I don't do it soon."

"I dinnae ken what a 'lady's man' is, but I am pleased to make ye smile. Now, go, lass. I will wake ye when we are ready to leave."

With a nod, Emilie gripped his cloak in front of her chest and hobbled carefully over to the fire, stepping on leaves rather than pebbles. The cloak was large enough to wrap herself in like a cocoon, and she did just that as the fire warmed her bones and lulled her to sleep. But only after she reminded herself that, no matter how chivalrous and handsome Goodwin was, she had to keep her emotions in check and ignore her heart every time it tried to take the lead. There was nothing between them and never would be. But, at least she and Lucas were alive and well, thanks to him.

USING HIS KNIFE, Goodwin cut a slice of apple and shoved it into his mouth while he guarded camp until the rest of their party returned. Queen Caitriona carried Lucas in her arms, refusing to put him down, and Goodwin didn't blame her. Everyone felt the terror of losing Lucas, but nobody could understand that pain more than a parent, which he hoped to be someday. But it appeared the fates were stacked against him. No woman in his village suited him, and he couldn't leave his king's service, not that he would ever consider such a thing. This was his life, and he was pleased by it. But the void he'd felt had only grown darker and deeper since Emilie arrived. If ever there was a woman he could see himself having a family with, it was her.

Goodwin thought back on the moment he found Emilie and Lucas in the forest. Just when he'd believed their search for Lucas and Emilie had fallen short, he'd heard the bairn's piercing cries and hurried toward the source.

He couldn't find words to describe how he'd felt the moment he'd seen Emilie huddled behind that giant oak tree's trunk, shaking and desperate as Lucas screamed in her arms. Now, she and Lucas were safe, and Goodwin felt a relief unlike any he'd ever felt in his life.

He didn't consider himself much of a religious man. His family had been caught in the conversion to Christianity from paganism, and soon his family died of illness, leaving Goodwin with little guidance or concern for higher beings. He was too busy surviving, training, and guarding the royal family. But finding Emilie and Lucas when he did felt like Divine Intervention, and Goodwin wondered for the first time in years if God was shining down on him. But, why would God allow an innocent bairn to be taken away by evil men? These were the thoughts that plagued him as he cut off another apple slice and shoved it into his mouth while he stared at the fire with Emilie's sleeping form at his feet.

"Ye ken ye dinnae need to hover over her like a specter," he heard Murielle say from behind him. He stiffened, knowing her keen observations were working against him.

"I amnae."

"Oh?"

"Oh," he responded calmly before popping the last slice into his mouth and turning away. "What is it with ye anyway? Why do ye keep hounding me?"

"Och, do I wear on yer nerves?" Murielle asked with a raised brow.

"Ye ken ye do."

"Then tell me the truth, and I shall leave ye be."

Sighing, Goodwin tossed the apple core to Boudicca, who stood nearby. She bent her long neck to pick it up and crunch it indelicately between her strong teeth. "Why do ye care? There is naught to say."

"I care because I care about ye, ye lout. Ye were my guard for eight years, my best friend. I grew up kenning I had to marry strategically, but ye always dreamed of a family. Yet ye jump from lass to lass and never look back. Then I see ye look at Emilie… it's different. *Yer* different."

"Murielle, just as I was ordered to guard ye, I was ordered to guard her. Ye imagine things with yer romantic nonsense."

"So, I imagined Emilie was outside the cabin in naught but yer tunic?" she asked, placing her hands on her hip.

"There are things yea cannae understand, Murielle. She was in yer chamber when the fight broke out, so we used the tunnel to escape to the cabin. It began to rain, which muddied her dress, which was already filthy from the tunnel. When we arrived at the cabin, her clothes and slippers were destroyed, so I found a spare tunic in the chest. She decided to wander down to the loch to bathe when she saw Arwyn's men and heard Lucas's cry. That's all there is to it, and none of that is yer concern."

Goodwin turned to walk away, and Murielle frowned. "If ye say I misread ye, and ye've no interest in Emilie, then I will let it be. I guess ye and I have drifted apart so much that I cannae tell what yer thinking anymore."

Stopping mid-step, Goodwin growled with frustration. There was too much to do to sit here and argue with Murielle and make her feel wrong about something she was so very right about.

Turning around, Goodwin glared at Murielle and ran a hand through his unbound hair. "We havenae drifted apart. Yer instincts are correct, but she is leaving soon, and I doubt she'd want anything to do with a man like me when she could be with one from her own time. Now, I need to pack up camp so we can leave immediately upon Brodyn's return."

Murielle nodded and smiled gratefully at him for opening up. "I appreciate yer honesty. I will say no more than this—I have kenned ye my entire life Goodwin Mac Dougal, and I havenae seen ye look at a lass the way ye look at her, and I doubt she looks at men in her time the way she looks at ye. I dream of the day I find a man worthy of looking at that way."

Goodwin smiled and, despite himself, felt a flutter in his chest. Could there truly be more than just attraction between him and Emilie? He wasn't sure how she felt, nor was he certain they'd have time to find out, but hearing Murielle's words set him at ease, and he was glad he opened up to her. "Ye mean, with all these kings coming across the land to visit ye, none of them make ye look at them like that?" he asked with a smirk.

Murielle made a gagging sound. "Nay, they are all terrible. Arwyn was the better-looking of them all and the youngest. I daresay I had no connection with the man yet had considered the match for our people's sake, but, well... I think he has shown his true colors."

"This isn't the end, ye ken. What he did will bring war upon us, I vow. And, I cannae help but fear that he hurt Emilie in some way. She willnae say and denies that he touched her. Still, I ken something happened."

Murielle frowned and looked at Emilie, sleeping peacefully by the fire. She sighed. "Unless she says, we may never ken what happened out there. But, Goodwin... she is safe. Lucas is safe. Let us focus on that and not what did or could have occurred."

Murielle's advice was wise, and though he knew he'd still worry, he gave her a nod and walked away to ready the horses and prepare the men to leave. He'd leave the fire burning until Brodyn arrived since Emilie looked so peaceful and warm sleeping beside it. She was courageous, intelligent, loyal, and stunningly beautiful. But, he reminded himself, the more his feelings softened toward her, the more dangerous she was to him. Dangerous to his heart, and his very being. He would never respond to another woman as he responded to her. Could he blame himself? She was beyond bonny, with soft, clear skin and rounded curves that made his—

Goodwin cursed under his breath when he realized he was staring at a tree while daydreaming about being naked with her again. "Ye arse," he whispered as he shoved a spare plaid into his satchel. Boudicca snorted at him, either confirming his words or offended by them.

"Not ye," he said wryly as he stroked her snout. But then her ears pricked and she pulled away, whinnying in distress. The forest floor began to shake as a rhythmic thundering shook the ground, and twigs snapped. He gripped the hilt of his sword, and the sleeping men roused, rolling to their feet with their swords at the ready in case the arriving party belonged to the wrong king.

Brodyn broke through the trees, and Goodwin sighed. "Brodyn!" Cait ran to her husband just as he dismounted and ran to her. They embraced, then she passed Lucas to him. Never in all these years had Goodwin seen his friend so physically distressed. His features creased, his skin blotched, and his eyes glittered with unshed tears as he clung to his beloved child. Even when Brodyn had thought he was going to die in their last battle, he'd kept his composure.

"Thank God," he murmured, hugging the child close. Looking at Goodwin, he bowed his head. "Thank ye, old friend."

"Thank Emilie. She kept Lucas safe when we couldn't. She's had an ordeal, and I suspect more happened than she is willing to say." Again, visions of Arwyn forcing himself upon Emilie plagued him, and he swallowed his rising bile, trying to remember Murielle's wisdom. He only hoped Emilie would confide in him, or even Queen Caitriona, if something had happened.

Brodyn looked at Emilie, who shifted beneath Goodwin's tunic and sat up when she heard the commotion. "I cannae ever thank ye enough for keeping my son alive."

"I'd never consider an alternative," she said, shaking her head. Despite the praise she received, Emilie genuinely appeared unaffected, confused why anyone would think her a hero simply for doing what she considered to be the right thing. To Goodwin, that was the most admirable trait anyone could have. Warlords killed for the glory. Kings killed to keep their people safe. Emilie would make a wonderful queen, but that would require her to marry another man, and that thought made his stomach sour and clench.

Walking over to her, Goodwin put out a hand to help her to her feet. She looked up at him with her yellowish-green eyes and reached up to accept his help. She winced when he grabbed her wrist, and he remembered her injuries.

"Och, sorry," he whispered as she hobbled onto her feet, using her other hand to clutch his cloak.

"I'm fine," she said with a smile. He smiled back and stared at her, overwhelmed by her beauty and courage—until she crinkled her brow and tilted her head. "Are you all right?"

He cleared his throat and nodded. "Aye. I thought there was an insect in yer hair, but 'twas a shadow," he lied to cover for his awkwardness. "Now that the others are back, we need to head back to the village. Ye can ride with me."

Emilie nodded and allowed him to carry her once again, as her feet were in deplorable condition. Carefully, he propped her onto Boudicca's saddle, trying not to be affected by the feel of her backside on his palm when she shifted out of his arms.

Once the party was packed and mounted, they headed north toward home, and Goodwin enjoyed the ride more than usual. The sun shone through the scattered branches, creating a dappled light as few clouds blocked the view of the cerulean sky. Birds chirped high in the trees, and leaves rustled in the gentle summer wind. Was this day finer than most, or was Goodwin simply seeing it through softened eyes? He had to admit that having Emilie nestled against him, and especially her round backside to his front, bolstered his spirits and made him hope for more with her in this lifetime, though he knew it was folly. Perhaps when they were back in town, he would have more time to speak with her and discover her intentions. Was she leaving, and if so, how soon? He longed to ask her now as she rested against his chest, with his arm around her waist to keep her steady, but he didn't wish to appear eager.

"Goodwin?" Emilie asked, leaning her head against his chest and turning so he could see her profile.

"Aye? Is everything all right?"

"Yes, but remember when I told you I had to do more to keep Lucas safe?"

Goodwin swallowed and tensed, clutching the reins. "Aye. Emilie, there is nothing ye can tell me that will make me think less of ye."

"Do you promise?"

"I vow upon Boudicca's life, for hers is worth more than my own."

"That's absurd. Don't say such things. You mean a great deal to a great many people... including me."

Goodwin raised his brows in surprise even though she couldn't see him. He was shocked to hear her admit such a thing, yet it pleased him greatly, for he felt the same way.

"Oh, aye? I'm glad to hear I've remained in yer good graces," he chuckled. "So, what is this task ye had to do? If he hurt ye or touched ye, be warned, Emilie. I will go after him, myself, and gut the man, king or no."

She hesitated but sighed and shook her head. "Surprisingly, he did not lay a finger on me, but I know he would have had I remained there any longer. But, he would have had a legal right to, as things are in this time."

What was she implying? Goodwin gripped the reins tighter and gritted his teeth. He didn't like where this was going.

"What are ye saying?" he asked wearily, trying to keep his voice steady.

"He was furious about traveling all the way from ... wherever he is from."

"Gwynedd," Goodwin said. "'Tis very far south."

"Right. He was angry that he was sent home without a bride. That's why he took Lucas. I think he meant to kill him as repayment. He said he would let Lucas go if he had a royal bride like he intended. He believes I'm Cait's sister, and he believes she is the niece of the Scots king, so..." she trailed off, as if unwilling to speak the truth of what had happened.

Goodwin's head swam as his skin heated and his stomach clenched. Nay, it could not be. "Dinnae tell me ye married the man, Emilie!"

"I had to!" she huffed. "What was I supposed to do? Let him kill Lucas?"

Goodwin sighed and felt unease settle into his bones. If Emilie was Arwyn's wife and Queen of the Britons, this altercation was far from over. Arwyn wasn't going to return home. Nay, he'd be coming for the Picts to retrieve his wife.

"Nay, I suppose ye had no choice," Goodwin relented. "But he willnae simply allow us to take ye. Ye ken he will be returning for ye. This means war with the Britons."

He felt Emilie shudder, and pity intensified his protective instinct toward her. He tightened his grip on her waist and said, "Dinnae worry, lass. Ye saved the king's heir with yer actions. Ye are the bravest lass I've ever kenned, though I begin to suspect ye have the worst fortune. If he promised to return Lucas after ye married him, why did ye flee and risk yer lives?"

"That's the thing. After what I assume was a handfast ceremony, Arwyn told me he never promised to return Lucas right away. He still planned to take us both south with him where he would hold Lucas for ransom. But the bairn was starving, and Arwyn was cruel and uncaring. He ignored my pleas to return him to Cait so he could be fed. I knew if I didn't flee, Lucas would perish." She paused and her breath hitched she audibly swallowed. "Arwyn slept beside me and awoke when I stood up, but he was so disgusted by Lucas's dirty nappy and crying, he allowed me to go to the stream to clean him up. That's when I fled. He told me he'd give me a few moments to return, or he would come after me."

Goodwin's blood boiled with hatred and rage. Arwyn ap Rhys was a filthy whoreson who deserved to meet with the end of Goodwin's blade, and suddenly, making that a reality was Goodwin's second greatest desire in the world. His first laid against his chest while he held her close, and suddenly he saw everything with clarity. Emilie was another man's wife, but not for long. Any man who would allow an innocent child to suffer and force a woman to marry him was not long for this world, if Goodwin had a say. Once he freed her from Arwyn's marital bond, she was free to stay or leave, but he knew beyond a shadow of a doubt that he wanted her to stay, and damn it all, he wanted her for himself. Forever.

"Ye will never have to see that man ever again, Emilie. He will come for ye, and when he does, mine will be the last face he ever sees."

Emilie nodded and sighed, nuzzling closer to him. Goodwin looked up to see Caitriona and Murielle watching him with smirks, and he shrugged. There was no point avoiding it any longer. He wanted Emilie, and whether she wanted him in return or not, he would protect her from any harm with his last breath.

CHAPTER EIGHT

"E MILIE, WAKE UP. We are home."

"Home?" Emilie murmured as she slowly opened her eyes and looked around. Wooden homes and thatched roofs surrounded her as chickens ran through the village and sheep bleated in a byre to her left. They had arrived back at Pinnata Castra, and Emilie looked over her shoulder into the intense amber gaze of Goodwin's eyes. Her breath caught. She could read his emotions in his gaze, and they mirrored her own.

When he dismounted, he gently lifted her from Boudicca's saddle and held her in his strong arms, refusing to place her on the ground due to her hurt feet, which she appreciated. It would be a rough couple of days of sitting around until they healed, but at least Lucas was safe. Nothing else mattered to Emilie.

As she held his gaze, her heart fluttered, and she resisted the urge to lean in and kiss him, especially with all the other riders surrounding them near the stables. Apparently, and most unfortunately, Goodwin mattered to her, as well. She had never felt such a strong connection with a man before, and Emilie wondered why she had to go over 1,300 years in the past to find it.

Goodwin walked over to Brodyn and Caitriona as he carried Emilie. "I will take her to yer home. Anya needs to clean and wrap the wounds on her feet. She cannae walk after her ordeal."

Cradling Lucas with one arm, Cait put out her free hand to lift Emilie's foot and look at the damage, frowning. "Oh, my sweet friend. You've had such an ordeal. The worst is over. Let's get you taken care of."

Goodwin shook his head. "I wish that were true, but I fear the danger is only beginning. We must have a serious discussion about what occurred out in that forest."

"Verra well," Brodyn said. "Head to the house. I will be there shortly."

Goodwin climbed the hill that led to the king and queen's house with Caitriona carrying Lucas behind them. Goodwin opened the door and placed Emilie on the bench near the fire. "She will need a bath and clothing, as well."

Caitriona glanced at Goodwin, then Emilie. "Okay. What's going on between you two?"

"Literally nothing," Emilie replied. "Your husband charged him to guard me, and that's what he's done. He's just very passionate about his job."

"Now I know you're full of crap."

"What is... crap?" Goodwin asked, raising a brow at his queen, and Emilie bit back a laugh.

"Shite," Cait said, putting a hand on her hip. "Goodwin. You cannot lie to your queen."

"I've said nothing but to say she needs a bath and clothing!" he huffed, putting his hands on his hip to match Cait. Emilie sat on the bench, enjoying their banter and watching Goodwin squirm. He could defeat any enemy, but he couldn't outmatch his queen.

"It's not what you said. I'm not stupid. You guys totally hooked up, didn't you?"

"What did I hook Emilie up to?" Goodwin asked in confusion, creasing his brow. "Ye make no sense."

"Leave him alone, Cait," Emilie laughed. "He saved your son and your best friend. Let the man go."

Cait narrowed her eyes at Emilie, and Emilie shrugged. She wasn't going to blurt out that she hooked up with Goodwin while he stood right beside her and clearly didn't wish for his queen to know. Besides, what was the point? He made it clear that he cared about her, but beyond that, Goodwin showed no intentions of pursuing a relationship with Emilie, and how could he? She was an outsider from a faraway place, sent here to save Lucas, and now she had. As soon as Emilie was healed, she could leave.

Though, she would not until Arwyn was no longer a threat. If she brought his army to Pinnata Castra's gates, she couldn't just scamper back to 2023 without knowing the outcome or helping in some way.

An alarming thought made Emilie worry at her lower lip. Had her decision to marry Arwyn changed the timeline's events? Emilie hoped she hadn't made a grave error, yet how could it have been a mistake if it was the only way to save Lucas, which is why she was sent back here to begin with?

There was no way to answer that question, and nothing she could do about it anyway. Her head hurt, and she dearly wished to bathe and sleep. She could start with that and worry about her concerns later.

Brodyn opened the door, kicking dirt off his boots before entering, yanking his cloak off his shoulders, and hanging it on a hook.

"What is the impending danger, Goodwin?" he asked without missing a beat.

"Arwyn will be arriving at our gates any day."

"How can ye be so sure of this? He kens he will never marry Murielle after this, and he failed to keep Lucas in his grasp. He should slink away to Gwynedd in shame."

"We have something... someone he willnae return home without."

"Who?" Brodyn groused, looking at Goodwin.

"His wife." Goodwin looked over at Emilie, and she hunched over, wishing to bury herself in the warmth of his cloak.

"What?" Brodyn and Cait shouted simultaneously, making Lucas shift and open his blue eyes before nodding back to sleep.

All eyes were on Emilie, and she had no choice but to explain the details that led to her becoming the enemy's wife and queen. "I'm sorry," she whispered once she'd finished telling the tale and looked away, afraid her friend's husband would explode.

The room remained silent for a moment before Cait walked over and sat beside her, placing a hand on her leg. "You did that for our son?"

"Why is that surprising? Do you think I'd ever allow anything to happen to Lucas? He's half of my very best friend. I love him."

Cait wiped away a tear and leaned her head against Emilie's. "Thank you," she whispered. "I'm so sorry you've been through this ordeal."

"I'm sorry you had to bear the agony of almost losing your son. I cannot imagine such a pain." Emilie and Cait looked at Lucas, who slept peacefully in his mother's arms.

"Emilie." Brodyn's authoritative voice pulled her gaze in his direction as he stepped toward her, towering above her like a mighty god who could easily strike her down.

But then he dropped to his knees before her and bowed his head, taking her hands in his. "Ye risked everything to save my son," he said with a raspy voice. "We shall risk everything to save ye from Arwyn. I dinnae recognize yer marriage to the enemy within these walls."

"Thank you, Brodyn," Emilie said with relief. She didn't realize how worried she had been that everyone would be angry with her until now. "You have a good man, Cait."

"Don't I know it." Cait leaned in to kiss Brodyn, and Emilie smiled, happy for her dearest friend yet longing to find that same kind of love. She resisted looking in Goodwin's direction. She dared not imagine such a life with a man she had just met, let alone a man she would soon never see again.

Anya walked into the room with her medical bag and came toward Emilie. "Lemme take a look at yer feet, lass."

"How did you know?" Emilie asked, cocking her head.

"I'm auld, not deaf."

"Right," Emilie murmured, stretching her feet out for Anya

to examine.

"Lordy, lass! Ye gone and torn up yer feet, ye did."

"I didn't exactly have a choice."

"How is yer wrist?"

"Not great, but better than my feet."

Anya nodded and looked at Emilie's forehead. "Ye still have some bruising, but ye are healing. First, let's get ye washed up, then we can remove any lodged debris and wrap them."

Nodding, Emilie shifted to get up, unsure what to do next. Goodwin stood aside with his back straight as he awaited orders from his king. With Arwyn and his men gone, Emilie no longer needed Goodwin's protection. This should have pleased her, but the sudden realization that whatever had developed between was over hit her like a swift punch to the gut—like the day in gym class where Aaron Richardson tried to pass her the basketball but instead threw it full speed at her belly. That same feeling now gripped Emilie as she found herself unwilling to part with his cloak, the one thing she still had left.

Pulling it closer to her, she looked at Goodwin. "Thank you for... everything, Goodwin. Might I return your cloak once I have proper clothing on?"

His gaze snapped from the fire to her, and the emotion she saw threatened to knock her off her feet. "Of course. Do ye need assistance up the stairs?"

"No, I will manage, but thank you."

Cait watched them interact with narrowed eyes, and Emilie knew she had to talk to her best friend once they had some privacy.

"Emilie can stay in one of the guest chambers now that they are empty. Thank you for everything, Goodwin. She will be safe within these walls now that Arwyn is gone."

A dark look crossed his crinkled brow. "Ye no longer wish me to guard Emilie?"

Caitriona looked at Emilie and back to Goodwin before looking to Brodyn for help to answer that question.

Brodyn's expression told Goodwin he also sensed his hesitancy to give up his station as her guard. Clearing his throat, the king said, "Though I cannae think of a threat to Emilie or Lucas now that Arwyn is gone, it wouldnae be smart to put our guard down now, especially since the man will want his wife back. While I believe Emilie is safe enough to stay with us, I will keep ye on as her guard, nonetheless."

Goodwin nodded, showing no sign of emotion. "Then I will sleep outside her door at night and trail her during the day."

"Can you not speak about me like I'm not right here?" Emilie huffed with annoyance. "There is no need for that, Goodwin. Surely, you'd prefer your bed."

"I'd prefer to do as my king commands."

"The king didn't say you have to sleep in front of my door at night," she pushed back.

"Listen, lass." Goodwin clenched his jaw and stepped closer. "Dinnae tell me how to do my job. I guarded Murielle for years, and one thing I ken for certain is that danger comes when ye least expect it. The enemy willnae announce himself readily." Narrowing his eyes at her, Goodwin crossed his arms. "I will return home to clean myself up while I ken ye are safe here. But I will return."

Looking at Brodyn, Goodwin nodded his head and left the house, leaving Emilie to gape as he walked away.

"Dear God in heaven," Murielle said with a laugh. "What have ye done to the man?"

"I have this effect on the male gender," Emilie mumbled before ascending the stairs.

"Ye make them fall in love with ye? Care to teach me how?" Murielle said dryly.

Emilie shook her head and grimaced. "What? No. I drive them mad."

Murielle smirked and nodded but remained silent. Caitriona followed Emilie closely as she climbed up to her chamber, wincing with every step.

"Go to the second floor and turn left. The best guest room is the second door on the right."

"This house is deceptively large," Emilie said. "Or maybe every step just feels like torture."

"Goodwin offered to carry you," Cait reminded her, but Emilie scoffed.

"The man has been carrying me around the entire Scottish countryside. I figured he needed a break from me and my injuries."

"That's not at all the vibe I got from him," Cait said suggestively, and Emilie knew she had to nip this all in the bud now, or else she'd be dodging the subject forever.

Reaching the second floor and turning left, Emilie stopped at the door Caitriona indicated and turned around to face her friend. "Fine. I had sex with Goodwin when we were in the cabin. Happy now?"

Cait furrowed her brow and pursed her lips. "I dunno. Are you happy about it? You don't seem to be."

Emilie shrugged. "I feel fine about it. You know I'm not the kind of girl who sleeps around, but we had a vibe, a connection. Here I am, 1,300 years in the past, and this sexy-as-all-hell warrior is ordered to guard me with his life... which he takes very seriously, by the way. There was just a lot of hormones and pheromones bouncing around. We're anthropology students. We understand this animistic attraction. That's all it was."

"Okay, if you say so."

"I *do* say so. And, once all this Arwyn nonsense is over, I have to return home, so what's the point?"

"Nobody said you had to rush home, Em."

"I can't stay here."

"I'm not saying you should or shouldn't. That's your choice. But, you do have a place here with us. You're family. But I won't have anything to do with guiding your decision. I'm just letting you know that you have options."

"Thanks, Cait. I appreciate that, but you came here because

your existence in this timeline literally saved all of Scotland. I have no such claim. If anything, I'm messing it all up with my marriage to Arwyn."

"You literally saved the heir to the Picts. I'd say you have a purpose here."

"Had, not have. I did what I came here to do. But I will consider it. I just really need to get clean and rest. And, beneath this cloak—"

"Goodwin's cloak," she reminded Emilie.

"Yes, beneath *his* cloak, I wear next to nothing. I will need something more appropriate."

"What happened to the tunic you wore yesterday?"

"It's still in the cabin…with my shoes."

Caitriona bit back a laugh. "You hussy."

"Shut your face."

"Get some rest. I will send some help to ready the bath." Smiling, Cait squeezed Emilie's hand in return. "I'm so glad you're here with me, even under the circumstances. Tonight, we will all celebrate the safe return of Lucas and his mysterious Auntie… I mean, the Queen of the Britons."

Caitriona stuck her tongue out at Emilie, who rolled her eyes. "Go be with your ridiculously adorable family. I will see you in a bit."

Emilie entered the room just as Cait turned to head back down the stairs. One small wooden-framed bed rested in the corner with a table beside it and a chair near the hearth. A small wooden tub with dried herbs at the bottom awaited the addition of hot water, and Emilie couldn't wait. She wanted a bath and sleep more than she wanted another go with Goodwin, and that was saying something.

With a sigh, Emilie shut the door, plopped on the bed, closed her eyes, and waited for her bath to be ready.

The situation was becoming much too complicated for Goodwin's liking. Obviously, pretending he wasn't attracted to Emilie wasn't working. Murielle and Queen Caitriona wouldn't stop giving him side glances as he stood sentry in front of her door. Keeping his features neutral, Goodwin looked straight ahead at the fire and ignored the looks he felt burning his skin. Emilie wasn't his, nor would she ever be, and he made a decision right then and there that any desire to pursue the lass ended now.

He didn't do complicated with women, especially one that would be gone soon. He'd be better off looking through her rather than at her. She could do as she wished, and he'd do his duty. He was strong enough to follow in her wake without succumbing to the weakness of emotions.

"Oh, Em! You look incredible!" Queen Caitriona gasped and ran toward the stairs. Against his better judgment, Goodwin flicked his gaze away from the fire to settle on another, one that burned brighter and hotter than any other.

Swallowing his reaction, Goodwin kept his features stonelike as Emilie descended the stairs in a light blue, silk tunic with a silver chain belt around her slim waist. The silk fabric shimmered in the firelight, clinging to her breasts and hips. Her hair was clean and dry for the first time in a while, sparkling like a wheat field on a brilliant summer's day. A healthy shade of pink tinted her smiling lips, and despite her need to hold onto the wall while she walked, she moved smoothly and gracefully, every step making her hips sway. That fertile body he'd held in his arms was enough to drive a man wild, but his vow to block out any desire for her remained fresh on his mind. He was a man of discipline. Surely, he could push down any feelings she triggered in him, physical or emotional.

Murielle took a moment to eye him, and he was pleased to give her no reaction. He would remain detached, silent, stoic. In fact, he found that reminding himself that she was now married to Arwyn and a queen in her own right helped him put up a very high, impenetrable wall. Aye, he understood the terms of her marriage and that Brodyn didn't recognize the union, but the fact remained that the lass had several complications surrounding her existence here, and Goodwin was better off enjoying the memory of what time they had shared.

"Doesn't Emilie look wonderful, Goodwin?" Murielle nudged him with her elbow, raising a brow at him, but he simply nodded and looked away.

"How are your feet?" Cait asked, coming closer to help Emilie down the final step.

"They've been better, but Anya is a miracle worker. After soaking my feet in the bath, she removed splinters, applied a salve to help them heal and numb the pain, then wrapped them in clean linen." For visual evidence, Emilie lifted the hem of her borrowed dress to show her wrapped ankles peeking through a new pair of matching blue silk slippers. "Thank you for letting me borrow another dress, Cait. I feel awful about the one left behind in the cabin."

Cait waved off her concern. "We will get it back. And, what's mine is yours, just like old times, right? We've always been the same size, except your boobs are clearly larger and straining to escape my dress," Caitriona said with a scoff.

Looking down, Emilie gripped the dress's neckline and tugged, trying to hide some cleavage but only succeeding in drawing more attention to her ample bosom.

Goodwin expertly guarded his features, staring through her and focusing on a chipped piece of plaster on the wall behind her. This was easy enough, he told himself. It would be a lot easier if he had time to find another distraction in the form of a willing lass, but with his duty to guard her at all times, Goodwin knew that finding himself female companionship would be impossible.

Looking straight at him, Emilie walked forward with a smile. "I appreciate that your duty is to guard me, but I really don't think it's necessary. There is no threat here."

"Threats are illusive by design," he grumbled. "They willnae show themselves until they strike. My gut tells me that Arwyn has a man inside the walls."

Cait gasped and clutched her chest. "Why do you think this, Goodwin? Have you told Brodyn your suspicion?"

"Not yet. It's a theory I've been considering since Lucas was taken. How was he able to access the bairn and get through the gates with the heir?" Goodwin shook his head and glared at the women in the room. "I dinnae believe we are without prying eyes and spying ears."

"Brodyn's men are loyal to the core," Murielle said, shaking her head.

"Are they? Men have a price. If Arwyn offered the right man the right price, he could buy his soul."

"Who was supposed to guard Lucas?" Emilie asked as she limped over, faltering in her step. Goodwin almost lunged forward to grab her, but he stilled himself, allowing her to find her own bearings. It went against his nature to let a lass stumble before his eyes, especially knowing the injuries she suffered and why, but any unnecessary contact with her could cause him to lose focus all over again. He had to remain vigilant and clear-headed. His success in guarding Murielle all those years was due to his lack of physical and emotional interest. That, and the fact that Murielle was so against being guarded that she found every way imaginable to make Goodwin's daily life hell.

Cait shook her head and frowned. "God, I don't even know. What kind of mother am I?" she wailed.

"Sister... dinnae say such nonsense. Brodyn doled out the commands. He made sure only the most trustworthy men were guarding his family. Ye were in distress and trusted that Lucas was safe. We will find my brother at the longhouse and find out who guarded who and go from there. Ronan was with me the entire time, and I trust him implicitly."

"Aye. Agreed." Goodwin knew without a doubt that Ronan was innocent. A name and a face came to Goodwin's mind, but he bit his tongue and decided to speak with Brodyn privately before throwing out his potentially problematic theory, especially when the person he considered was female.

"Shall we go? Brodyn has roasted the best boar for the occasion, and I am starving!" Murielle said, more upbeat than necessary. She was trying to keep everyone calm and spirits high, which Goodwin appreciated. There was no room for panic. As long as the women and children stayed calm, the men could do their duty and keep a watchful eye out for trouble.

As they walked through the village toward the longhouse, Goodwin walked directly behind Emilie, forcing his gaze straight ahead rather than on her perfect, swaying backside. Eyes straight ahead. Head up. Discipline.

Delicious smells and joyful sounds wafted toward them as they drew closer. The entire village had gathered to celebrate the safe return of their future king. Goodwin wished he felt as secure as the rest of the village, but there were too many concerns surrounding Lucas and Emilie's abductions to allow him to relax. His duty was to be ever vigilant. He would rest when he was dead.

"Emilie, tonight we will party like it's 699!" Queen Caitriona shouted, putting her arms up as she swayed to the music just before stepping inside the longhouse.

"Heck yes!" Emilie said, copying her friend and shaking her hips. Goodwin had no idea what they were talking about, but he wondered if Emilie intentionally goaded him with erotic movements that made her enticing dress cling to her curves.

Just before they entered the rowdy longhouse, Goodwin impulsively reached out to grab Emilie by the arm. It hadn't been planned, but a sudden need to speak with her overtook his better senses. A look of surprise crossed her face just before she crinkled her brow with confusion.

"Before we go inside, I wish to speak with ye."

"Oh, sure," she said, allowing him to guide her to the side of the entrance as the rest of their group entered, causing the crowd to roar with enthusiasm as King Brodyn entered carrying Lucas.

"Now that ye and Lucas are safe, I want to clarify a few things between us."

Emilie nodded and looked up to his height, awaiting whatever he had to say. She was beautiful beyond measure, and that was the problem. He had to cut any ties now before he became overly attached. "I enjoyed our time together, but ye were right. It was an attraction and nothing more. I will better serve as yer guard if we agree that what happened was a mistake."

Emilie frowned and pursed her lips together. "Sure, Goodwin. That's a smart idea."

"So, ye agree?"

"Yep." She responded quickly, too quickly, and he wondered if he had offended her. He wasn't trying to hurt her. He was trying to protect himself. If she wrapped her arms around his neck right now, declared her intention to stay in this time, and leaned in for a kiss, Goodwin wouldn't hesitate to throw her over his shoulder and take her back to his bed. But, she didn't. Instead, she agreed and turned away, walking through the entrance before he could take back his words or change his mind.

It was for the best, or at least that's what he told himself. If Murielle and Caitriona both felt the connection he shared with Emilie, then things had gone too far. He was her guard. Nothing else.

Walking in behind her, Goodwin sat beside her at the head table, where she leaned in to chat with Caitriona and Samuel, who had just returned to the village after a visit to his own time. He had Murielle, Caitriona, and Emilie enthralled in whatever tale he told, and Goodwin stood sentinel behind Emilie with his hands behind his back. Ronan stood behind Murielle and Lawrence behind Queen Caitriona, which told Goodwin that Brodyn expected more trouble. Had he considered a corrupt guard? With all of the commotion, Goodwin had yet to speak privately with his king, but he would as soon as they returned to the house.

Musicians played as food was placed on the tables. Roasted venison with rosemary accompanied carrots and turnips, beans, cheeses, and fresh bread as garlic wafted in the air. Emilie turned around on her bench and looked up at him. "Come." She patted the small space between her and Queen Caitriona. "Eat with us."

Goodwin shook his head. "I cannae guard yer back if I'm sitting beside ye."

Emilie frowned and put her food down. "Then I'm not eating, either."

"Dinnae be a stubborn lass. Ye need to eat."

"As do you."

"And I shall once ye are safely in yer chamber."

Emilie gave him a look that told Goodwin she believed he was the stubborn one, but she had no idea how quickly a blade could slide through someone's spine. From talking to Queen Cait, he knew that in Emilie's time danger didn't lurk around every corner and men didn't openly kill kings and queens for power. Ignoring her scowls, Goodwin looked straight ahead again, focusing on a dark stain on the wooden-planked wall. He remembered the day that stain was made. Brodyn's brother Talorc accidentally bumped into the wall while carrying mead, and the stain remained, a morbid reminder of the man who tried to kill his own twin brother for the title of king.

On the other side of the table, Ronan stood behind Murielle but constantly flicked his gaze over to Emilie, and from this angle, Goodwin knew it was not her face the man admired.

Goodwin growled and gritted his teeth, glaring at his fellow warrior and friend until the man felt his burning gaze and looked up. Goodwin narrowed his eyes and shook his head, mouthing, "Don't even think about it."

Ronan shrugged. "Want to trade?" he mouthed. Goodwin clenched his jaw so hard that he could have cracked a molar. His stone-cold stare would have frightened most men, but Ronan only chuckled and looked away.

"Emilie, after the feast, I must speak with you privately," Samuel said from beside Murielle. Emilie took a bite of buttered bread and nodded, but Goodwin shook his head.

"She willnae meet with anyone in private."

Once again, Emilie turned to scowl up at him, but Samuel nodded in understanding. "Of course. I fully expect you will be there to watch over here while we talk, but I do have important updates for her that I'd prefer to discuss before she returns to her chamber."

"Verra well," Goodwin said.

Emilie huffed with irritation. "He is my friend, my boss, and my mentor. He's been alone with me many times since I was eighteen. He is trustworthy."

"I ken that. Nonetheless, 'tis my duty always to be wherever ye are."

Emilie huffed again and turned back around to finish her meal, laughing at some jest the queen made about college and a car. He was surrounded by time-travelers whose conversation made not one bit of sense to him.

Meanwhile, the rest of the village was clueless that the queen and her companions were from an entirely different world. Goodwin wasn't sure how they could all be so oblivious. These people may as well have traveled from a distant star in the sky. Even that notion was unbelievable, but Queen Caitriona once told him that a man had walked on the moon, that the stars were physical balls of gas in the sky, and that the sun was also a star.

Goodwin shook his head. Part of him wished to sit beside Emilie and ask her a million questions about the world. She was slightly younger than him, yet she knew more about the world and everything beyond it than any person in his time. But, to be alone with her would be to tempt himself beyond a limit he couldn't pass.

As people finished their meals and guzzled their libation of choice, the music intensified, and Emilie grew restless in her seat. "We should dance, ladies! Come on!"

"Ye dinnae need to ask me twice!" Murielle said, shooting from her seat so fast that she nearly knocked the top of her head against Ronan's jaw. King Brodyn stood in the corner holding Lucas as he chatted with villagers, so Cait nodded and stood from her bench, taking Emilie by the hand.

Goodwin followed them to the center of the longhouse, where they attracted attention from other men and women, who gathered to join the dancing. Goodwin hated dancing. It was a nonsensical waste of time and energy, yet he knew he was a minority in this belief.

Unlike Goodwin, Ronan had no issue with dancing, and he stepped up to Emilie with a smile. "Might I trouble the hero of the day for a dance?"

"Oh!" Emilie perked up and smiled, flushing. "I am no hero, but I am glad to dance with you."

Taking her hand, Ronan pulled her closer, wrapping an arm around her waist while they both ignored Goodwin's rigid presence beside them. "How do ye dance where ye are from?" Ronan asked her.

"Uh, quite similarly to how you dance, I'm sure," she said cryptically, avoiding a direct answer. Ronan accepted her response and guided Emilie in a few steps that she was unfamiliar with, but she clearly enjoyed the experience as she tilted her head back to laugh. Goodwin felt the perpetual knots in his stomach tighten.

"Ronan, ye arenae watching Murielle."

"Then, I'm sure ye can manage that. I've got Emilie. She's safe with me."

Emilie looked at Goodwin and smiled, her cheeks rosy and her face alight. "Oh, yes!" she said. "Goodwin, that's a fine idea. You guarded Murielle for a long time before. I'm sure Ronan can watch me just as well as you."

Goodwin couldn't tell by her upbeat tone if she was sincere or trying to get rid of him. Either way, he was not leaving her side. Ronan smirked at him triumphantly, and blood boiled in Goodwin's veins. He was losing his temper, doing everything in his power not to grab Ronan by the neck and choke him in the middle of the longhouse floor.

"My king commanded I guard ye, and I will continue to do so until otherwise commanded," he said with a dangerous edge.

"Great, then I will speak with Brodyn tonight and arrange the change in guards," Emilie said, turning her back on him as Ronin continued to spin her on the dance floor.

Enough. All thought, all reason left Goodwin as unfamiliar emotions pushed to the surface. Later, he'd blame it on his unwavering loyalty to his duty, but he recognized the constriction in his lungs and clenching in his stomach. He was damned jealous, and he'd not the strength to fight it.

Goodwin reached out and grabbed her arm, yanking her into his chest. She squealed with shock, looking up at him with confusion in her yellow-green eyes. "I've got this from here, Ronan. Keep an eye on yer charge."

Ronan scowled at Goodwin but knew he had no say in the matter. For all his apparent interest in Emilie, his king had commanded him to watch Murielle, and Ronan was a man of his word.

"What is your problem?" Emilie hissed at him, trying to push away.

He pulled her closer, feeling the heat of her body against his, every curve through her thin silk dress driving him to the point of dizziness. "Ye are my problem. Ye are stubborn, defiant, and naïve. Ye have no idea the sort of dangers that lurk in this time."

"Something tells me you are my only danger in this room."

Goodwin's nostrils flared as he took a deep breath and gripped her waist so tightly that she winced. "Ye may be right about that, but I willnae take that chance."

And, before every person in the entire village, Goodwin leaned in and slashed his mouth against hers, slipping his tongue into her sweet mouth as she turned to mush in his hands, yielding all her strength but for her grip on his biceps.

Goodwin wasn't certain how long he kissed her, for his head floated in some unrecognizable world he had never before visited, a world where only he and Emilie existed and everything else faded away. All he knew was, as far as the village was concerned, Goodwin Mac Dougal had just claimed Emilie Wilshire as his own.

And, he had no regrets.

CHAPTER NINE

T HE CROWD WHOOPED and hollered at the scene, making Emilie snap out of the moment and look around. Hundreds of eyes watched them, most with amusement, but a few younger women appeared disappointed or angry.

Embarrassment threatened to pull Emilie under, but instead, she straightened her back, turned away from Goodwin without looking at him, and slowly walked toward the door.

"Em!" Cait ran up to her and grabbed her wrist. "That was... public. Are you okay?"

Swallowing, Emilie nodded but kept walking, unsure what to say or do. It wasn't the dramatic nature of the kiss that had her upset. It had been hot, romantic, and had made her stomach flutter with possibilities. But Goodwin clearly only kissed her to push Ronan away. That was fine with her. Emilie hadn't been on the hunt for a man. Earlier, Goodwin had made it clear he wanted nothing to do with her outside of his duties. Then, within an hour, he had his tongue down her throat in front of the entire village. Was he so possessive that he'd claim a woman he didn't even want just to be the alpha male? Emilie hated that sort of macho behavior, and her insides seethed that he would use her for his own means.

She knew Goodwin would be on her trail. After all, that was his duty, right? The cold night air slapped her in the face as she crossed the threshold, and the thin silk of her borrowed dress did little to stave off the chill. Goodwin's cloak remained in her chamber because this California girl wasn't used to stepping outside in the summer and being enveloped in freezing winds.

"Emilie." Goodwin's deep voice rumbled from behind her, but she took a few more steps into the dark before turning to face him.

"What the ever-loving crap was that?"

"Why do ye and Queen Cait keep calling things 'crap'? Are people in yer time obsessed with shite?"

"No! But we call out the 'shite' when we see it, and that was shite! Goodwin, what *was* that?" she yelled, grappling with her hair as the wind blew it in every direction.

"I kissed ye. And I may not be the smartest man in the world, but I'm fairly certain ye kissed me back."

"I'm not the one who, just an hour ago, said I didn't want more between us!"

"I never said I didn't want more!" he shouted back, hands on his hips. God, he looked good when he was frazzled.

"You said it was only attraction," she reminded him. "Then why stake your claim on me if there is nothing more than attraction? I have no interest in Ronan, and surely you know this. Was this your way of ensuring no other men come near me? If so, I'm sure you succeeded."

"That's not what that was, Emilie. Ye have me in knots! I cannae tell if I want to strangle ye or kiss ye, so I chose the more enjoyable option!"

"That's really freaking romantic, Goodwin!" she scoffed, stepping closer. "Do me a favor. Stop using me for your own purposes. Whatever this rivalry is between you and Ronan has nothing to do with me!"

"There isnae a rivalry! But aye, seeing Ronan with his hands all over ye made me sick. Believe it or not, there was no motive behind that kiss. It was pure instinct. Isnae that how we ended up in bed together before? We cannae seem to control ourselves."

Emilie shook her head and jabbed a finger into his hard chest. "No, *you* have no control. You said you were done with any relationship with me, and I accepted that. I controlled my emotions, even if it hurt. I didn't maul you in front of a room full of people!"

"It hurt ye when I said I didnae want more between us?" he asked, his eyes and voice softening.

"Nobody likes to hear that someone they slept with wants nothing more to do with them, Goodwin. We've known each only a few days, but in that time, we've experienced some traumatic things together. I suppose I felt a stronger connection to you because of that. I realize now that this is nothing new for you, growing up in this time. But in 2023, women are not abducted by vengeful kings and forced to marry them to save another king's heir. That's the crap we read about in novels or see in movies, but don't experience in real life."

"I dinnae understand half of that, but what I do understand makes sense. Emilie, none of this is normal here, either. And nothing about the way I feel about ye is normal for me. I havenae ever done that with any other woman."

"So, that's why half the young women in the village scowled at me," Emilie murmured. "You really are a heartbreaker, aren't you?"

He frowned and shook his head. "Nay. I never once in my life made a woman believe there was more to be had than a night in my bed. Any hope they harbored is not on me."

Emilie scoffed. "Spoken like a true player."

"I dinnae ken what any of what you're saying means!" he roared, throwing his hands in the air. "Heartbreaker! Player!"

"It means that you hold more power over women than you think. You have relations with them, then never look at them again. It hurts them, Goodwin!"

"I have nothing more to offer them than that. Protecting my king and his family to the death, if necessary. This is my life. They ken this well, and it isnae my fault if they hoped for more when nothing was promised."

Emilie pursed her lips and looked at the ground beneath her

feet, toeing a small white rock that stood out against the darker, smaller rocks surrounding it. She sighed and looked at the sky, seeing the North Star shining brightly again. Where was it leading her now? If she followed it to the edge of the world, would it lead her astray?

She was already lost, she decided. "I want a new guard."

"What? Nay!"

"Goodwin, you are incapable of keeping a level head around me. If this is all just attraction, then I don't know what love looks like to you."

"Love?" Goodwin furrowed his brow and opened his mouth before snapping it shut when he couldn't think of anything else.

"Oh, for God's sake. I'm not suggesting you're in love with me! I'm saying you're an intense dude with intense emotions. Oh, 'dude' means 'man.' I need you to remember that because I say it a lot. And, 'hella.' It's a Nor Cal thing."

Goodwin looked at Emilie like she was crazy, and maybe she was, but after that kiss, there was no way to be in his constant presence without losing her mind, especially if neither of them could decide how they truly felt and what they truly wanted. Hell, she still wasn't sure if she was coming or going.

"Ye make no sense to me, lass, but I find I want to ken everything about ye," he whispered, stepping closer.

"I wonder if you're fascinated with me because I come from another time, just as I am fascinated with you for the same reason. I spent my entire life studying your world, your culture. And, here you are, flesh and blood, the very object of my lifelong obsession. It's not *you* that I'm interested in, Goodwin. It's what you represent. It makes sense now that I think about it."

She meant none of that. It hurt even to speak those words, and it hurt more when she saw the look of despair shadow his face. But, this was an unusual situation, and if they could rationalize that a fascination with the unknown was what pulled them together, the faster they could both move on from this. She wasn't going to achieve that with him hovering around her day and night.

Stepping even closer, Goodwin towered above her. Something hard dug into her hip, and she quivered before looking down to see it was the hilt of his sheathed sword. Wisps of cold breath floated from his parted lips, mingling with hers as he leaned in.

"If assigning ye a new guard is what ye want, then so be it. Ye may be confused about what ye want, but make no mistake, Emilie. I ken that I want ye. I want more than yer body," he said, looking down at her pebbled nipples. She crossed her arms and inwardly blamed the cold, though she knew his proximity was the true culprit. "Though I cannae lie. I do want yer body. Verra, verra badly."

Swallowing hard, Emilie struggled to keep her features neutral, refusing to admit how much he affected her. The lilt of his voice melted her insides, making her knees weak.

"I want yer mind. I want to ken everything about ye. I want to spend time with ye, not because I'm ordered to, but because 'tis my greatest desire to spend every moment in yer presence. But, most of all, I want yer heart, for I've given ye mine without even kenning it."

Closing her eyes, Emilie felt the ground beneath her slipping away, crumbling until she felt like she floated on air. How had this ancient warrior captured her in mere days when modern men hadn't ever made her feel this way after months or even two years of dating? There was a rawness to his words and neediness in his grip on her waist. He fought for self-control with every nerve in his body. She felt the tension in his rigid stance and his tightened grip.

Opening her eyes again, she saw the anxiety in his eager gaze as he awaited a response from her. Words floated in her brain, but none came close to doing justice to the moment. Some things were better said with actions, and at that moment, there was only one thing Emilie could think to do.

Reaching onto her tiptoes, Emilie slid her arms around his

neck and looked into his amber eyes, once again reminded of the one treasure she owned in her entire life, a gift from her adoptive mother. Now, that same calm she felt when she held the amber in her palm radiated through her as she looked into his eyes.

Emilie closed the short distance between their lips, gliding hers across his, slowly, gently. They had kissed a few times before but never with so much emotion and angst hanging between them. Their first kiss had been born of intense attraction, their second a product of Goodwin's instinct to claim what he wanted. This time, the kiss was intentional, loaded with unspoken words, consumed with uncertainty and hope.

Goodwin groaned as he pulled her closer and their tongues met, slowly exploring, savoring one another. This time, the hardness she felt against her pelvic bone was not the hilt of his sword, but she tried to focus on her emotions above her physical needs. She had hastily jumped into bed with him, and though she didn't regret it, this situation had escalated beyond attraction.

Her mind floated with possibilities. Was she staying here or going home? Was there anything to go home to aside from her nearly empty flat? Her life had been her work and Caitriona. But, Emilie couldn't bring herself to participate in archaeological digs after the trauma she experienced previously, and Cait was here now. Emilie's existence had been reduced to staring at genealogy websites, trying to trace any record of Caitriona. Someone or something propelled her back to this time for a reason. She assumed the reason was to save Lucas but was there another reason? Was Goodwin her destiny, or was Emilie allowing herself to get too wrapped up in the moment? Would she regret it forever if she left this time, especially if the veil closed on her permanently?

She had a lot to consider, and though every day here made Emilie lean toward staying, it wasn't a decision easily made. One thing was certain: if she stayed, it was for herself, not for a man. Emilie sighed as Goodwin placed both palms on her cheeks and softly stroked his tongue against hers. She was putty in his hands, and logic swirled with fantasy in her overactive mind.

A throat cleared, and Emilie gasped and pulled away from Goodwin, but he kept a tight grip on her waist, unwilling to let her slip away so easily. What was the point? Everyone in the village had already seen Goodwin stake his claim. He may as well get a flag and tie it to her waist for everyone to see.

"Sorry to interrupt." Brodyn stood with his eyes narrowed and large arms crossed while Cait stood beside him, holding Lucas. Murielle and Sam stood behind Brodyn with cheeky grins that only made Emilie more embarrassed. "You want to tell me what that was in there?"

"I... I'm sorry," Emilie squeaked, hoping she hadn't insulted Cait's husband somehow.

"Nay. Not ye," Brodyn said. He pointed at Goodwin and narrowed his eyes. "Ye ken ye cannae get attached to yer ward. Yer mind will become addled and compromised. I'm taking ye off her guard. She needs a man who will keep his hands to himself."

Goodwin raised a brow, not appearing affected at all. "Verra well. I was going to suggest the same."

"Ye were?" Brodyn cocked his head and rose a brow.

"Aye. It's become obvious to everyone, including myself, that I have grown fond of Emilie. I willnae lie to her or my king. I require a position that will keep my head on straight."

Brodyn pursed his lips and nodded. "Battle is impending. I wish to catch Arwyn before he returns to Gwynedd or shows up at our gates. His men will be weakened and exhausted from travel. Now is the time."

"Agreed, my king. I'd like to believe he wouldnae be mad enough to show up at our gates with so few supplies, but he has proved himself emotional and reckless. I believe, worst of all, there is a corrupt guard amongst our ranks. 'Tis the only way Arwyn's men could have gotten to Lucas."

Brodyn nodded. "I have considered the verra same, and I spoke with Lawrence, who guarded my wife and son, but he is innocent of foul play. He came to my aid when the fight broke out near Murielle's chamber. I believe that someone told Arwyn about the tunnel beneath her chamber. He intended to break in and take Murielle by force, but it was Emilie inside the chamber. In the commotion, Lawrence left Allen in charge of Lucas to fight in the corridor. Now, Allen is conveniently missing."

"That son of a bitch," Goodwin growled. "All of this is his fault?"

"I cannae say for certain until we find the man and get some answers. Lawrence will guard Emilie. He, unlike ye and Ronan, seems able to resist her charms."

Goodwin looked at Emilie with relief in his gaze, and she knew he was glad that Lawrence and not Ronan would shadow her. She felt her face flush as the men spoke about her like some siren luring men to their demise.

"And what of me, my king?" he asked. "Shall I ready the men for battle?"

Brodyn nodded. "Aye. We leave at dawn. I ken this gives us little time, but I wanted to boost morale within the village and celebrate Lucas and Emilie's safe return. But, the celebration ends, and the battle begins the moment the sun creeps over that horizon," he said, pointing to a distant mountain range to the east.

"Aye. I will tell the men now and begin preparations."

"We must also seal off all escape tunnels leading outside the village. If Allen betrayed us, Arwyn could access our tunnels."

Alarm showed in Goodwin's widened eyes. "Aye. I will send men out immediately to board up the tunnels from the forest side." Goodwin began to walk away, but before he did, he turned back to Emilie with a heat in his gaze that threatened to catch her on fire. "We arenae done here. I will speak with ye before I leave on the morrow." Before she could open her mouth to say a word, Goodwin pulled her to him and slashed his mouth against hers again. "Now, if I fall in battle, I will die with a smile, kenning I kissed the most beautiful woman in this time and any time before or after."

He stormed toward the armory, leaving Emilie flustered and swerving where she stood.

"Damn," Cait said, stepping up to Emilie. "Goodwin is smitten."

"I've never seen him like this," Murielle said, wide-eyed and mouth agape.

"Surely, he has been this way before," Emilie said, trying to cut the tension. "A man like him is just passionate. He likely is this way with every woman he fancies before he moves on."

Murielle scoffed. "Not accurate."

"Nay," Brodyn added. "He's never kissed a woman in public like this. He means what he says, lass. Ye have some thinking to do. And I have a battle to prepare for." He took a few steps toward the armory but turned on his heels and took Cait in his arms, dipping her backward just before slipping his tongue into her mouth. Surprised, Cait squealed but melted into him, wrapping her arms around his neck as he kissed her senseless. When he pulled away, he winked at his wife. "I couldn't let Goodwin show me up."

"Ye never could," Murielle said, rolling her eyes.

Brodyn stormed off this time and didn't look back. "Are all men like this in this time?" Emilie asked, watching the men disappear into the armory.

Murielle slowly nodded. "I havenae found one. Mayhap 'tis ye women from the future that drive them mad. I should take a few lessons."

Samuel had remained quiet throughout the night's events, and Emilie looked at him, wondering what he was thinking. When he saw her pondering him, he cleared his throat. "King Brodyn is right, Em. Soon you must decide to return home or stay here. That's what I wished to speak to you about earlier."

Emilie looked at Cait as she held Lucas on her hip and booped him on the nose, making him giggle.

"Oddly, I think I've already made my choice." She smiled at Cait, who lit up with a blinding white smile.

"Em, I'd love nothing more than for you to stay, but you need to decide if it's what you want. Don't make the decision based on anyone else. This is your future, your life."

Emilie smiled. "Cait, if you knew how I spent my days alone in my flat in Edinburgh, you'd understand why this is an easy decision for me. You and Samuel are my family. I spent my entire life studying an ancient civilization I now find myself in, and you and Samuel are here. How can I leave this behind?"

"I don't stay here, Em. I come and go," Samuel reminded her.

"I know, but Edinburgh is far from where you are even in my time. I never saw you. I'm staying, but I suddenly realize that I do have some affairs to put in order in Edinburgh."

"Such as?" Cait asked.

"Such as paying my final rent to the landlord and breaking the lease. He gave me a home when I had nowhere to go. I can't just disappear on him. He has kids to feed."

"Then, I will safely escort you back to the cave," Samuel said.

"Ye are a fine woman, Emilie Wilshire. I see why Goodwin loves ye," Murielle said with a kind smile.

Emilie furrowed her brow and looked sideways at Murielle. "Goodwin isn't in love with me!"

Murielle raised a brow and shrugged. "One of us has kenned him for three days. One of us has kenned him for 20 years. I'd usually laugh in the face of anyone who said love could be found in three days, but that's before I saw Brodyn with Cait. If this isnae love, it sure is on its way to becoming love. But, I agree with Cait. If ye stay, dinnae do it for a man."

"I would never." And Emilie knew her words to be true. No matter how she felt about Goodwin, she simply could not, would not give up her life for a man she had just met. "But, I've known Cait for the past eight years, and I know that some kinds of love are worth sacrificing everything for."

Cait leaned in to kiss Emilie's cheek just as Lawrence's bulky body stomped over to her side with crossed arms. "I see ye've requested yer favorite guard?" he said with a smirk. "Tired of

Goodwin trying to eat yer face?"

Emilie rolled her eyes. This coming from the man who hog-tied her when he found her wandering the land beneath their hillfort. "Just don't bind me ever again, and we will be fine." Emilie hugged Murielle, Cait, and Lucas before walking toward the house. She was exhausted and needed sleep, but she wasn't sure that would be possible after all that had occurred tonight. Aside from Goodwin being unable to control himself around her, Emilie had essentially brought on a battle that Goodwin and other men might die fighting—at least she blamed herself even if she knew, deep down, none of it was her fault. Not only did that weigh on her soul, but if Goodwin died because of her, she would never forgive herself.

"It's not your fault!" Cait shouted to Emilie as she walked away. Stopping to look at her friend from over her shoulder, Emilie saw the look on Cait's face. "This is Arwyn's fault. He made his own choice to kidnap Lucas. You did what you had to do to save my son, so don't you dare blame any of this on yourself!"

"How… how did you know what I was thinking?"

"I know you better than you think. Now get some rest. I love you."

"Love you more!" Emilie shouted to her best friend as Lawrence lumbered behind her, looking too much like a flesh-colored Shrek for Emilie's comfort. She was definitely safe from falling for him, but the knots in her belly made her question if it was too late to spare her heart from falling for Goodwin.

EVEN IN THE dead of night, with the wind stirring the leaves at his feet, sweat dripped down Goodwin's bared chest as he loaded supplies onto wagons, preparing for departure. Nobody had mentioned the scene he had created hours before, and he was glad for that. There was too much running through his mind and too much to do for him to knock out someone's teeth right now. Though, he was itching to spar with someone, to loosen up his stiff muscles before they left. The sun would rise in an hour, and he would be gone. There was no telling which direction Arwyn's men had traveled. Would they be found on their way to Pinnata Castra, or would they be halfway to Gwynedd?

If the journey took an entire cycle of the moon, so be it. There was no length Goodwin wouldn't go to make Arwyn pay for his many transgressions against those Goodwin called family. Ronan entered the armory and gathered a handful of arrows to add to the supply cart, checking Goodwin in the shoulder as he passed.

Goodwin wiped the sweat from his brow and glared at his friend. "Are we going to have problems?" he snapped at Ronan. He didn't want to fight with Ronan, but he was done with his friend's petty behavior and pouting all night.

"Aye, we have a problem. Ye kenned I was interested in Emilie, so ye humiliated me by grabbing her and kissing her in front of the entire village, claiming her for yer own without regard to her feelings or mine. Mayhap she prefers me."

"She doesnae," Goodwin huffed, picking up several bows to load in the cart.

"Ye cannae ken that," Ronan shouted, pushing Goodwin from behind and making him drop the bows with a clatter.

"Aye, I can!" Goodwin pushed him back. "Dinnae do this, Ronan. We are on the same side. We need to focus on the battle, not a woman."

"Easy for ye to say when yer so certain she will choose ye when ye get back."

Cracking his neck to the left, then the right, Goodwin straightened his spine and stepped up to Ronan, his equal height and weight and a damned good sparring partner. "I dinnae ken if she will even be here when I get back. Dinnae forget she is a visitor. There may be no future with her for either of us, especially if we die in battle. Can we focus now?"

Goodwin bent over to collect the bows he dropped, but Ronan pushed him again, this time making him fall forward into the dirt. Filth mixed with his sweat, caking his chest in a muddy mess. Scrambling to his feet, Goodwin roared and plowed into Ronan, knocking the man on his arse.

"If ye want to brawl, then we will brawl, but make it a fair fight, not when my back is turned!"

"Fine!" Ronan got to his feet and threw a fist, but Goodwin dodged, throwing a right hook into the man's stomach. Ronan grunted but retaliated with a shot to Goodwin's jaw, making his head snap back.

"Ye bloody arse!" Goodwin knocked Ronan to the ground and connected with his nose just before he felt someone grab him from behind and pull him away. Looking over his shoulder, he saw Lawrence scowling at them.

"Why are ye here? Ye're supposed to guard Emilie!" Goodwin shouted, wiping a trickle of blood from his lip.

"He *is* watching me." He heard Emilie's voice and froze, wiping more blood from his lip.

"What are ye doing here?" Goodwin asked as he bent over to help Ronan off the ground. His friend accepted the help with a hesitant grunt, turning away before he had to face Emilie.

"I couldn't sleep. I've been up all night worrying about the battle," she said. "I wanted to see you before you leave."

"Why is that?" he asked.

She looked him up and down with a frown. "You are covered in dirt and blood. Why were you fighting Ronan?" A hint of anger laced her tone.

"It seems he is displeased with me." That was all he wished to say on the matter, and her frown and nod told him he needed to say no more.

"All of this is my fault. The battle, your fight with Ronan. I don't even belong here. I'm causing too much trouble."

"Dinnae say that, Emilie." He couldn't help but be near her.

He took her hand in his and pulled her closer as Lawrence took over, helping to load carts with supplies. "Arwyn was in the village when ye arrived, remember? Murielle wasnae going to marry him. He was always going to be sent away without a wife, and he was always going to steal Lucas in retaliation. None of that was yer doing. Ye showed up and risked yer life to save him. I dinnae wish to be bold in saying this, but I hope to be the man to make a widow of ye."

Emilie bit her lower lip to prevent a small smile, but he saw the amusement in her eyes. "I welcome widowhood. If you make me a widow, I will repay you with a kiss."

"Oh, aye?" he asked, perking up and pulling her closer. "But, I cannae have a kiss now?"

"Perhaps," she said with a shrug. "I wouldn't wish to deprive a warrior of a kiss on the eve of battle."

Goodwin leaned in, his heart pounding in his chest, desperate to taste her sweet lips again. Instead, he was met with her hand against his mouth. "But first, I wish to speak with you."

"Can we kiss, then talk?" he asked, flashing her his best seductive grin, but she smiled and shook her head.

"Talk first," she insisted. "I wanted you to know that I will return to my time while you're away."

His heart dropped to his toes, and he felt all the blood drain from his face, leaving him dizzy and unstable. "Ye decided to leave?" He tried to mask his despair, but he knew she saw his distress.

"Only for a while," she added, giving him a wee burst of hope. "I have decided to stay in this time with Caitriona and Lucas. They are the only family I have. There is nothing in my time worth ever leaving them again. But, I have some business to deal with before settling in. Samuel will guide me back there."

Relief flooded Goodwin's chest, and he took a deep breath of fresh air. She was staying. Nothing she said reflected a desire to stay for him, but that was fine. He understood it was a great decision, and though they shared a bond, she didn't know him well enough to stay for his sake. But, it gave him time to woo her and prove his worth. That's all he needed. "Kenning that ye will be here when I return will sustain me on my journey. Now I ken I willnae perish, for I have too much to look forward to. That is, if ye are willing to give me the chance to prove my worth."

"Oh, Goodwin." Emilie wrapped her arms around his waist, placing her head against his sweaty, muddy, bared chest. "You are the sweetest man I've ever met. There is so much we don't know about one another. I wish we had more time before you left."

"Come with me." Goodwin took her hand and dragged her away from the armory, pulling her beneath a willow, its long vine-like branches hiding them away from the chaos just feet away.

"What are we doing?"

"I have one hour before I leave. I wish to spend it with ye, and I just want to talk. No kissing."

"No kissing?" she asked, feigning shock.

"All right, mayhap a wee bit of kissing, as well. But I want to ken all I can about ye. Right now. Tell me everything."

"Oh... it's hard to summarize twenty-six years of my life, but I will try. But then, it's your turn."

Goodwin nodded and sat on the grass beneath the tree, pulling her into his lap. She wore a thin white tunic with his cloak wrapped around her shoulders, making his pulse quicken and his stomach flip. Seeing her in his cloak was almost as wonderful as seeing her naked. *Almost.* "Ye have yerself an agreement."

"Okay," she sighed, nestling into his lap to get comfortable. "My full name is Emilia Jean Wilshire. I was born in a place called California. It's very warm and sunny there almost all of the time. I'm an orphan. I know nothing about my parents except that they gave me away, so I figured they weren't worth knowing. My adoptive parents were amazing, but both died by the time I was ten. I spent my life in foster care—which means living with different families until I finished school... my education," she said to clarify. "And I went on to college, where we learn certain trades. That's where I met Cait. We lived together and were inseparable since we were eighteen—until the day she disappeared through that cave."

Goodwin listened, trying to make sense of most of her words. "That must have been verra frightening."

"It was the very worst time of my life. I thought she was dead. All I did was cry and search endlessly for her. Then one day, she showed up again, and I received a call that she was in the hospital. That's where people go when they are sick. Then, she found out she was pregnant with Lucas, and she came back here, and I've been all alone ever since, spending my days on the internet, trying to find anything about her."

"Internet?" he asked as he scooped her blonde hair behind one ear and tilted his head in confusion.

"There is not enough time to explain what that is. Maybe once you return. What it comes down to is my life has not been great, at least not until I met Cait. She's my family. Where she goes, I go. I tried to follow her here many times. The cave wouldn't let me through. Then one day, I woke up here. Maybe *she's* my soulmate." Emilie laughed at that, and Goodwin couldn't help but slide his hands beneath the cloak to rub her back in comfort.

"Yer life isn't too different from mine. In fact, I daresay they are nearly identical in some ways," he said. "I am 27 years old and also an orphan. I was raised by Brodyn's family. That's why I tried to tell ye that I'm not in love with Murielle. Many people, including Brodyn, have thought the same because we are so close, but she is my sister. My life has been nothing but training, guarding the royal family, and fighting battles. Until ye showed up, I had nothing to look forward to, nothing to live for." He realized at that moment that he may have said too much, but he was open, raw, and vulnerable around her. He may very well not make it home, and if he died on that battlefield, he wanted nothing left unsaid to the bonnie woman in his lap who made his heart pound, his cock hard, and his blood rage. More than that, she made him hope for something more.

"I admit, I find hope in this, too, Goodwin. I'm too afraid of getting hurt. Everyone I care about always leaves me. Even Cait did, though I would never blame her. She found her soulmate, and I am beyond happy for her. Still, part of me wishes it was my turn."

"Maybe it is. Emilie, I have never cared about a woman the way I care about ye, so quickly, so deeply."

She nodded, and he felt that she wanted to return the sentiment but was too afraid. He understood that feeling, also. Being vulnerable was scarier for him than any battle. "What's yer favorite food?" he asked to lighten the mood.

"Easy. Twinkies." Goodwin creased his brow. What, by all the pagan gods, was a Twinkie? She giggled and smacked his leg. "Don't look at me that way. It's a disgustingly delicious treat, like a cake filled with cream. My adoptive mom used to buy them in bulk and hide them from my dad because she knew they were not good for her. So, we would hide in the closet and eat them together until we felt sick. It's one of my only memories of her. That and an old piece of amber she once gave me that had an insect trapped inside. It's my only remaining piece of her."

"I wish I could try a Twinkie," he said with a smile.

"Oh, they are hella good, dude."

Goodwin laughed at her ridiculous words. She had warned him. "My favorite food is an apple," he said. "They only grow once a year and are so sweet and juicy…. Just like yer lips."

"That is so cheesy," Emilie said, smiling at him.

He frowned. "Nay, apples dinnae taste like cheese."

Emilie tilted her head back and laughed. "This feels like speed dating. In my time, you can meet someone you don't know and have only a few moments to get to know them and see if you like them."

"Oh, aye? And, do ye like me?" Goodwin asked, pulling her slightly closer, burying his nose into her golden hair. It smelled like roses and cinnamon, and he saved it to memory in case he never got the chance to smell her again.

Emilie looked up at him with her eyes, the color of moss mixed with sunshine, and a smile spread across her bonnie face. "I more than like you, Goodwin."

When her words processed in his mind, Goodwin's smile slid from his face as he looked down to study her features. "I more than like ye, too, Emilie. Might I kiss ye now?"

"Since when do you wait for permission?" she asked with mischief crinkling in the corners of her eyes.

"Since ye got angry at me the last time."

Looking at him, Emilie twisted in his lap to better face him. "I want nothing more than to kiss you right now," she whispered, placing her hands on the sides of his face.

"Lass, I want many things more than a kiss, but I will take whatever ye are willing to give." He knew she felt his desire pressing against her backside, but he couldn't help his body's reaction whenever he was this close to her.

On a sigh, Emilie placed her lips on his, slowly at first, lingering, exploring. He followed her lead, savoring the passionate slide of her tongue against his. When her pace quickened, and she rocked against his groin, Goodwin groaned and slid his hands lower beneath the cloak, cupping her sweet backside as Emilie fisted his tunic.

Goodwin tore himself away from her kiss, panting as he grappled for control. "By the gods, how do ye affect me this way? If we dinnae slow down, I cannae control where my hands wander next."

Emilie heaved for breath and nodded. "I know. You have the same effect on me. But, you're right. You have to leave here soon, and your men need you. I don't want to take any more of your time."

"I wish to give ye all my time," he murmured against her lips. "But I ken ye are right."

"You will come back to me, Goodwin. Do you hear me? You can't come into my life like this and not come back."

"I vow I will return. Kenning ye await me is the greatest motivation to survive."

"Good. Now, finish helping your men, and know that I'm thinking of you every moment while you're away."

Goodwin swore he'd float away if not for her weight pinning him down. He wanted to carry her home and never let her go, but that wasn't reality. He had things to take care of, and so did she. But when they came together again, he vowed to win her over entirely.

Together they stood up and kissed one last time before Lawrence ambled over with crossed arms. "Ye done sucking her face off there, Goodwin? We gotta get moving."

Emilie gripped his hand and squeezed. "Come back to me."

"Nothing will stop me. Not even the devil himself."

Slowly, her hand slipped from his, leaving him feeling empty without her touch, but his heart was full as he watched her walk back to the house with Lawrence by her side, feeling a heaviness in his chest that made him almost sick. "So, this is love," he whispered beneath the willow tree. It was singularly the most wonderfully painful sensation he had ever felt in his entire life. Sweeter than the juiciest apple yet deadlier than the sharpest blade. Now he understood why men killed for love. He would kill Arwyn not only for what he did to Lucas but for forcing Emilie to marry him.

And, when he returned, he prayed he'd be the next and last man ever to call her wife.

CHAPTER TEN

WITH THE CORAL and lavender-streaked sky still fighting off new rays of sunlight as clouds shifted with the wind, the entire village came out to say goodbye to the men who would risk their lives to keep everyone else safe. Husbands hugged wives, and fathers hugged children. Brodyn and Cait huddled in a corner together with Lucas between them, and Emilie stood beside Murielle, watching the men ready to depart. Goodwin shoved a few more sacks of food stores into one of the carts before walking toward Emilie, and her heart thumped wildly against her chest as a gorgeous grin lit up his face.

"Goodwin is a lost cause," Murielle said with a sigh. "Ye ken, many women in the village are devastated."

Emilie had no time to respond before Goodwin took her hand and pulled her to him. "'Tis time for me to go, but I shall return."

"You promised," Emilie said, laying her ear against his chest, listening to the beat of his heart.

"Aye, and I always keep my promises." Goodwin placed a finger beneath her chin and tilted her head to look at him. "I love ye, Emilie."

"W-what?" she asked, stumbling on her words as shock and warmth radiated through her skin like a roaring tsunami of emotion. Nobody had ever said those words to her and hearing them roll off his tongue so smoothly made her stomach flutter. In the deepest recess of her heart, she knew she already loved him, too, even if it felt too soon to admit openly.

"Ye dinnae need to respond. I just couldnae leave for battle without ye kenning my heart."

He kissed her forehead affectionately while she stood as still as a statue, processing his words. With a nod, his dark waves of hair blew in the wind like some ancient version of Fabio but ten times hotter. Still, she stared blankly back, unable to make her mouth move.

He turned toward Boudicca, who munched on grass near the carts, and tied his satchel to her saddle.

"Go, Emilie," Murielle said with a nudge. "Do ye love him?" Emilie looked at Murielle, then Goodwin, and back. Swallowing hard and feeling a pinch in her chest, she nodded. "Then go. Tell him. He can promise to return all he wants. Every man here has promised the verra same to his family, but some of them willnae return. Nothing is certain. Ye dinnae ken because ye didnae grow up here, but when the men leave, some never return. Dinnae have any regrets."

Nodding, Emilie lifted her skirts and dodged some fresh rain puddles as she pushed through the crowd of weeping women and children. "Goodwin!"

Just before he mounted Boudicca, Goodwin's head turned toward Emilie's voice, and she plowed into him, gripping his strong arms as she looked up at him. "I love you, too." His dimple flashed, and she clung to him to keep herself steady.

"Ye dinnae need to say it simply because I may not return. Only say it if ye feel 'tis true in yer heart."

"It is," Emilie whispered. "It scares the crap out of me, but it's true. I've fallen in love with you, Goodwin."

He dipped her backward and kissed her senseless as the wind blew through her hair. It felt like a scene from a romance novel. She was living her very own love story, and she clung to him, desperate to commit this moment to memory, to allow it to sustain her as she awaited his return.

"Ye have made me the happiest man alive, Emilie Wilshire. If

I return, I hope ye will consider becoming Emilia Jean Mac Dougal."

They sure didn't waste time dating in the year 686, but life here was tumultuous, and women were married and breeding by the age of sixteen. Compared to most of the single lasses in the village, Emilie was ancient and considered no longer of marriageable age. None of that mattered to her. She just cared about following her bliss. Besides, she had dated Thomas for two years and never felt this way about him. Sometimes, it wasn't the amount of time spent with a person. It was the quality of time spent. Every second with Goodwin felt like the greatest moment of her life.

She nodded and kissed him gently once more. "Just focus on coming home so we can discuss our future when you return. But, I do like the sound of that."

He flashed her another smile as the train of men began to depart. With the ease of a seasoned rider, Goodwin mounted Boudicca and sent her a final wink before taking off down the hill, speeding up to flank Brodyn.

Emilie stood and stared as he rode away, wondering if her years spent devouring romance novels had turned her into a sap, but she didn't care. Her man rode off to battle, and the knots in her belly tightened with every clop of Boudicca's hooves toward the gate.

A hand gripped Emilie, making her turn to see who dug their claws into her flesh. A small woman, perhaps a few years younger than Emilie, scowled at her with blue eyes, her red hair blowing in the wind. "Ye think ye can keep his interest? Every lass in the village has failed, and ye will, too. Mayhap ye should go back to whatever hole ye crawled out of before ye find yerself in an unpleasant situation."

"And you are?" Emilie asked, raising a brow and jerking out of the girl's grip.

"Sarah, the woman he was courting before ye showed up."

"Huh, he never mentioned your name to me. Something tells

me your feelings for Goodwin were not reciprocated. You can blame me, but he decided against you before I stepped foot onto this soil."

"I was in his bed the night before ye showed up!" the lass hissed. "I could carry his child!" Emilie scowled, unsure if she should believe this woman, but even if her words were true, she spoke of a time before Emilie even knew Goodwin existed. She wouldn't be jealous of his past, even if it was only days ago.

"Goodwin is a big boy. He can make his own decisions. Neither of us speaks on his behalf. Now, if you will excuse me." Emilie stormed off, feeling deflated. She should have known something like this was bound to happen. Sarah may not have been encouraged to speak up while Goodwin was present, but now that he had left, Sarah seemed determined to cause trouble. Good thing Emilie was best friends with the queen.

"Aye, he can make his own decision—unless ye are a witch who placed a spell on him," Sarah threatened with malice in her tone.

Emilie kept walking, doing her best to ignore the angry woman. She wasn't certain how serious a witch accusation was in this time. She'd need to speak with Cait and make sure nobody started to build a pyre. These people only converted to Christianity two generations ago, so many still valued their pagan roots, and pagans didn't believe in witches in the same manner Christians did. Emilie only prayed the pagan origins of these people kept them from starting a witch hunt.

Murielle stood by the house talking to Samuel, and they seemed deep in conversation, so Emilie walked past them on her way back to the house.

"Em! Wait!" Murielle lifted her skirt and trotted toward Emilie, a grim look on her face. "Believe nothing Sarah says. She's a loose woman of looser morals. She is willing to do anything to get what she wants, and for the past year, she's decided she wants Goodwin."

"She said as much," Emilie said. "I trust him and his word. If he wants to be with me, I trust there is nobody else. Sarah doesn't scare me. Okay, so her witch threat wasn't great."

"What?" Murielle shook her head. "That lass needs to watch herself. For all she kens, ye are the queen's sister. How dare she threaten ye?"

Emilie shrugged. "I'm not too concerned. Goodwin asked me to consider marriage..." Emilie leaned in to whisper in Murielle's ear, so Samuel didn't overhear. He seemed preoccupied, now talking to Cait and holding Lucas, but Emilie wanted to keep this knowledge between her, Murielle, and Cait.

Murielle shook her head, her blue eyes widening. "By all the saints!" Murielle squealed. "I kenned he was in love with ye, but even I am surprised at how quickly this has progressed."

"Yeah, it's scary," Emilie said slowly. "My logical side says this is insanity, but my heart says this is the real thing. He's it for me."

"Of course, he is. Anyone can see that. Why do ye think Sarah is so angry? She failed to win him over despite many, many futile attempts. Ye show up, and less than a sennight later, Goodwin is a changed man, considering marriage. I do believe ye have Cait to thank for some of this," Murielle said, beginning to walk back toward the house. Emilie followed, cocking her head.

"How so?"

"Before Cait arrived, both he and Brodyn were grouchy, brooding warriors who wanted nothing to do with love. Brodyn forced Cait to marry him, thinking she was a lass sent to form an alliance. He had no interest in marriage beyond political gains, and he certainly didnae expect to love his wife. I think Goodwin was satisfied with his position in the king's guard and casual encounters with women. But, Cait swept Brodyn off his feet, and Goodwin saw how happy he was. I ken for certain Goodwin has changed since she arrived. He hasnae bedded any lasses... I ken this because if he had, we'd all hear about it. These lassies discuss their conquests with the pride of men charging into battle."

"Sarah said she was in his bed the day before I arrived."

Murielle laughed as she opened the door to their home and stepped inside with Emilie behind her. "She probably was, though she was most certainly not invited. He was with Brodyn and me the entire night before ye arrived. We were busy with Arwyn and his men. Goodwin guarded me that night and slept outside my chamber door. I ken he wouldnae have left his post."

Somehow, a weight lifted from Emilie that she hadn't been aware she carried. Though she wasn't intimidated by Sarah, Goodwin had said it had been a while since he slept with another woman, and Emilie wanted to believe that Goodwin was an honest man. He had nothing to gain by lying about such things.

For now, aside from worrying about Goodwin every second, Emilie had her own life to tend to, and if she was going to stay here with Cait, she needed to know a few details—like how to survive in this time and where she would live if she didn't marry Goodwin. Again, she reminded herself that she would stay for herself and Cait, but not a man. That included making arrangements for herself that didn't include him. If things worked out, which she hoped they would, then she could discuss those details with Goodwin. For now, she needed a plan.

Emilie found Cait over by the fire, nursing Lucas as she spoke with Anya, who chopped vegetables on a wooden slab. "So, if I'm going to stay, I need a purpose here. I have no idea how to do anything."

Cait looked at Emilie and laughed. "I understand completely. We don't have grocery stores or malls here. We make our own food, shelter, clothing... everything."

"In theory, I know how all of it was done. I've read about making fabric on the loom or using plants and piss for dyes, but I have no idea how it's actually done."

"Well, there is no time like the present to learn," Cait said, shifting Lucas to the other breast.

"Ye can start by chopping these carrots for tonight's stew," Anya said, signaling Emilie to take over.

"I already know how to chop carrots," Emilie said, picking up the knife.

"I figured as much. But I'm 99 years old, and damn it all, I need to sit."

Emilie chuckled as Anya shuffled over to a bench and kicked up her feet. "I amnae long for this world, lassies. I feel my spirit growing weary. Without Edwin here all these decades, I've awaited death. 'Twas death that brought him to me, and in death, we can be together again and start our next life. But my cursed flesh willnae release me."

Emilie frowned at the old lady, hearing the pain in her voice. She remembered Caitriona telling her that Anya arrived in this time during the Second World War, hiding from dropping bombs in a cave. But when she left the cave, she met Edwin, who ended up being her soulmate through many lifetimes. The same story was true for Caitriona. If only Goodwin had been Emilie's destined mate throughout every lifetime, this decision might be easier to make. Cait knew without a doubt she belonged here with Brodyn. For Emilie, she had to follow her instincts to make the best choices. There was freedom in that, and she was determined to make the best of this, even if Sarah was determined to make her miserable.

"I find the best way to pass the time while the men are away is to consume myself in chores," Caitriona said.

"Spoken like a true Pictish woman," Emilie said with a smile. "I'm more than ready to earn my keep around here. I'm not sure when Samuel is returning to our time, but hopefully, it won't take me too long to return here."

"Assuming the veil allows ye to cross through again," Anya said from behind her.

Emilie paused chopping the carrots and looked over her shoulder at the older woman. "I hadn't even considered that. What if I can't go back? Or, worse, I go back and can't return here?"

"'Tis possible," Anya murmured. "Samuel and I can pass through as needed because our role in this time loop mess required it. I was able to aid the Picts with my medical knowledge and gather modern supplies. Samuel was meant to bring Cait to Brodyn to prevent the destruction of what will be Scotland someday. But if ye were brought here solely to save Lucas, yer task is done."

"Unless there is another reason she was sent here," Murielle added, walking over to the chopping block to snag a few pieces of carrots. "What if she is meant to stay here with Goodwin and have his bairns?" She waggled her brows before popping the carrot pieces into her mouth.

Emilie pursed her lips. "I don't think I'm destined for much of anything," she confessed. "But hey, at least I can say I'm the Queen of the Britons for now," she said wryly.

"Emilie, you weren't ever able to pass through the cave after I left, were you?" Cait asked. Frowning, Emilie shook her head. "I fear you won't be allowed back if you leave."

Emilie hadn't thought of any of these details, but now she wasn't sure she should try to head back to 2023 if there was a risk she couldn't return. Now that she had decided to stay, leaving Caitriona, Lucas, and even Goodwin seemed impossible.

"We will think about the options, Em. Why don't you follow me outside? I will show you how everything is done—making dye, making fabric, dying the fabric, gutting fish, and plucking chickens. Even making soap and candles."

"Maybe I should go back to 2023, after all," she quipped, and Caitriona stood up, handing Lucas over to a young nursemaid.

"It's not so bad. You get used to the labor. There is beauty in a small village working as one to sustain life. You can be a part of that."

"Okay, I'm convinced. Let's go." Putting down the knife, Emilie followed Caitriona into the new day, ready to learn how to be a proper Pict woman. As Caitriona properly introduced Emilie to the people they passed, the reactions ranged from wary to amused. Everyone had seen the claiming kiss the village's champion warrior planted on her last night, and many of the young lassies were not pleased. Many backs remained turned away from her, making their lack of acceptance well-understood without words. Apparently, mean girl cliques weren't just a modern experience, and based on the daggers Sarah shot at her from the center of her mean-girl circle, Sarah was their Regina George. *Great.* Emilie did always have a way of pissing off the wrong person.

"Forget them," Caitriona said, waving them off. "They are all jealous. None of them could keep his attention for more than thirty seconds despite years of trying. You showed up, and he claimed you immediately. They will get over it when another handsome warrior flashes a grin at them."

"I hope so. I didn't fall 1,300 years into the past to be cast out by yet another popular group. I've had enough of that for one lifetime."

"Well, if it ain't the new lass who stole Goodwin's heart," A plump woman wearing a kerchief in her hair said with a smile, her ruddy cheeks glistening with sweat from the steam rising from several barrels. "Have ye come to get yer hands dirty?"

"Indeed, I have," Emilie beamed, glad to have at least one member in her welcoming party.

"Grab yerself a stick. See those bundles of wool? They need to be dunked into the vats of dye and allowed to soak overnight."

Emilie walked over and bent over to grab a stick, being re-pelled backward when the pungent smell accosted her nostrils. "Good lord," she hissed as her eyes watered and her nose stung.

"Och, aye. 'twas a nasty batch of urine this time."

"Where does it come from?" Emilie asked, trying not to ap-pear overly affected by the stench of steamed piss mixed with powdered dyes.

"From everyone. We piss in the chamber pots and pour them all into the vats. Ye can do many things with a good vat of urine." The lady gave Emilie a crooked smile as she tossed bundles into what looked like an orange-colored dye. "I sometimes forget that ye and yer sister were raised in a royal household. Ye had servants for these chores. Ye ken nobody would expect a royal lass to do this."

"If I stay here, I want to do my part," Emilie said, hesitantly tossing more wool into a purply-blue dye.

"Och, ye are staying? How wonderful! Has it anything to do with a certain warrior?"

Emilie shook her head, feeling her hair frizz from the steam." No, no. I want to be with my sister and my nephew. We have no other family left."

"Family is all that matters in this world, lass. Pay no attention to the young ones over there giving ye grief. They dinnae like not being the center of everyone's attention."

Caitriona raised a brow and helped stir the wool floating inside the barrels. "They weren't very welcoming to me, either, but they accept me now."

"You're their queen! They have to, or else Brodyn will stomp them into pancakes. They have no reason to accept me."

"What is a pancake?" the plump woman asked with a cocked head.

"Uh…" Emilie really needed to watch what she said around here. "It's a delicious sort of cake we make in Dal Riata," she added quickly. "You mix finely-ground wheat with butter, eggs, and milk."

"Like an oatcake but with flour? It's like bread?"

"Yes! Yes, like bread but without the yeast. It stays flat in the pan. So, it's called a pancake."

"Well, mayhap ye and yer sister can show us this pancake some time," the woman said with a smile.

Time passed quickly as Emilie stayed busy helping the women around the village with all manner of chores. She made candles and soap, worked the loom, and before she knew it, her back ached, her injured feet throbbed despite the magical salve Anya applied to them, and it was time for dinner in the longhouse.

"This day flew by!" she said to Cait as they headed home to

clean themselves before their meal.

"Oh, they really do. It's easy to get lost in the work. We Picts work hard and play hard. But with the men away, you will find a more subdued environment in the longhouse. No dancing and minimal laughter. The women honor the men's sacrifice by saving the ale and celebrations for their return."

Emilie felt a warmth in her heart for these people. They truly were a community and shared their burdens. It was so unlike the big cities she'd grown up in. When they returned to the house, Murielle pulled Emilie into her chamber.

"Em! Get ready in here. I already have some warm, scented water. We cannae take a full bath, but we can clean ourselves up while we get to ken one other more."

"Sure!" Emilie gladly entered Murielle's chamber but paused when she looked beneath the bed, where the secret door was.

"Dinnae concern yerself with Arwyn," Murielle said, reading her mind. "I ken our guards have all left for battle, but they wouldnae have left us without protection. The gates are well-guarded, and the tunnel exits in the forest have been boarded up. Even if Arwyn kenned about the tunnels from one of the guards, they cannae enter them."

Nodding, Emilie entered the room and removed her smelly overtunic, leaving on her sheer white undertunic and rolling up the sleeves. Murielle handed her a clean cloth, and together they wiped away the grime from the day.

"I must confess to being verra intrigued by yer time," Murielle said before scrubbing her face until it glowed a healthy pink color. "Caitriona has told me that women have equal rights in yer time."

"For the most part, yes. But, it's still a battle, and one women have fought for centuries. We can work all the jobs as men, but we get paid much less for the same work."

Murielle crinkled her brows and pouted. "That's unfair."

"Yeah, it is. It's still a work in progress, but we aren't forced into marriages, and we have a lot more rights than we used to."

"My greatest desire is to see yer time, but I fear I cannae cross over, and worse, if I did, I wouldnae be able to return."

Emilie scoffed and nodded. "I understand completely."

"Mayhap ye can ask Samuel to help with yer chores in yer time. Ye may not be able to go back and forth, but he can."

"True, but he has no access to my bank accounts... that's where we keep the money... like coins, where it's safe. He is my beneficiary. That means he gets all my money if I die since I have no family. I signed everything over to him. Oh, he doesn't know that. Don't tell him. He'd protest. So, Samuel can't pay my landlord with my money unless I'm declared dead. There is nobody there to notice I'm gone except my landlord and maybe a few people at the museum."

Saying that out loud made Emilie feel hollow inside. She truly had been all alone. Had anyone even noticed she was gone? More than ever, she knew staying here was her best choice.

"What can ye tell me about Samuel?" Murielle asked casually as she looked in a distorted mirror that made Murielle look like Quasimodo. How could she adequately groom herself with such a junky mirror? Had she any idea how truly beautiful she was?

"You have interest in Sam?" Emilie asked with a wide grin.

"Shh! Keep yer voice down! People listen. I'm a princess. 'Tis my place to marry a king. We've had so many men coming and going from the village, and because of me, Arwyn stole my nephew. Who I am interested in doesnae matter. But, aye. I find him handsome, intelligent, mysterious, intriguing... alas, I have no choice but to marry a king. Not that a man like Samuel would have any interest in an ancient lass such as myself when he can have a modern woman." She sighed and picked up a brush to comb her hair.

Holy crap! A Pictish princess was in love with Sam! Suddenly, Emilie felt pangs of guilt in her belly. She'd been so busy blaming herself for what had happened with Lucas that she hadn't considered how Murielle felt about this war with Arwyn.

"Murielle. I think I need you to look me in the eye right now and listen carefully to what I'm about to say." Murielle lowered her brush and looked quizzically at Emilie. "You are an extraordinarily beautiful woman. Not only in this time but in our time. Any man would be lucky to have you, including Samuel."

"Nay, ye flatter me, but no man has ever paid me the attention that Goodwin pays ye or Brodyn pays Caitriona. Ye are beautiful women. I am a hag." She lowered her head, and for the first time, Emilie realized how insecure Murielle was despite her outward strength.

"That mirror you have is rubbish, Murielle. That is not how you look. That is not what others see. Men may not look at you the way you wish because you're the king's sister and destined to be with a king. The men in this village know they have no chance and that your brother will destroy them for so much as winking at you."

She laughed and nodded. "Aye, that is true, at least."

"All of it is true. Arwyn is an ass, but he's handsome, and he wanted you very much. Not just because he was desperate for a wife or an alliance, but because he'd never find another woman as beautiful as you."

"Except that he did." Murielle looked at Emilie and gave her a sarcastic look.

"I suppose neither of us sees what others see in us. It's the lot of women. We always underestimate ourselves. I was certain Goodwin was in love with you when I arrived because... how could he not be? You're easily the most beautiful woman in the village. I'm glad he sees you as a sister, or else I'd never stand a chance. Samuel is a busy man who keeps his nose in books. He goes back and forth to continue teaching and working because he is passionate about what he does. But, once Cait was married to Brodyn, he could have left. He was freed from his responsibilities in this time loop mess. He keeps coming back. I often wondered why, assuming he was simply enthralled with this time period, but now I wonder if he isn't coming back over and over because of a certain woman."

"Do you really think?" she asked, taking Emilie's hands in hers and squeezing.

"The last thing I want to do is meddle. You have to marry a king, and Samuel hasn't said a word to me. But, now that you've brought this to my attention, I'm not a bit surprised that whenever I see him here, he's near you."

"Oh! Even if I cannae marry him, the hope of just having his affection sustains me!" Murielle continued to comb her hair using that awful mirror, and Emilie smiled at her excitement.

"All right. How do I look?" Murielle asked with blushing cheeks and a genuine smile.

"You look breathtaking, truly," Emilie said. And she did. Emilie wasn't kidding that she was glad Goodwin grew up with Murielle and had no romantic feelings toward her. It made Emilie realize just how much she hoped things worked out here with Goodwin, not only because it would be very awkward living here with him if things went poorly, but because, in such a short time, Goodwin had grown to mean more to her than even she could understand.

"Do ye want me to wait while ye change into a clean tunic?" Murielle asked, placing the mirror carefully onto the table.

"Oh, no. You go ahead. I still need to comb my hair and run to my chamber to get a new tunic." Nodding, Murielle squeezed Emilie's shoulder and headed out the door, leaving Emilie alone for the first time all day. Her feet ached, and her lower back could use a good soak from the day's many chores, but Emilie never felt so fulfilled. She was used to hard, physical work as she dug into the earth to find memories of times long past, but being here now and helping to make clothing, soap, and candles for the very people she studied for years left Emilie with a glowing feeling of accomplishment. She found herself excited to tell Goodwin all about it when he returned, another sign that she had grown to enjoy sharing her life with him.

"Emilie Jean Mac Dougal," she said to herself, picking up the funhouse mirror poor Murielle was forced to use daily. Her hazel eyes appeared different sizes, and her nose looked crooked. Emilie laughed and shook her head as she put it down. No wonder Murielle didn't understand her true beauty. Nobody could use this mirror daily and feel confident.

With a sigh, Emilie sat down on the bed to rub her aching feet for a moment before returning to her room to find something to wear. When she heard a shuffling sound beneath the bed, she gasped and stood up, stepping away and holding her breath to remain quiet. The shuffling stopped, and after a moment, Emilie released her breath, deciding it must be rodents within the tunnel below. There was no way anybody could access the tunnels from outside the village, she reminded herself.

Opening the door to leave the room, Emilie shrieked and stepped back when she faced Sarah's scowl.

"Excuse me," Emilie said softly, trying to pass by, but Sarah blocked the doorway. She shoved Emilie back into the room and quickly shut and barred the door behind her.

"What the hell are you doing?" Emilie shouted, tired of this childish behavior.

"I dinnae like ye." Sarah narrowed her eyes and continued to back Emilie into the room, toward the bed.

"I'm not particularly fond of you right now, either," Emilie groused, shoving Sarah back.

"Everything was fine until ye arrived. I had a plan, and ye ruined it all."

"Well, I'm sorry my presence ruined whatever plan you had, but if it involved Goodwin, it was never going to go well for you. He isn't interested in you whether I'm here or not."

"Ye ken nothing!" Sarah hissed. "Ye show up here and claim the best man in the village after a single day! Some of us have been waiting a lifetime for him! Once Murielle marries, Goodwin will move on and start paying attention to the rest of us! After many kings came and went, I took it upon myself to make a deal with Arwyn."

Emilie shrank back, realizing Sarah was more unhinged than

she ever imagined. "*You* plotted with Arwyn? Did you have anything to do with him stealing Lucas?"

"What? Of course not! He was only meant to take Murielle through the tunnel while she was in her chamber! The cursed woman would continue to reject every suitor until she was an old hag if someone didnae force it! Not only do our people need that alliance with the Britons, but I needed her gone so I could finally catch Goodwin's eye! But ye... ye show up with yer odd words and odder behaviors, catching his eye without any idea how long some of us have awaited our chance!"

The woman was wild-eyed, flushed, and clearly not of sound mind. Worst of all, she was a danger to everyone in this village for telling the enemy how to use the tunnels. Suddenly, a realization sent icy dread trickling down her spine.

"Sarah... is there a man inside the tunnel right now beneath this chamber?"

A terrifying grin spread across Sarah's face, one Emilie had only seen in horror movies, never having faced a criminally insane human until now. "Aye. Only this time, he awaits ye. When the fight broke out in the corridor, it was meant to be Murielle in that bath, not ye. The fight was a distraction. Arwyn meant to sweep into this chamber and force Murielle out before anyone noticed. He would have been long gone and had her wedded and bedded before King Brodyn or Goodwin could stop him. But, the bath I helped fill went to ye instead, and when Goodwin guarded the chamber, I kenned the plan was ruined. Murielle was elsewhere, and Goodwin ran to protect ye rather than join the fight. That's when I kenned *ye* were in my way, not Murielle."

A memory flashed in Emilie's mind, and suddenly she remembered where she first saw Sarah. "You were one of the women filling the tub in Murielle's chamber. You're one of her servants, and you betrayed her!"

Sarah shrugged. "We look out for ourselves, those of us beneath the rest of ye. Goodwin was my chance to raise my rank, to be in the king's inner circle, to be a fearsome warrior's wife. Ye ruined that for me with yer witchery! Arwyn killed the guard who watched Lucas and stole him out of revenge when the plan didnae work, but he kenned where the tunnel led. I believe he intentionally rode past that area with Lucas to lure ye and Goodwin out. It worked, and now ye are Arwyn's wife, thanks to yer selfless act. See, Emilie? The right thing doesn't always pay off. Ye sacrificed yerself for the Pictish heir, but now ye are married and cannae have Goodwin. Yer husband awaits ye."

"You're insane!" Emilie shouted. Nobody was left in the house to hear if she screamed, and she suddenly realized Sarah had her literally against the wall. "You can't make me go to Arwyn! He's preparing for a battle somewhere!"

"That is true on all accounts. I cannae force ye down that tunnel, and Arwyn is occupied, preparing to fight to have ye back, but..." Sarah lowered her voice and stepped even closer to Emilie, fear suddenly glazing her eyes. "His target isnae King Brodyn. If he doesnae have ye by his side when the battle begins, he is prepared to slaughter Goodwin. Neither of us wants this. So ye see, Arwyn has me in a bind, as well. If ye dinnae go to him, Goodwin dies, and we both lose."

Emilie's stomach clenched and churned as she fought to breathe. Sarah hadn't planned for Arwyn to turn on Goodwin, but he was a shrewd man who understood emotional manipulation. If Goodwin died, Sarah lost everything. So did Emilie. "How have you communicated with Arwyn if he isn't within the tunnels?"

"He has other men to do his bidding," Sarah offered as an explanation, but this time her voice shook, and fear laced her tone. She was a scheming bitch, but clearly, she never meant for Goodwin to become the target. Now, Emilie had no choice but to return to Arwyn if she wished to save Goodwin. This was no fairytale or romance novel. There was no happily-ever-after awaiting Emilie. She either remained Arwyn's wife to save Goodwin, or she returned home, which left everyone at risk and offered no promise that Goodwin would be safe. Either way she faced this situation, Emilie saw only one conclusion. She had to protect Goodwin or die trying.

"I will go to him." Emilie narrowed her eyes at Sarah, who exhaled loudly with relief. "I do this for Goodwin. Not you."

"I do this for Goodwin, not ye, either. Ye will go to Arwyn, and I will marry Goodwin upon his return. Now that I see it isnae Murielle he loves, I have my chance. I can sway him. I ken it."

Emilie chewed her lower lip, wondering if she dared to disillusion this young woman. In the end, she decided to let it go. The lass would likely end up an outcast or worse after all she had done to betray her people. She had sealed her own fate, and those consequences would soon fall upon her head without Emilie pointing it out.

Looking down at her sheer undertunic, Emilie cringed and sent Sarah a pleading look. "I will do what I must and go into that tunnel. I only ask for a little compassion. Do not send me down there without proper clothing and shoes. Woman to woman, you wouldn't allow me to be exposed, would you?"

Sarah visibly swallowed and narrowed her eyes as she skimmed Emilie in deep thought. Without a word, the lass walked over to a chest near the end of the large four-poster bed and opened its lid, making the old, rusted hinges creek ominously. Shuffling through the contents, Sarah removed a worn pair of brown leather boots and a faded green tunic, tossing them both at Emilie's feet. "Put these on, then it's time ye leave and never return."

Nodding, Emilie clenched her jaw to stave off her fear as she slipped her sore feet into the boots, grateful that they fit her well enough, then pulled the tunic over her head. "Thank you," Emilie whispered, wrapping her arms around herself protectively.

"Well, if Goodwin happens to see ye with Arwyn, I dinnae want him seeing more of ye than necessary." Sarah grabbed Emilie's arm and jerked her toward the bed. "'Tis time." Sarah stomped her booted foot three times against the wooden floor. A hand came out from beneath the bed and grabbed her ankle, making Emilie scream in terror as she tried to run. Instead, she lost her balance and fell onto the floor with a painful thud. Never had Emilie suffered more ridiculous injuries in such a short time until she arrived here. Her elbows took most of the impact and began to throb.

A man shouted from beneath the bed. "I cannae see in this cursed hole, and the dead guard's body has a foul stench! Send her down!"

Sarah scowled at Emilie and nudged her side with the tip of her boot. "Go on. Climb down. I ken ye've done it before. Only this time Goodwin isnae there to catch ye. 'Tis a wee bit of a drop. Dinnae step on Allen's corpse. Arwyn's men killed him and hid him in the tunnel, so it appeared he betrayed Brodyn and fled. I had naught to do with it, but sacrifices must be made," the woman said, so casually that icy dread slid down Emilie's spine.

Emilie looked at Sarah and shot her one final dirty look as if it would do anything to better her predicament. And then, flat on her stomach, Emilie pulled herself toward the faceless man beneath the bed. With only about a foot between the opening in the floor and the bottom of the bed, she had very little room to climb down. Now she understood why Murielle's bed was so high off the ground. It must have been designed to allow access to the tunnel... but just barely.

Turning so her feet dangled over the opening, Emilie yelped when she felt the man on the other side grab her ankle again and drag her down. Before she knew it, she was crumpled on the tunnel's cold, dark earthen floor just as the boards slammed closed, enveloping them in utter darkness. She had been afraid the last time she was in this tunnel, but she'd known Goodwin would protect her. Now, she was trapped with Arwyn's guard and knew he'd do anything to bring her back to his king. The acrid smell of death assaulted her nostrils, and Emilie gagged, knowing somewhere in this darkness was the body of the guard who had been watching Lucas before his kidnapping. She cupped a hand over her mouth and nose, but it did little good.

When she felt the guard's hot, sweaty hand grab hers as she got to her feet, she yanked it back and dared to pull rank on him. "Do not touch your queen! I will tell King Arwyn how you've treated me, so be mindful."

She said it with all the authority she could muster, praying the man didn't laugh in her face, enough if he couldn't see her. Fortunately, he muttered, "Aye, my queen," and released her. "I only mean to guide ye back to King Arwyn. He has ordered me not to harm ye. He kens the king's men captured ye and took ye away. His revenge is for yer captor, not ye."

She wanted to shout that Arwyn was her captor, not Goodwin, but this man was doing nothing but performing his duty, as all men did in this place and time. She was at his mercy and would be until she arrived at Arwyn's camp. What she would do when she arrived was undecided, but Emilie had learned quickly that little about this situation was within her control. She needed to think on her feet and decide what to do as every moment shifted her circumstances.

Placing her hand along the rough dirt wall to her right, Emilie began to walk, blindly following the path, glad to remain in the dark, for she preferred not to see what critters shared her space.

CHAPTER ELEVEN

T HE AFTERNOON SUN beat down on Goodwin and the men as they came to a halt in the middle of a grass valley with summer wildflowers sprinkled across its green blanket like specks of rainbow fallen to the earth.

Shielding his eyes with his hand, Goodwin squinted into the distance as their scout rode toward them with haste. When he approached, the scout halted his horse so swiftly that it reared and kicked its forelegs in protest.

"What did ye find?" Goodwin asked as he shifted in Boudicca's saddle. He knew by the look on Simon's face that something was amiss.

"Arwyn's camp remains in the same place."

"He never left?" Brodyn asked, looking sideways at Goodwin with a frown. Goodwin clenched the reins in his hands, knowing Arwyn must have a plan if he stayed, rather than returning home for supplies or attacking Pinnata Castra to get Emilie back.

"It seems so, my king," Simon said, heaving for breath. "I went unnoticed, but that means I couldnae see beyond the brush. But, men roamed the area, and smoke billowed from a fire. They are there."

Brodyn looked up to the sky and gauged the sun's position as he shaded his eyes. "We have approximately two hours until sundown. Do we wait or attack now?" He looked at Goodwin for guidance, and Goodwin closed his eyes, thinking about every scenario in his mind. Usually, they would wait for nightfall to bombard the enemy, but this enemy clearly expected Brodyn to come to him, and he also seemed confident that he wouldn't need well-rested men or supplies to survive this battle. He must have known Brodyn would seek revenge on Lucas and Emilie's behalf, yet the man remained. Why?

"He kens we will come. He kens we willnae attack or else he'd have sought high ground or fled, for his men have nothing. So, what does he have on us?"

Brodyn tensed in his saddle. "Could he have taken Lucas or Caitriona?"

"I dinnae ken how. We boarded off all the tunnels."

"Have we discovered who betrayed us?" Brodyn asked through clenched teeth.

Goodwin shook his head. "Ronan and Lawrence were with ye during the corridor fracas, and Allen has yet to be seen, but I dinnae believe he would betray us. I fear he was killed when Lucas was kidnapped. Whoever told Arwyn about the tunnels was not a guard. So, who else kens about the tunnels?"

"Anyone with access to Murielle's chamber or the other royal chambers with escape tunnels," Brodyn said warily.

"Servants." Goodwin looked at Brodyn. "Any of the servants would ken they exist. But they are so well-treated by ye and Queen Caitriona. Who would dare betray ye and risk losing their position?"

Silence fell between the men as they thought. One face continued to manifest in Goodwin's mind, the face of a lass who continuously tried to get into his bed or woo him whenever he was near. But, what motivation would she have for such things?

"Sarah," Brodyn said with a growl that made Goodwin's head snap up.

"I was just considering her, but why? What has she to gain in such a terrible act of betrayal?"

"I dinnae ken, but no other servant would dare. She has always been in love with ye. Would she have plotted with Arwyn to kidnap Murielle that night? If Murielle was gone and forced to marry, Sarah would believe she had a chance to win yer heart."

Goodwin scoffed at the theory but immediately frowned as he considered its plausibility. "Sarah was in Murielle's chamber that night, helping to fill the tub. However, Emilie took a bath in the chamber when the fight broke out, not Murielle. I ran in to protect her by using the tunnel."

"If Sarah made plans for Murielle to be taken from her chamber, there wouldnae have been time for her to alert Arwyn that Murielle wasnae there before the fight broke out. When they broke into her chamber, it was empty, which prompted Arwyn to kidnap Lucas instead." Brodyn looked warily at Goodwin, and Goodwin felt his blood run cold in his veins.

"This is all just a theory. We cannae ken any of this is true."

"Nay, but ye've told me enough about Sarah for me to ken she'd go to great lengths to have ye. Did she not recently climb into yer bed while ye were away, hoping ye'd finally have her?"

Goodwin grimaced and nodded. "Aye. Stark naked she was. I threw a blanket at her and told her to go home. She wasnae pleased. That was only two days before Emilie arrived."

"And ye took to Emilie immediately. Everybody noticed, especially Sarah."

"Aye." It was all Goodwin could say. Arwyn didn't have Emilie. He couldn't possibly. Still, he had something that made him confident enough to stay put and face his enemy without resources, and whatever it was, or who it was, Brodyn's army had no choice but to surge forward and discover what Arwyn was planning.

"We attack. Now." Brodyn popped his knuckles, cracked his neck, and straightened his back.

"Agreed." Goodwin turned toward their warriors, who patiently awaited orders updates or orders. "Arwyn has neither retreated nor advanced. He remains in the same camp that Emilie and Lucas escaped from. Without supplies, his men will be tired, hungry, and unable to defeat us."

The army cheered and raised their fists, but Brodyn stopped

them by raising his own. "Nay, this is not a victory. He has a plan; of that we are certain. No king keeps his men unprotected, kenning his enemy will seek immediate revenge. Something has made Arwyn confident, and we must ride toward his camp immediately to discover what it is. We willnae charge or attack, for it may be one of our own he uses as leverage. We shall approach cautiously, but only Goodwin and I will advance into the camp until ye hear our signal. If he has taken another member of our tribe hostage again, I will kill him myself!" Brodyn roared, his army following in his battle cry.

Goodwin leaned into Brodyn's ear. "If he has Emilie, he dies by my sword."

"I'd expect nothing less," Brodyn responded. "Let's pray he has nobody in his grasp, for it means we've truly been betrayed by one of our own."

With that, Brodyn turned in the direction of Arwyn's camp, and Goodwin did the same, urging their horses forward, moving swiftly through the trees as their men followed. Goodwin's heart constricted inside his throat as thoughts of Emilie or anyone in his village being held hostage again. It couldn't be, he told himself repeatedly. Whatever Arwyn had planned, it couldn't be kidnapping Emilie again. Could it? And while Sarah was intent on having him, she wouldn't betray her own people, would she?

When they reached a clearing far enough from Arwyn's camp, but close enough to call Brodyn's army if needed, Brodyn and Goodwin slowed their horses, and their men did the same.

"We move forward alone from this point," Brodyn told his men. "Unless ye hear my signal, stay here."

Together, Goodwin and Brodyn rode toward the camp, seeing smoke billow into the sky before they saw Arwyn's men.

"They kenned we'd come," Goodwin said when they approached and found the camp guarded on all sides. "Simon came and went unnoticed, and he didnae mention the guards. They must have just surrounded the camp."

As they slowly approached, shouts rang out from the guards

as they stepped forward carrying their swords. The men appeared weary, filthy, and exhausted but still at Arwyn's command.

"We wish to speak to Arwyn," Brodyn demanded as he dismounted his horse. Goodwin did the same, not wanting to bring Boudicca into a trap.

"He kenned ye would come," one of the guards said, and Goodwin immediately recognized him as one of the main guards who covered Arwyn while at Pinnata Castra. "He has something to show ye." The man's yellow-toothed grin sent a chill of dread up Goodwin's spine, and his hand instinctively went to his sword.

The guard shook his head. "I wouldnae draw yer sword if I were ye. Ye dinnae wish for our king to harm her."

"Her?" Brodyn's voice was deep and menacing as he stepped closer.

Goodwin grabbed Brodyn's tunic and pulled him back. "It's not Caitriona he has, Brodyn."

Brodyn looked at Goodwin and frowned. "Emilie."

Fire ran through Goodwin's veins, and he clenched his fists to prevent from unsheathing his sword and running every man in this camp through.

"Bring us to him," Goodwin growled through clenched teeth.

"King Arwyn was correct. Ye *do* fancy his wife. She came to him willingly, ye ken."

Goodwin scowled and shook his head. He knew not what this imbecile meant, but he knew Emilie would never have run back to Arwyn. The man was trying to deceive him, but it wouldn't work. Too much was at stake for Goodwin to fall into mental traps.

Goodwin repeated his command. "Bring us to him."

"Verra well. Hand me yer weapons."

"My army awaits my signal. Ye willnae take our weapons, or ye will have hundreds of Picts—well rested, well-fed Picts—slicing open yer guts. I ken yer men are weakened and have no supplies. Our fight is with Arwyn. Bring us to him, along with our swords. We arenae stupid enough to take on yer army alone, but we willnae be brought in for the slaughter."

The guard popped his knuckles, and Goodwin heard the man's stomach growl. "Have ye any food?"

Slowly, Goodwin reached into the satchel attached to Boudicca's saddle and pulled out a handful of oat cakes, willingly handing them over to the man, who promptly tossed them toward his fellow guards, each of them devouring the cakes without a second thought.

"Ye follow a king who allows ye to starve," Brodyn said, shaking his head. "'Tis not how I'd treat my men." The guard looked at Brodyn briefly before sinking his teeth back into his final piece of oat cake.

"Ye may pass," the guard said, waving them in as he led the way. He escorted them through the brush as men stared at them from all directions. Some looked angry, but most looked tired and defeated, weary of battle. Goodwin didn't believe good men should die for a king who allowed them to suffer, but that decision lay in Arwyn's hands.

Stopping in front of a large tent, the guard turned to look at Goodwin. "Ye did me a favor, so I shall do ye the same. Ye have a snake in yer midst. A servant lass named Sarah. She isnae to be trusted." With that, the man whispered to another guard in front of the tent, who nodded and entered. A moment of silence passed before Goodwin heard a woman shriek from within the tent, and he immediately drew his sword.

"Emilie!" Panic consumed his senses, guiding his actions as logic fled his mind.

Brodyn pulled him back. "Goodwin, nay! Stand down!"

Goodwin did as his king commanded, an instinct honed over two decades of training despite his newer instinct to protect Emilie at all cost. Still, he couldn't control his mouth. "Emilie! If ye hurt her, I'll kill ye!" he shouted, clenching his fists and straining to keep the last of his restraint in check.

The tent flap opened, and Arwyn came through with a smug smile as he dragged Emilie behind him. Relief washed over him when he saw that she was unharmed, but rage quickly replaced his relief when he noticed her state of undress. Aside from Arwyn's large fur cloak covering her body, she appeared to wear nothing else. His ears rang, and he closed his eyes, willing himself not to vomit or draw his sword.

"Of course, I would never harm my wife," Arwyn said with a feigned offense. "She is my greatest treasure, arnae ye, my sweet?" Arwyn pulled Emilie into his side with a grin and forced his lips onto hers, slipping his tongue between her teeth as she struggled.

"She truly is the bonniest woman I've ever seen. How is it ye Picts are surrounded by such beauty? I was disappointed to leave yer stronghold without Murielle as my wife, but as ye can see, I have found myself a much better mate. She will make a wonderful queen and mother to my bairns."

"Emilie... did he touch ye?" Goodwin couldn't focus on anything else, not Arwyn's ramblings or the dozens of armed men surrounding him. All he saw was the pain in her eyes, her disheveled hair, and her state of undress. She shook her head, but Goodwin wasn't convinced, especially when he noticed the red mark covering her left cheek. Why else would she be wearing nothing but the man's cloak if he had kept his grubby paws off her, and why had she yelped just as they approached the tent?

"Young man," Arwyn said, furrowing his brow. "Is it traditional for a king's guard to ask another king's wife about their intimate relations?"

"It is when ye forced her to marry ye!" Goodwin shot back, spittle flying from his mouth. He was beside himself with fury, hatred, and a desire for revenge.

"Emilie came to me willingly. Ye saw that for yerself when she left ye on the shore to ride with me. She wants a powerful man between her thighs, not a common, pathetic guard. For every one king, there are a thousand men such as ye who believe ye deserve the best lassies in the land. They arenae created to love men such as ye. The sooner ye learn this, the better off ye'll be.

Stick with that lass... what's her name?" Arwyn looked at Emilie with a grin, then back at Goodwin. "Ah, aye. Sarah. Now there is a lass with ambition, one of yer station. Might I say, she is also quite clever with her mouth if ye ken my meaning."

"Enough, Arwyn," Brodyn said, sounding bored. "Ye ken as well as we do that Emilie married ye to save her nephew's life. What have ye to gain in this game? Ye kenned I'd come for ye, and yet ye didnae prepare yer men."

"My wife came willingly to me. If ye dinnae believe me, ask her yerself."

Goodwin's gaze shifted to Emilie's, and she shrank back with humiliation. It didn't matter. He knew Emilie, knew her soul. If she allowed herself to be willingly brought back to Arwyn, there was a greater explanation.

Brodyn looked at Emilie with sorrow in his eyes. "Is this where ye want to be, lass?"

"I..." Emilie looked from him to Goodwin, then to Arwyn, who narrowed his eyes warningly at her. "I belong with my husband," she whispered, diverting her gaze.

"Ye've threatened her!" Goodwin growled. "Ye've threatened to kill me if she didnae comply, didnae ye?"

Arwyn's forced smile slid from his face, and his cheeks turned red with rage. "Ye think my wife would care to spare yer life?" Arwyn stepped closer, nearly Goodwin's match in height and weight, but Goodwin stood his ground.

"Ye think a woman like Emilie would be with a man like ye if not for threats?" Goodwin shot back.

"Release my wife's sister from this forced marriage or die." Brodyn's calmly spoken words made Arwyn snap his gaze away from Goodwin.

"Ye will have to kill every one of my men if ye wish to kill me."

"Spoken like a true coward," Brodyn mused, crossing his arms. "A fight. One to one. The winner takes Emilie home. If ye refuse, I will signal my men. Ye dinnae stand a chance. Every one of yer men will die, including ye."

"Ye wish to fight me for yer wife's sister?" Arwyn said incredulously. "Are ye in love with her?"

"Nay, but I am," Goodwin said, stepping closer to Arwyn. "Ye already deserve to die for harming Lucas, but ye will die by my hand today for forcing yerself on Emilie."

"She is my wife! My property! I can do whatever I wish with her, and 'tis none of yer concern!" Arwyn snapped.

Goodwin balled his right fist and slammed it into Arwyn's face, feeling cartilage break as the man staggered back with a wail. The second Arwyn released his grip on Emilie, she ran into Goodwin's arms with a sob, burying her face into his chest. "He threatened to kill you if I didn't come back," she whispered through her sniffles. "I had to... to save you."

"Enough now. Enough of this," Goodwin whispered, carefully pulling her off of him and pushing her toward Brodyn, who gave a piercing whistle that echoed off the trees and sent birds soaring into the sky.

With a roar, Arwyn lunged toward Goodwin but met with his fist once more, this time in the pit of his stomach." The man grunted and crumpled to the ground.

"Get up!" Goodwin spat. "Fight me, ye piece of shite!"

"Guards! Get them!" Arwyn yelled and pointed at Goodwin and Brodyn, but before any man could make a move, the thunder of hooves rumbled the earth beneath their feet as Brodyn's army tore through the campsite, horses plowing through tents and kicking over supplies. Chaos broke out as Arwyn's men scattered, too tired and outnumbered to pick up their swords.

"Yer surrounded, Arwyn!" Brodyn shouted. "Ye die by my hand or Goodwin's. There is no escape. Choose yer fate."

Wiping blood from his nose, Arwyn narrowed his eyes and spat blood on Goodwin's tunic before unsheathing the sword at his side.

"Finally!" Goodwin roared, withdrawing his own trusted sword and getting into a battle stance. With his free hand, he beckoned Arwyn to take the first swing. Staggering forward, Arwyn swung, but Goodwin stepped aside. With a growl of frustration, Arwyn cracked his neck and lunged again, this time easily blocked by Goodwin's sword.

"She... is... mine!" Arwyn huffed when he straightened his back. "My wife! My men stand as witnesses!"

"Then I will be pleased to make her yer widow," Goodwin hissed, gripping his sword's hilt with both hands, wishing it was his enemy's neck. "She ran from ye the second ye let go. If ye have to keep a hold of yer wife, she isnae truly yers."

"Ye wish to raise my bastard? That's what will happen if ye slay me, I vow! In nine months' time, she will give birth to my son! Are ye willing to raise my child as yer own, reminding of me plowing her every time ye look into his eyes?"

Those words nearly undid Goodwin, but he hardened his features and steeled his resolve to kill the man. Goodwin swung his sword, never so distracted or emotionally motivated to kill a man. His aim was off, and instead, he caught Arwyn's arm, making him shout with pain as he took a step back.

Blood flowed from his wound, but Arwyn raised his sword higher, narrowing his eyes. "She relished my cock in her mouth, moaned her pleasure when I slipped inside her, bucked her hips with need when my seed filled her!"

Arwyn played a dangerous game, but it would be his last. With a mighty roar, he charged forward with his sword held high, ready to cleave into Goodwin's head and split his skull in two.

"Goodwin! No!" Emilie shouted from the side, and a glance in her direction showed Goodwin that Brodyn struggled to restrain her as she flailed in an attempt to break away and run toward him.

She loved him. That was all he needed to know to continue this fight. But, that moment of distraction cost Goodwin greatly as Arwyn's sword caught his shoulder, and an intense, searing pain radiated down his arm.

He refused to give Arwyn any satisfaction despite Emilie's

distressed wails. Goodwin bit back the pain, even though he knew the wound would kill him if not properly treated, just as Arwyn's wound would kill him.

Emilie loved him. Because of that, Goodwin was determined not to die. Nay, he was going to destroy Arwyn, marry Emilie, and have two dozen bairns, and he would enjoy creating every single one of them while he made love to his wife.

Men circled around, but none dared to disturb a fight to the death. No other men needed to die this day, so long as Arwyn's blood flowed through the soil. Cocky and overconfident, Arwyn smiled with victory as he thrust his sword at Goodwin.

It was time to end this man before Goodwin bled to death here along with him. With all his strength, with all the desire in his soul, he pushed through and dodged Arwyn's attack, then thrust his blade through Arwyn's heart, hearing the crack of bone and sinew as his opponent's face blanched and his eyes widened with surprise. He dropped his sword to the ground before he followed it.

A swift, mostly painless death. It was more than Arwyn ap Rhys deserved. If only his uncle had an heir, this bastard would never have inherited the kingdom of Gwynedd, and none of this would have happened. The man had sealed his own fate, and the usual sorrow that plagued Goodwin after a kill escaped him. He felt nothing but love and concern for Emilie, who broke free and ran full force toward him with tears streaming down her face.

"Oh, my God!" she cried. "You're bleeding so much! Help! Get me a cloth, fabric... anything!" she shouted. Ronan moved forward with his knife, slicing off his tunic sleeve and tossing it to Emilie, who quickly wrapped it around his arm and tied it into a knot. He hissed with pain but immediately felt the blood flow begin to stop.

"Goodwin, are you all right? Oh, no, no, no," she whispered. "I love you! I love you so much! And... and, he lied! I didn't touch him! He tried, but I bit him. He slapped me, but I don't care. All I care about is you. I'd never have relations with another man! But he threatened to kill you if I didn't come back, and you were on your way here, and I knew he'd do it!"

Emilie's frantic words and fussing over him only made Goodwin smile. His injury didn't matter. Only she mattered. "I ken that already, love. I ken ye wouldnae willingly bed him. I only worried that he forced ye."

She shook her head, and Goodwin wiped a tear from her cheek with the hand attached to his uninjured shoulder. "I love ye," he whispered. "Ye never need to explain yerself to me."

Emilie wrapped her arms around his waist, and his heart pounded against his ribs. Men scurried about, some to remove a dead king, others to commend the living king, but only he and Emilie existed in this space.

"We need to get ye to Anya so she can fix yer wound."

"Ye said 'ye.' Ye are starting to talk like us now," he said with a grin.

"Then I guess that means I'm a Pict now."

"Not officially. Ye must marry one first."

"If only I could find a handsome Pictish dude who would have me." Emilie looked up at him with flushed cheeks and a smile that melted his heart.

"If only," he murmured before lowering his lips to hers. It was gentle. It was all-consuming. It was perfect—just like Emilie.

CHAPTER TWELVE

T HE WIND HOWLED, and rain pelted the earth just as they reached the village gates. Emilie sat in front of Goodwin as he rode Boudicca through the entrance. She sighed as relief washed over her. They were home, and they were alive. Nothing else mattered to her at the moment, aside from getting Goodwin's wound cleaned and stitched up.

Though he gritted his teeth against the pain and shrugged it off, it was a nasty wound that would take weeks or even months to heal. He would be fortunate if he ever had full use of that shoulder again.

Immediately upon their arrival, Caitriona rushed toward them, mud caking the bottom hem of her skirts. "Oh, thank God! Where is my husband?" The fear glazing her eyes broke Emilie's heart. After nearly losing Brodyn last year in a battle, Cait was forever scarred. She'd never send her husband to battle without reliving that fear.

"I'm here." Brodyn rode through, and Caitriona gasped, running to him as he dismounted. Their love was inspiring, but Emilie wasn't jealous because she had her own love made just for her.

Turning to look over her shoulder, Emilie looked at Goodwin, whose skin was ashy and covered in sweat. "We need help!" she cried, gripping his uninjured arm as he teetered precariously in his saddle. She told him he wasn't strong enough and had urged him to ride in a cart, but he'd refused. Now, it appeared

Goodwin was ready to collapse. Brodyn and Lawrence ran over to Boudicca, carefully pulling Goodwin from the horse as Emilie followed, feeling helpless.

"What happened?" Cait asked, matching Emilie's frantic pace as she hurried for the house to find Anya.

"He killed Arwyn but received a bad blow to his shoulder. I pray he hasn't lost too much blood or gets an infection."

"Oh, no!" Caitriona ran ahead of the men, and Emilie stayed near Goodwin.

"He doesnae look well," Lawrence grunted as he supported his weight.

"He just needs to be patched up," Brodyn said confidently. "He will recover, or else I will kill him myself."

Goodwin had enough strength to grunt at his friend. "Ye cannae kill me. I have too much to... live for," he said weakly, looking at Emilie.

"Just focus on getting better, mate," Lawrence said.

As Brodyn walked past prying eyes and frantic villagers searching for their husbands and fathers, he shouted loud enough to be heard without stopping. "All of yer men are safe and approaching the gate. No men fell."

A collective sigh of relief moved through the crowd as many ran toward the gates.

Approaching the house, Emilie saw the door wide open as Caitriona stood beside Anya and the servants. Sarah stood beside the others, looking concerned when she saw Goodwin's condition, then going white when she saw Emilie. Had she really expected her plan to work? That everybody else would simply allow her to leave with Arwyn while Goodwin returned home brokenhearted so she could pick up the pieces?

"Ye bitch," Goodwin cursed when he made eye contact with her. "Ye lying, scheming, pathetic bitch!"

"Calm down, Goodwin," Emilie whispered, worried he would waste what little energy he had left on a woman most unworthy of it.

"She is at fault for all of this!" he continued.

"Lawrence, seize her. Take her to the holding cell while I decide what to do with her," Brodyn commanded with cold calculation in his tone.

"Wh-what is all this about?" Caitriona asked, looking between them all for answers.

"She plotted it all," Brodyn growled. "She told Arwyn about the tunnels and plotted to have Murielle kidnapped because she thought Goodwin was in love with her, then Emilie when she discovered Goodwin loved her. She is a traitor! We could have all been killed!"

Caitriona's features turned to stone. Emilie had never seen her friend look so cold, so fearsome. Stepping up to Sarah, Caitriona narrowed her eyes. "You put my family at risk? Our people? Our village? All for a man who doesn't want you?"

Sarah flushed and looked away in shame, but Cait grabbed her face and forced her to look at her. "Did my son get taken because of you?"

"I didnae mean for that to happen! I vow, my queen! I'd never harm wee Lucas!"

"But you'd risk harming everyone else in this village by allowing our enemy intimate knowledge of our defenses? You tried to have Murielle taken, which led to Lucas being taken and Emilie marrying our enemy to save him! Then you forced Emilie back to Arwyn?"

"He threatened to kill Goodwin if I didnae make Emilie return to him!" she cried. "Emilie went willingly to save Goodwin!"

"And how, exactly, did you hope all of this would turn out?" Cait growled, squeezing Sarah's face as tears and snot dripped down the lass's face. Emilie almost felt sorry for Sarah, but not enough to intervene. Caitriona had every right to be furious with the woman who put her family and her village at risk. "Tell me!" she shouted, making Sarah jump.

Lawrence led Goodwin to a chamber on the first floor while their queen berated Sarah, and Anya followed. More than anything, Emilie wanted to be by his side, but he was in good hands, and her friend was ready to unhinge. Brodyn stood by, but he knew better than to intervene.

"I… I hoped Emilie would be forced back to Gwynedd with Arwyn so I could have G-Goodwin," Sarah stuttered through her pursed lips.

"Ah. So, you decided *your* happiness was more important than the safety of my family? You'd have my sister sent away, my son taken, my husband killed in battle, and Goodwin nearly killed, so you may have a chance to be with him?"

Sarah remained silent, shaking her head, but she did not need to respond. The evidence was mounted against her. Slowly, Caitriona removed her vice-like grip from the pathetic woman's jaw, and just when Emilie thought Cait was going to turn away, she raised her hand and struck Sarah across the cheek, sending the girl crumpling to the floor, holding her face as she broke out in uncontrollable sobs.

"Did I not treat you well enough? Did I not give you everything? I did everything to make you feel appreciated and cared for because I did appreciate and care for you! But no more. You're dead to me."

Caitriona only stopped when Brodyn walked over and placed a placating hand on his wife's shoulder, which caused Cait to break down into tears and bury her face in his chest.

Silence fell over the room as other servants glared at Sarah with spite, moving several paces away from her in a show of support for their queen. Murielle walked through the door and stopped in her tracks, looking around the room.

"I see I missed the best part. Did my brother give it to her?"

Emilie shook her head. "Cait did."

A wide smile splayed across Murielle's face. "Even better." Ronan walked in behind Murielle, back to guarding her as usual with his rigid stance. He glanced at Emilie before looking straight ahead.

"Ronan, take Sarah to the cell," Brodyn said calmly as he

rubbed his quaking wife's back. "I'll deal with her later."

"Aye, my king." Ronan did as he was commanded, gently lifting Sarah from the ground by one of her arms and escorting her toward the stairs leading down to the dank cells that Emilie was glad to never have seen. Why did pity war with anger inside her heart? Sarah absolutely deserved everything she got, but Emilie still felt a niggle of guilt for being the one to show up and win Goodwin's heart overnight while Sarah sat in the shadows. Still, only a person with an evil heart would act in such a manner, and Emilie needed to remind herself of that. Unrequited love was a part of life that many faced, yet they didn't respond so dramatically.

With Sarah locked away and Brodyn comforting Cait, Emilie decided to slip away and find Goodwin. All she had to do was follow the hissing sounds he made as Anya cleaned him up. When she stepped into the chamber, her stomach churned at the sight of his wound. Inflammation turned the damaged skin an angry shade of red as blood seeped through the gaping tear.

Anya looked up at Emilie and signaled her closer. "Pour alcohol on yer hands, then come press this cloth to the other side of the wound while I continue stitching. He is losing too much blood, and I cannae see where the wound begins or ends."

Without hesitation, Emilie did as she was told, picked up the small vase Anya had indicated, and poured alcohol over her hands before grabbing the cloth and coming closer. When she pressed the cloth against his shoulder, Goodwin groaned and gritted his teeth.

"Sorry," Emilie whispered. He closed his eyes as more sweat dripped from his brow. She wanted to hold and comfort him, but there would be time for that later. Anya worked quickly, pouring more alcohol on the wound, making him growl with pain.

Soon, he was stitched up, and Anya fashioned a sling for him before handing Emilie a modern pack of capsules with a drug company's logo on the package. "I take it ye'll be caring for him as he heals?" She nodded and took the tablets. "Give him one of these every morning and night to keep the infection away."

Emilie looked at the package and read the label. "Amoxicillin?" She eyed Anya and smiled.

"Aye, I told ye I can get supplies when I cross through. 'Tis why I am always gone. But mark me, I willnae last long, and someone else will need to obtain these."

"Is this not meddling with the timeline?" Emilie asked, raising a brow.

Anya shrugged. "Way I figure it, I was brought here for this purpose. Been saving these dolts for decades now. If God, or whoever sent us here, didnae want us to meddle, they shoulda thought of that first."

Emilie chuckled and nodded. She couldn't argue with that logic. "I will make sure he gets the pills. Thank you for taking care of him."

With a nod, Anya walked away and shut the door with Lawrence trailing behind her. Alone with Goodwin, Emilie sat beside him in silence, allowing him to rest. His dirt-streaked face might have been wan, but he was still as handsome as ever. With his eyes closed and his bared chest rhythmically rising and falling as he lay on the bed, Emilie slowly stood up to move toward a bench near the hearth.

Goodwin's uninjured arm shifted as his hand reached out to grip her wrist. "Already tired of me, lass?"

"Never," she said, brushing stray strands of his dark hair away from his sticky forehead. "I was going to move over to the bench so you had more space."

"I dinnae want space from ye. I always want ye near." He patted the bed, indicating Emilie to lay beside him, and she smiled, more than happy to do so. "Are ye going to feed me one of Anya's magic capsules?"

"Yes, but it's not magic. It's science."

"I dinnae ken what science is."

"I will explain it later. Here," She slipped a pill between his lips and handed him a clay mug of water, which he happily drank down so fast that it began to run down his chin.

Emilie used a spare cloth to wipe his chin and dirty cheeks while she was at it before snuggling into his right side, away from his injured shoulder.

"Ye women from the future have no end to yer tricks, dinnae ye?"

"Nope. Just wait and see. So. Many. Tricks."

Goodwin forced one eye open to look at her, sending her a cheeky grin. "I cannae wait," he said with a grunt.

"I didn't mean it like that!" she said with a laugh.

"I did. Now, come lay with me, love." She moved toward him, but he shook his head and put out a hand. "First, I need ye to remove that dead man's cloak. I cannae stand seeing ye wearing that a moment longer."

Emilie looked down and grimaced. She'd been so concerned for Goodwin this entire time that she hadn't stopped to remember that she wore Arwyn's cloak and nothing else. Humiliation washed over her as she remembered how she became unclothed.

"I don't have anything else on beneath it," she whispered.

A scowl distorted Goodwin's face as he understood her circumstances. "I'd run him through a thousand times over for what he did to ye if I could. Did he hurt ye, love?" She shook her head, not wanting to speak about it more than necessary.

Yes, Arwyn had attempted to force her by tearing her tunic over her head and leaving her naked, but she fought back and earned herself a sound smack across the face for her insolence. She would have lost the battle had Goodwin and Brodyn not shown up when they did. When a guard entered Arwyn's tent to announce their arrival, he'd tossed his cloak at her just before dragging her outside to use as bait. Hearing him goad Goodwin while they fought had given her shivers and an ominous glimpse into what would have been her fate had they not shown up in time.

The cloak was a reminder of that experience, and though she longed to burn it, she had nothing else to wear, which was becoming a never-ending problem for Emilie. Every time she borrowed a new tunic, it got destroyed one way or another. Between the weather, travel, escaping danger, and a monstrous man, Emilie had lost them all.

Still, this was a cloak she would happily lose. Slowly, she untied it from around her neck and walked over to the hearth to shove it into the fire. And then she faced Goodwin, naked and vulnerable. Obviously, he'd seen her naked before, but that had been her choice to bear herself. Now, she was naked because another man had tried to violate her. The look on Goodwin's face told her he understood without her explaining it.

He patted the bed beside him and lifted the covers for her to climb beneath. "Ye are safe now, love. Ye ken I'd never hurt ye. But I will hurt any man who ever touches ye against yer will again."

Emotion lodged in her throat, and repressed tears stung her eyes as she nodded and walked over to the bed, wanting nothing more than to nestle beside Goodwin. There was something profoundly intimate about lying beside a man while naked, all the while knowing neither of them expected to do more than sleep.

Careful not to jolt his arm, Emilie carefully climbed into the bed and under the covers, feeling warmth radiate from the inside out as he pulled her against him, kissed her temple, and quickly fell asleep again. She closed her eyes and forced her wandering mind to shut down, simply grateful to be here with him, feeling his heartbeat against her cheek. So long as it continued to beat, she'd be a happy woman.

A FAMILIAR VOICE drifted to her ears as Emilie stirred. Cracking open her eyes, she felt Goodwin's heavy arm draped across her waist and turned to look at him over her shoulder. His eyelids shifted as he slept, his mouth slightly ajar, but at least there was no drool. He looked innocent with his flushed cheeks and peaceful features.

When she heard voices again, she recognized Samuel's and decided to sneak away for a few moments to speak with her friend. It had only been two days since she saw him, but so much had happened in that time, and she felt a need to be in his calming, level-headed presence. Had he been back in 2023, and if so, had he been able to arrange payment for her landlord?

Slowly, Emilie lifted Goodwin's arm and sat up in the bed, pleased when he didn't stir. He needed all the rest he could get. She couldn't very well leave the chamber without clothing, but there appeared to be no chest in this chamber containing spare clothing. Looking around, she spotted a neatly folded blanket at the edge of the bed, and she decided it was her only option. She'd wrap it around herself as a makeshift tunic, ask Caitriona for another tunic to borrow, and prayed it remained clean and intact.

Stepping out of the chamber disheveled, barefoot, and wrapped in the blanket, Emilie walked down the empty, cold corridor and followed the voices to the main living area. Cait and Brodyn sat in their usual seats with Lucas nursing as he seemed to do all day long. Murielle flushed and smiled as she looked at Samuel, who spoke as enigmatically as ever about whatever topic he rambled on about. Murielle seemed engrossed, and Emilie wondered if she was genuinely interested or simply enjoyed listening to Samuel blather. Either way, a smile spread across Emilie's face as she approached.

"Em!" Caitriona shouted, spotting her friend. "You look like shit!"

"Thank you. I feel like shit," she muttered.

Cait frowned and looked down, putting a finger in Lucas's mouth to gently break his suckle so she could cover herself and pass him over to Brodyn. "I'll get you another tunic."

"I'm sorry I keep ruining your tunics," Emilie mumbled.

"Oh, stop. You've been through hell." Cait walked up and touched Emilie's arm, leaning in to whisper. "I don't know what happened to you out there, and I feel terrible that I was so distracted when you all came back that I didn't think to ask. I just saw that you were okay, and that's all I needed to know at the time. But, based on your level of undress when you arrived, it's obvious that something happened. I won't make you tell me, but if you ever want to talk, I'm here."

Emilie nodded at her best friend. "Thank you. I'm okay, I promise."

"Since you're planning to stay, I figured you'd require a new wardrobe. You'll find several new tunics in your chamber above stairs." Cait headed toward the steps, but Emilie stopped her.

"You've already helped me enough. Stay down here with your family. I'll run up and change." Cait opened her mouth to protest, but Emilie stopped her. "I need to change either way. I can check out my new clothes while I'm up there. I'll be right back." Before Cait could get a word out, Emilie bolted for the chamber, desperate to be fully clothed again. Entering her room, she walked over to the chest and opened it, shocked to find it nearly spilling over with new clothes. Cait hadn't been kidding! A few pairs of leather slippers accompanied new leather boots at the base of the chest, and Emilie began to dig through the clothing pile, admiring the many colors to choose from and knowing firsthand how much work went into their creation.

Most of the fabrics were bold in color. Purple, blue, green, yellow, orange. But a light blue tunic caught her eyes, and she carefully pulled it from the chest, holding it out to admire its finer details. Long flowing sleeves hung from the bodice, with intricate knot patterns sewn into the neckline and bottom hem, sparkling with silver thread.

Why was this particular dress so fancy compared to the others? Shrugging, Emilie admired it for another moment and decided to put it back, saving it for a special occasion. Instead, she pulled out the yellow tunic, needing something light and cheery to raise her spirits. Quickly slipping it over her head, Emilie grabbed a silver chained belt to link around her waist and slid her feet into a pair of leather slippers before bolting back down the stairs, desperate to hear if Samuel had any news for her.

When she approached, she noticed Murielle had stepped aside to bounce Lucas on her hip while Cait chatted with Samuel. Guards and servants cluttered the room, and she wondered if Brodyn was paranoid about the tunnels leading into his home.

"Emilie," Samuel sighed, hugging her as she walked over to him and Cait. "Cait told me about your ordeal. I'm so terribly sorry I was away when this all happened. I feel like I've failed you somehow."

Emilie frowned and shook her head. "None of this is your doing. You couldn't have prevented any of this, Sam."

"I suppose that, since I'm the one who guided Cait here last year to fulfill her destiny, which led to you arriving here, I bear some guilt in the matter."

"Please," Emilie said dismissively. "Cait was meant to be here. She had to come, or history as we know it would have been forever changed. And you didn't bring me here—a banshee did," she said calmly, wondering how she had gotten to a point in her life when discussing time travel and banshees was part of casual conversation. "I'll take 'things I never thought I'd say' for 200, Alex," she murmured to Samuel, making him chuckle.

"I suppose. I'm just glad you are all right, at least in this time-line."

"Uh…" Emilie's brow creased at Samuel's odd statement. "Care to explain?"

"I went back to 2023 and, as promised, looked into your situation. I ended up having to fly to Edinburgh on a red eye when I saw the news. Em, your flat and the entire building were destroyed in a fire the night you disappeared. It happened at two in the morning, which means everyone in the building perished, except for Mister Morgan who lived just above you, because he left to take his dog on a potty break."

Emilie felt the blood drain from her face as she grew dizzy. She clung to Samuel to keep her balance.

"Oh, my God! Emilie! You would have died in that fire!" Cait cried, staring at Emilie in horror. Words escaped Emilie. Her poor neighbors. She hardly knew any of them, but that didn't make the news any easier. Thank goodness Mister Morgan and his sweet Pug, Lulu, were out of the building.

Swallowing her bile, Emilie gripped her stomach. "Everyone thinks I'm dead?" she whispered.

Samuel nodded. "To them, you are dead. There is no body or sign of you. They declared you dead, and... well. It wasn't far-fetched since the fire blazed so hotly, they found next to no remains for most of the people, and what they could find was unidentifiable. It was an electrical fire that started in the basement and virtually exploded. I'm so sorry..."

So many things ran through her mind, and she fought back the panic. She didn't want to be dead! Yes, she planned on staying here anyway, so the life she left behind was useless to her, but there had been a solace in knowing she could exist in both worlds. "At least there is nobody there to mourn me," she said with sadness in her heart.

"That's not true, Em." Samuel took her hand and slipped something into it. When she looked down, she gasped and felt instant tears flood her eyes.

"My piece of amber from my adoptive mom. But... how?"

"You had a fire safe in your flat. This was the only thing in-side of it. Your landlord, Duncan, was very upset, but not for the reasons you'd expect. Yes, his property was destroyed, but losing all those lives left him in shambles. He was particularly upset by losing you. He said you were the only person in that building who ever stopped to say hi and treat him like a human being and not just a landlord. He grieves for you."

A sense of guilt, or maybe grief for her landlord gripped her heart. He would never know that she lived. Tears ran down her cheeks, and she didn't bother to wipe them away, for she knew more would continue to fall. "So, to the people of 2023, I'm dead."

"But you're not dead!" Caitriona exclaimed and grabbed Emilie, pulling her into a tight embrace. "You're here, damn it! And you didn't want to go back anyway! It was a horrifying accident, but you avoided it because—"

"Because of the banshee's warning." Emilie looked up at Cait and then at Samuel, who slowly nodded.

"It appears someone, or something, was looking out for you," Samuel said.

"It's proof you were supposed to come here, Em. You belong here just as much as I do," Cait said.

"I thought the warning was meant for Lucas," Emilie said, shaking as she tried to control herself.

"It could have been for both of you. You survived by falling through those stones instead of returning home, and then you saved Lucas."

"That's a busy banshee," Cait said, trying to make Emilie laugh. It worked, making Emilie crack a smile, but it quickly faded as she found her way to a bench and slowly sat down to process the news.

"So, the one man who grieves me has lost everything he has and now cannot afford to feed his kids."

Pursing his lips, Samuel walked over to the bench and sat beside Emilie. Brodyn and Murielle also came over, huddling around Emilie with support.

Samuel cleared his throat. "Do you recall who you listed as your beneficiary with your bank?"

Her head snapped up, and her eyes grew wide. "Yes! You! It was Cait, but when she left, I changed the paperwork to your name."

He nodded. "I have your things, Emilie. Your boss from the tour company found your phone near the vault you disappeared through, and your purse was still in the locker. I have to go back soon to sign some paperwork, but I wanted to know what you want me to do with the money, though I suspect I already know."

"It's yours now, Sam. It's worthless to me. Keep it."

"I think I know a certain landlord who could use the money more than I can," Samuel whispered and gripped her hand.

More tears dripped from her eyes as she broke down all over again. "You'd do that?"

"I don't want the money I inherited from my 'dead'—" he put the word in air-quotes—"friend, especially because I have the pleasure of knowing you are alive and well in a time that I cannot divulge to others. Never been one to have my cake and eat it, too," he said with a smile.

"You don't even like cake," Emilie said with a chuckle as she wiped her tears away. Murielle disappeared and reappeared with a handkerchief, and Emilie gladly accepted it to wipe the snot dripping from her nose.

"It was meant to be, Emilie," Murielle whispered. You gave up everything to save us all and ended up saving yourself."

Emilie looked up at Murielle and felt gratefulness flourish in her chest for the life she had created here in such a short time.

"Thank you, to all of you. You're so right. I planned on staying here anyway." She looked down at the piece of amber in her palm which reminded her of Goodwin's beautiful eyes and smiled. "I'm where I belong. My heart just hurts so much for all those people. I can't tell you what to do with the money, but I agree Duncan could really use the help. So could Mr. Morgan."

"Consider it done. I'll handle everything when I return. They're planning a memorial for you all."

Emilie put up a hand. "I'm sorry, but right now, I just cannot handle anymore."

"I understand. Here are your belongings." Samuel handed her a leather satchel filled with her things. "I put everything in there so your fancy name-brand purse didn't draw suspicion. I also charged up your phone. You obviously can't use it, but I thought you may want one last look through all your photos."

"Thank you, Sam." Leaning in, Emilie took the bag from him and kissed his cheek. Opening the satchel, she saw her purse, unzipped it, and pulled out her wallet. "Here." She slid a wad of twenty-dollar bills out of her wallet and pressed them into Samuel's hand. "Take it. Maybe next time you're in our time, you can bring back more medical supplies since it's becoming too taxing for Anya."

He nodded and stuffed the money in his own satchel tied to his belt.

She put the wallet onto the table and then began rifling through her purse—random receipts, a hairbrush, a dried-out tube of lipstick, a few pens. An emergency stash of Twinkies in the side pocket. She'd save those for later. And... "Murielle, I have something for you, as well."

Murielle tilted her head with curiosity, wondering what Emilie could possibly have from the future to give her. She found the object she searched for at the very bottom of her bag, wondering how purses always seemed to swallow the one item she desperately searched for. "Here. Open this."

She handed Murielle a round, metal compact decorated with enamel thistles on its front. She'd found it in a small Edinburgh shop and fell in love with it. Now she loved it more, but only because it would enable Murielle to see her true self.

Hesitantly, Murielle turned the circular metal item over, running her thumb over its embossed surface. "This is utterly enchanting," she murmured. "Your time has wonderous objects." Her thumb slid over the small button in the front, making the compact pop open with a start. She gasped and nearly dropped it when she saw the mirror inside. Samuel dove forward to catch it mid-air, handing it back to her. Murielle's gaze widened when she stared at her own blue eyes in the mirror. "Is this... me?"

"Yes. That's you," Emilie said with a satisfied grin. "I'd say it's a bit of an upgrade from that mirror in your chamber that makes you look like a Picasso." Cait laughed at that, and Emilie was glad someone understood her reference.

Murielle carefully touched her face, testing her reflection to verify it was her. "I dinnae look at all how I expected."

"You're stunning," Emilie said. "I told you."

"Och, I dinnae ken about that, but I cannae believe I can finally see my likeness with such clarity."

"You do not give yourself proper justice, Murielle," Sam whispered from beside Emilie, but nobody else seemed to hear it. Emilie gave Sam a side glance, wondering if he meant for her to hear his softly spoken remark, but she decided to pretend she never heard it. Whatever was brewing between him and Murielle was between them.

"Thank ye, Em, a thousand times thank ye. This is beyond the most precious trinket I have ever held in my hands."

"You are very welcome, Murielle. I hope it serves as a re- minder of your true beauty. It's very fragile. Do not drop it, or it will shatter into a thousand pieces."

"As would my heart." Murielle clutched it to her chest, and Emilie couldn't help but smile. She'd known the mirror was a treasure when she found it, but never had she expected to gift it to a friend 1,300 years in the past.

With a sigh, Emilie stood from the bench. "I'm going to go back into the room to make sure Goodwin is all right. I've already left him for longer than I wanted to. It's just—I didn't expect to find out that I'm dead."

"We're here if you need anything, Em." Cait hugged her and pulled back to look her in the eyes. "Everything is going to be all right. I absolutely promise. We're together again, and you have a pretty amazing man here who is head over heels in love with you."

"I know," Emilie replied, feeling slightly lighter than before. She wandered away from her friends in a daze as she shuffled back to Goodwin's room, glad to see he was still sleeping. Plopping on the bench near the hearth, Emilie sighed and began to thumb through her photos.

CHAPTER THIRTEEN

PAIN LANCED THROUGH Goodwin's body when he shifted awake. Where was he, and why did it feel like the fires of hell fed on his shoulder? It all rushed back to him in a single flash. The battle, Arwyn's blade slicing through his left shoulder, his blade sliding through Arwyn's guts, Emilie standing in nothing but the cursed man's cloak.

Emilie. Her sparkling yellow-green eyes, her long wavy blonde hair, her striking smile and perfect teeth. Her perfect, round arse and perky breasts.

"Emilie?" He pushed himself into a sitting position in spite of the pain it caused and looked around the room. "Emilie!"

"I'm here." Suddenly he felt the bed move beside him, and Emilie was there in a beautiful yellow tunic that shone dully against her glowing skin and golden hair. "Are you all right?"

"Are ye an angel? Have I died and gone to heaven? Mayhap those Christians kenned what they spoke of all along..."

Her soft hands ran through his damp hair soothingly just before she placed her other hand on his chest, gently urging him to lay back down. He did as the angel commanded, looking at her in a daze. "I think I must be dead, but I cannae tell if I'm in heaven or hell... or mayhap the Otherworld. There are far too many religions."

Emilie chuckled before swiping hair away from his forehead and stilling, her smile fading as her face blanched. "You're burning up!"

"I ken that. 'Tis why I thought I was in hell until ye hovered above me."

"Anya!" He heard her yell and felt her rush from the bed, wondering why his angel was yelling so loudly. His temples throbbed, and his skin burned like he was covered in embers.

Blackness consumed his vision as he fell back into the depths of, wherever he had been, before he heard voices surrounding him once again.

"Goodwin? I think he fell back to sleep."

"He was talking about angels and religion. He thought he was dead."

"He will be if this fever doesnae break."

He heard the voices, mostly understood the words, but couldn't respond. He was too far away, stuck in a chasm where voices danced and echoed but barely reached his ears. Something cold and wet landed on his forehead, and it felt like falling through a frozen lake, instantly sending painful chills over his aching flesh. He cried out but wasn't sure if anyone heard him.

"Emilie." He knew the name he spoke. He knew the face he longed for, but he couldn't piece it all together, couldn't remember why he longed for her. "Emilie."

"He won't stop saying my name, but he doesn't seem to know I'm here."

"He's in a bad way, lass."

A deep voice entered the chasm, its rumble vibrating against Goodwin's temples. "He was fine last night."

"Fevers tend to worsen overnight. They also break overnight. We need to cool him down and find a way to make him swallow his next pill."

Goodwin thrashed as something pried his mouth open. A bitter object touched his tongue, but before he could spit it out, cold water flooded his mouth, and his jaw was tilted upward, forcing everything down his throat. Curse these demons in hell who tortured him. What had he done on this earth aside from protecting his king and loving a good woman? "Emilie." That was her name. That was his angel who hovered over him. If only he could see her again, but his damned eyes wouldn't open.

"I'm here, Goodwin. I won't leave your side. Even if you cannot see me, I'm here." He felt something soft grip his hand, and he squeezed back, which cost him dearly. With no more strength, he fell back through the dark passageway, and the voices faded.

This pattern seemed to go on for an eternity, where he felt Emilie, heard Emilie, but soon slipped away, dragged back down into the darkness by invisible claws, scorching his flesh until he passed out from the pain.

"ANY CHANGE?" EMILIE looked from Goodwin to Cait and shook her head. With every passing day, Emilie lost hope. Two days of this fever. Two days of forcing pills down his throat, wiping his skin and hair down with cold water, trying to talk to him but receiving no response.

"I'm so… scared," She couldn't hold back the anguish any-more. "I'm going to lose him, aren't I?"

Brodyn stood in the doorway, looking more angry than sad. "Nay. He's not going anywhere. I willnae allow it."

If only one could will a man to survive, then lovers would never die. Would he ever be more to her than that, or would he fade away and lose this battle before she could ever have the chance to be his wife? In such a short amount of time, she had fallen in love with him. The thought of marriage, though swift, only ever made sense with Goodwin. He was everything she ever wanted in this life, and now he couldn't even say her name like he had the first day. Slowly, he was slipping away.

"Don't lose hope, Em. Miracles do happen."

"Not for me. Never for me. Everyone I love leaves me," she cried with a pathetic hiccup. Looking over her shoulder, Emilie reached out for Cait's hand. "I don't mean that toward you. I understand why you left. I just can't take any more loss."

"I understand." Cait squeezed her hand. "I'm sorry. I still have hope. In my short time here, I've seen worse wounds and worse fevers. Lawrence suffered a similar fever after the last battle and look at him now."

"He's like if Frankenstein mated with Wolfman," Emilie said with a frown. "Huge, stiff, clumsy, hairy, rough, and... slow."

Cait shrugged. "Apt description, but he was like that before the accident."

Brodyn creased his brow as he always did when they spoke of things he couldn't understand. "I'll explain it to you later, love," she said. "Em, holler if you need anything at all."

They left the room, and alone with Goodwin, Emilie leaned across his bared chest. It helped her to feel his breathing, even if shallow, and hear his heartbeat, even if weakened.

"Come back to me. Please don't leave me. I love you." Her tears coated his skin, soaking into the spattering of dark hair across his chest. He didn't stir, but she prayed he could at least hear her words and that they offered him some comfort while he remained trapped between worlds. He straddled life and death, and the very thought made Emilie feel nauseous, but she had nothing left inside her stomach. Everything she ate came right back up.

Closing her eyes, she allowed her tears to fall as sleep tugged at her eyes. The only sleep she'd had since his accident was crying herself to sleep, but she preferred the oblivion of nothingness to the painful reality that Goodwin was dying, and there was nothing she could do to save him. Could fate be so cruel as to pull her through time to save her life, only so she could fall in love and live here in misery without him?

Darkness surrounded her but looking up, she saw stars twinkling overhead, brighter than any Exploratorium she'd ever visited. They were even brighter than when she first appeared in the year 686 and followed the North Star toward Pinnata Castra.

Where was she? Her conscious mind knew she'd fallen asleep. This was obviously a dream, but never had she dreamed and known what it was.

Looking around, she realized there was nothing at all but the stars above. Orion's belt twinkled, and Ursa Major winked, but the North Star shone brighter than all the others, a glittering hot white beacon calling her to it.

"Emilie!" she heard his voice call her name, echoing all around, vibrating through her.

"Goodwin!" she cried, wanting to run to him but having no idea where to run in this place so devoid of life and light.

It was just a dream, and her logical brain knew this, but the desperate, clawing, aching need to run toward him outweighed logic. There was no logic to love. People had done insane things in the name of love since the dawn of time, and Emilie was no different. If some whimsy told her to run through dark nothingness toward Goodwin, then she would do it.

Looking up once more at the North Star, she did the only thing she could think to do and walked toward its light.

"Emilie!" His call grew louder and more frantic.

"Goodwin! Where are you?" she cried as she began to run full speed in the same direction.

"I dinnae ken! 'Tis so dark!"

His voice seemed closer, so she kept running. "Stay still and keep talking!" she cried as she ran.

"I have nowhere to go, so I willnae move!" She smiled at his awkward words. Obviously, he was just talking to be heard, which was all she needed from him. "So, I will keep talking, but I dinnae ken why ye want me to do this. Am I dead? Are ye dead? I was hot, but now I feel nothing, 'tis as if—"

Emilie plowed into something large and invisible, falling backward with a grunt. The object grunted also, and Emilie scrambled to her knees. "Goodwin?"

"Was that ye? Ye plowed right into me!"

"I can't see you!" Of course, she wouldn't be able to see him with the absence of light. That thought had escaped her as she struggled through this odd dream. Since when did dreams follow the laws of physics, anyway? Feeling around the area as she crawled on hands and knees, Emilie finally felt something soft and smooth against her palm.

"Is that ye, love?"

"Do you feel that?" she asked with hope blossoming in her chest.

"Aye, ye have my arm." She felt his hand clasp hers, and she was suddenly propelled forward, crashing against his chest as his hands slid around her waist.

"Goodwin! Where are we? Is this a dream?" She felt around until she found the stubble on his face that had grown into more of a short beard over the last few days.

"I think we are dead, love," he gripped her closer, clinging to her in the darkness, and she did the same.

"No, we aren't dead. I don't know what this place is, but I think it's a dream. I just needed to feel you again, to hear you and know you hear me too."

"I've heard everything ye said to me while I was here."

"Is this what you've seen this entire time?"

"Aye, just darkness. Emilie," she felt his grip tighten on her waist. "I love ye. I dinnae want to live without ye."

"It's me who is at risk of living without you, Goodwin. You need to fight this! You need to find a way out of this! You're dying!"

"I've tried, but 'tis an endless darkness! I want ye to ken how much I love ye in case—"

"Don't you dare finish that sentence and give up on me!" Emilie slid her hand down to his and gripped it. "I followed the North Star when I first arrived in your time, and it led me to you. I followed it again in here, and it led me to you, again."

"I dinnae ken what the North Star is."

"The brightest star in the sky, Goodwin! Look up!"

"I dinnae see any stars!"

"Then follow my lead!" This was all madness. Maybe he was right; they were both dead, wandering in purgatory. Either way, she had nothing to lose. Holding Goodwin's hand in a crushing grip, Emilie ran toward the brightest star in the sky, terrified he'd turn into a puff of smoke and disappear forever.

A bright light flashed and blinded Emilie, causing her to jolt upright with a start. Blinking, she looked around and realized she was back in his chamber, sitting on the bed. And Goodwin still laid beside her with his eyes closed, unmoving. His skin was cold.

It had only been a dream. Letting out a blood-curdling scream, Emilie released all her pain, all her rage, sadness, and fear as she clenched her fists and roared until she ran out of breath. The door flew open, and a crowd of people ran in. Brodyn led the way, followed by Cait, Murielle, Ronan, Samuel, and Anya.

"Em... is he..." Cait wouldn't finish the sentence, but there was no need, for they all understood what was at stake.

"It was only a dream! I found him! I had him! He was with me, but I woke up, and he was still unconscious! I can't save him!" She shook with emotion and collapsed back down onto his chest. "He isn't gone, but I think I've lost him," she whispered.

"Emilie!" Goodwin shouted her name, making her sit up with a start, clutching his uninjured shoulder as she shook him, but his eyes remained closed.

"Goodwin! Come back to me! Do you hear me?" she pleaded, placing her hands on both sides of his head as she stared down at his still face. "Look at me, damn you!"

His amber eyes popped open with a start, and he sucked in a deep breath, looking right at her as awareness dawned on him. "Emilie, oh, thank God!" He tried to embrace her before wincing when he moved his shoulder.

Everyone in the room gasped and moved forward, hovering above them both, but Emilie was only focused on Goodwin. She knew they were all just as stunned as she was and loved him very much.

Emilie pushed him back down and laughed with unbridled

bliss as her vision blurred from the unshed tears threatening to fall. With all of her inner strength, she fought back those tears. She would look into his eyes without any obstructions, and she would memorize this moment with crisp detail, not through blurry vision.

"Your fever broke! I thought I was going to lose you!"

"I'm not too sure you didn't," he croaked, his voice raw from disuse. "Ye... came for me."

Emilie creased her brow. "You remember that? But, it was a dream."

"Ye pulled me out of the darkness, lass. Ye've done so more than once since I've kenned ye."

Even after looking death in the eye, Goodwin still had a way with words that melted Emilie from head to toe. She shook her head. They must be thinking of two different things. He was out for nearly three days. Clearly, he wasn't thinking straight.

Anya pushed through the crowd. "Move aside. I need to check his wound." Placing a hand on his forehead, Anya nodded encouragingly. "Fever is gone. Ye were in another world for a few days, lad." Next, she shifted to the other side of the bed to gently remove his bandages. She'd changed them several times while he lay unconscious. Though angry and swollen, the injured flesh would heal now that he'd overcome the worst of the infection. Even now, as he winced when the fabric pulled away from his stitches, Emilie saw that the wound had crusted over with a healthy scabbing and no sign of pus.

"Looks like ye are gonna be all right, lad. Yer a fortunate man. I've never seen a man so deep in the fever come out the other side."

"I had an angel on my side." Goodwin offered a weak smile and took Emilie's hand in an even weaker grip.

Anya didn't seem interested in his nonsense, likely used to men hallucinating with fevers. "I will leave this jar of salve and clean linens on the table. Rub this into the skin twice a day when ye change the bandages."

Emilie looked at the jar. "Why didn't we use this before? Is it for infection?"

"Nay, 'tis for pain and is hard to come by. There was no point in giving it to an unconscious man. Now that he is awake, he will be feeling the pain." Anya looked at Goodwin and gave him a firm nod. "Good to have ye back. Ye had us all worried sick, ye dolt."

She turned and shuffled through the crush of people before disappearing through the doorway. The old lady cracked Emilie up with her blunt honesty and deadpan humor.

Brodyn stepped up and gently smacked Goodwin in his uninjured shoulder. "Ye had us all scared out of our minds."

"I'll try harder not to die next time," Goodwin said, flashing his devastating dimpled grin.

"I dinnae ken if there will be a next time. We will see how yer shoulder heals."

"Ye cannae mean to take my sword."

"I mean to have my fiercest men on the field. One weak link can equal defeat. Ye ken this well enough. But, as I said, we shall see."

Goodwin obviously didn't like his king's command, but he didn't argue for he understood the logic. "Then I will have to work my way back to being the best."

"Second best." Brodyn winked and smacked his arm one last time. "Come, everyone. Leave Goodwin to rest."

Never one to listen to her elder brother's demands, Murielle pushed past Brodyn and Cait to sit beside Emilie on the bed. "Ye two holler if ye need anything. And dinnae scare us like that ever again." She leaned down to kiss Goodwin on the cheek before squeezing Emilie's hand. Then, standing from the bed, Murielle headed toward the door.

Not so long ago, seeing Murielle kiss Goodwin would have made Emilie certain they were in love, but now she understood their lifelong bond, and she was glad Goodwin had so many people who loved him. Above everything, Goodwin deserved love, and he could add Emilie to the top of that list. Even Psycho Sarah, as Cait now called her, loved the man.

Once they were alone, Emilie laid down beside him, finding great peace in the silence as she and Goodwin held hands and looked into one another's eyes. She didn't bother mentioning her dream, for she was certain that's all that it was, and his awakening immediately after was a mere coincidence.

"Em?"

"Hm?" she smiled and ran her fingers over his face, pleased to see his skin a healthy shade again.

"What happened?"

She pursed her lips, wondering if he was still somewhat in a daze or if he'd suffered short-term memory loss. "Well, you got hurt fighting Arwyn, and your blood became infected. You were lost to me for nearly three days," she said, hearing emotion crack in her voice.

"I mean in the darkness," he whispered, stroking her hair. She squinted in confusion, not quite sure what he meant. "You showed up in the darkness and pulled me out. You told me to follow the brightest star in the sky."

Emilie popped up to a seated position and looked down at him, too stunned to speak for a moment. Had they somehow synced dreams? She'd heard stories of people dreaming the same thing on the same night but always thought it was a ridiculous notion. "You remember that?"

He nodded. "Dinnae ye remember?"

"I do. I just thought it was a very intense dream. When I woke up, you were still unconscious for a few moments."

"Ye disappeared, and I was alone again. I couldnae hear nor feel ye. But when I looked up, the stars glittered overhead for the first time since the darkness started. And, I did as ye said. I followed the brightest star, just ran full speed toward it, unsure where I was going until I woke up beside ye. The stars led me back to ye, Emilie, just as ye said they first led ye to me."

In stunned silence, Emilie regarded Goodwin for a long moment without a logical thought to offer. It seemed impossible, and yet, his retelling was exactly how it happened. Had she somehow slipped into whatever plain of existence he was trapped in? She rejected that idea outright. And yet, she was here beside Goodwin because she slipped 1,336 years into the past simply by falling through a pile of stones that were hundreds of miles away from this coast. Perhaps it was time for Emilie's scientifically trained brain to accept there was another side to this existence she may never understand. And while Emilie had spent her entire life in the pursuit of knowledge, she decided to let this one remain a mystery. In the end, the whys, hows, and ifs didn't matter. She was here now, and he was by her side.

There was only one mystery that had been on Emilie's mind that she'd be glad to have an answer to. She must have remained silent with a puzzled look on her face longer than she realized. Goodwin snapped his fingers in front of her face to pull her out of her daze. "Ye all right, Angel?"

"Are you really going to keep calling me that?"

"Yer a beautiful woman who came out of nowhere and saved my life. I may not be a great man of faith, but I hear what the Christian priests and monks have to say about such matters, and I may be a changed man because of ye."

"Well, don't go expecting any miracles from me," she said with an airy chuckle, but his features grew serious when he sat up in bed. Emilie put a hand out to stop him, but he shook her off and straightened his back.

"Ye are my miracle, Emilie. When will ye ever understand that?"

Leaning in, Emilie gently placed a kiss on his cracked lips and looked into his eyes. Though she was grateful to have her piece of amber back, Goodwin's eyes were all the amber she would have ever needed. "Then we have that in common. Because you are my miracle."

"What were ye in deep thought about a moment ago?" he asked, leaning in to kiss her again.

"Huh? Oh!" She nearly forgot with all the talk of angels and miracles. "I was thinking of the moment right after Arwyn sliced your shoulder. There was an odd look on your face before you retaliated. You almost looked happy. I've wondered what you could possibly have been thinking of to make you smile while you bled!"

Goodwin grinned ear to ear and reached out with his good arm to bring her closer. "Och, I *was* happy. But not because I was ready to make ye a widow. Nay, killing men never excites me. But the thought I had right before I killed him excited me greatly."

"Which was what?" she asked, finding herself insanely intrigued to discover what would excite him just before a fight to the death.

"That I was going to kill Arwyn, marry ye, and get two dozen bairns on ye… and enjoy every second of it." He waggled his brows, and Emilie's eyes widened as she playfully pushed her hands against his chest.

"Two dozen children? I thought you loved me! That sounds painful, not to mention insane!" she grimaced, but warm tingles flittered through her body to know that Goodwin wanted a family with her. She found she wanted that with him beyond measure, as well.

"Mayhap, I was being over-enthusiastic. I'll settle for a dozen."

"Four. Final offer."

"Five," he pushed back.

Emilie cringed. "Let's just agree that we both want children and leave it there for now."

His features sobered, and he visibly swallowed, pulling her into his lap with one hand. She'd never underestimate his strength. The man moved her around as if she was but a plush doll, even in his weakened state. "Before we can have bairns, we need to marry. And, I want bairns immediately."

"Then, I guess that means we should marry immediately,"

she said with a grin. "But I'm only twenty-six. I had hoped to wait until I'm thirty to have a child."

"Thirty?" he nearly shouted. "Are all mothers old in your time?"

"Thirty is not old! Rude! We just live much longer, and many of us pursue jobs and educations first."

"It's old for having bairns. Lassies have bairns at fifteen!"

"And that's called statutory rape in my time and is not only disgusting, it's illegal, thank God." Emilie scowled and shook her head.

"I always thought the practice of marrying lassies off young was... as ye call it, disgusting. All right. We come from two different times. Fifteen is way too young. We both agree on this." Emilie nodded emphatically. "And thirty is much too old to begin having bairns if we are going to have a dozen."

"Four."

"Five," he insisted.

Emilie crossed her arms defiantly but gave him a small smile. He was adorable when he negotiated, even if it was her womb he bargained with. "I guess we should just meet in the middle, which is..." Goodwin scrunched up his face and counted on his fingers. "Ah. Twenty-two. So, ye owe me three bairns by now."

Emilie laughed and shook her head. "Your logic is lacking, but I see your point. If we want to have four bairns—"

"Five," he interjected.

She paused and glared at him playfully. "Then I suppose I can agree to have bairns immediately."

"Ye really are an angel, love." Leaning in, Goodwin kissed her thoroughly and deeply this time, no small pecks or gentle grazes of their lips. She felt him grow hard against her thigh and wondered how he could have strength enough for that after his ordeal.

Pulling away, Emilie shut it down. "I didn't mean we'd make a bairn right now, Goodwin!"

He laughed and laid back down in the bed. "I ken, lass. I

cannae help myself near ye. But I really should rest. Emilie?"

"Yes?"

"Will ye marry me?"

"Didn't we just discuss this?" she raised a brow.

"Aye, but, Queen Caitriona once told me that men don't tell a woman to marry him in yer time, they ask."

"You discussed marrying me with Cait?"

He shrugged. "I had to ken my odds." Taking her hand, Goodwin looked her in the eye. "Will ye marry me, love? I cannae take another breath until I ken that yer my betrothed."

Goodwin sucked in a deep breath and held it with his cheeks puffed out, and his eyes widened, looking like a fool. But he was her fool, and she loved him and his ability to be deadly serious one moment and act like a clown the next.

"Yes, yes!" she said, laughing. "I will do anything if it means you stop making that ridiculous face! I will marry you!"

Goodwin let out the air with an exaggerated huff, wincing when the act caused his shoulder pain. "I love ye, Emilie. As soon as my shoulder is healed and I am able to carry ye over the threshold of our new home, we will marry."

"Oh! I have the perfect way to celebrate!" she said, standing from the bed as she wandered over to the satchel containing her purse filled with personal effects from her time. Goodwin watched with curiosity as she returned with a cylindrical yellow item in her hand.

"What is this?" he asked, looking at the clear wrapping with wide eyes.

"It's a Twinkie! My favorite food, remember? Samuel brought my purse back with him during his last visit. I forgot that I'd brought this with me to work that night. Here." Opening up the wrapping, Emilie carefully split it in half. Goodwin flinched when the crinkled wrapper touched the bed.

"What the devil is that? It's clear like air, yet I can see it. I dinnae like it!" Goodwin flicked it off the bed, and Emilie laughed as it floated to the floor.

"It's just a wrapper!" she laughed, handing him his half of the sweet treat. "Here. You will love this. I've been waiting for you to wake, so I can see you try it."

Apprehensively, Goodwin took his half in hand and stared at Emilie. She nodded encouragingly, and when he popped the entire piece in his mouth, his eyes widened again before closing. "Och, what is this magic?"

"Isn't it the best?"

"Aye, 'tis... my new favorite food," he said with a mushed-up Twinkie in his mouth.

She laughed. "I told you! Here, have the other half, too. That's how much I love you, Goodwin. Get some rest. I will inform Cait of our formal betrothal and start preparations."

With a nod, he blew her a kiss, popped the other Twinkie into his mouth, and closed his eyes, drifting back to sleep. This time, Emilie was confident he'd awaken again.

CHAPTER FOURTEEN

G OODWIN'S SWORD FELL to the ground with a clang, and he shouted curses into the blue sky. The sun shone, and birds chirped, and Goodwin wanted to curse them, too.

After three weeks of being stuck in bed as he recovered, Goodwin had spent another week in the lists, doing nothing but train and exercise his stiff shoulder. It was more than stiff. It was stuck. Rotating it upward sent shocks of agony through his entire sword arm, making his weapon clatter to the ground every time. If he couldn't be a soldier, if he couldn't protect his people or his future wife, who stood in the sideline, cringing, he was worthless.

"It's all right, Goodwin. It's going to take time to recover."

He knew she meant well, but he had no patience for false hope and pretty words that equated to nothing. His reality was that he had lost years of skills because she'd distracted him during his fight with Arwyn. Spinning around to glare at Emilie, Goodwin picked up his sword and stormed toward her. "Dinnae ye have anything better to do than hover over me?"

Emilie frowned and took a step back. "I was only trying to encourage you."

"I don't need your encouragement! I need honesty! I'm a broken man! The only thing I was ever good at has been taken from me! Because of y—" He stopped short of saying the words. Blaming Emilie would be the worst thing he could do. The logical part of Goodwin that hid behind his anger knew she was innocent of everything his emotional brain accused her of. He just needed space. Space to overcome this injury, space to heal, space to come to terms with the loss of his hard-earned skills.

Too late. Sometimes an entire thought need not be spoken for the whole message to be delivered. He saw Emilie flinch, and he swore he saw tears brimming her eyes before she turned to look elsewhere. "I will leave you alone, then."

She walked toward the byre, where she had been busy milking the cattle so she and the other women could make more butter. Emilie had truly assimilated with the village and never shied away from any task, no matter how messy. She often sat around the fires at night with the wee children, telling them stories she called "classics," and spent all day helping everyone with every task, eager to learn as many skills as possible. She'd also stayed by his side every night while he recovered, occupying him with stories from her time and showing him the oddest images he'd ever seen in his life, something she called *photos* on the object she called her *cell phone*. It terrified him, and he still couldn't understand how this small item captured one's likeness without stealing their soul.

Around Emilie, he felt ignorant, feeble-brained, and archaic. *He* was archaic, he reminded himself. He wasn't good enough for her, and the more time he spent with her, the more he realized how much she gave up to be here. He didn't like feeling that way, which led to him pushing her away more and more. The only problem was that she busied herself planning their wedding every day. The only thing Goodwin wanted more than Emilie was her happiness. And, with him being injured and worthless, how could she be happy with him? It was safer to close himself off and push her away, even if it hurt them both. She'd made it clear she was staying in this time for her own purposes, not for him. And with news of her supposed death in 2023, she couldn't leave here even if she wanted to, which only worsened Goodwin's mindset. Was she only marrying him because she was stuck here?

Again, his logical brain told him that was ridiculous, but the insecure monster eating away at his guts told him she was settling. He'd rather be alone forever than with a wife who settled.

"Emilie..." he called to her as she walked away, but either she didn't hear him, or she ignored him. She disappeared into the byre in a swirl of dark green skirts, and Goodwin cursed himself, this time throwing his sword down with all his strength, kicking dirt up into the wind.

His fellow warriors stopped to look at him sideways, but they knew better than to say a word. Not a single one of them would feel less distressed than he if they lost their sword arm. "Brodyn, spar with me," he snapped, walking toward the middle of the field, expecting his friend to follow. When he turned, he found himself alone as Brodyn remained in the same spot, eyes narrowed.

"Ye are too angry to spar with anyone. Go take a dip in the loch to cool down."

"I dinnae need to calm down! I need ye to spar with me so I can properly train!"

Brodyn continued to glare at him. Goodwin was being an arse to everyone he loved, but he had a rage in his soul he couldn't wade through, so thick was its festering essence. He was drowning in his own emotions, which he'd never experienced before.

Slowly, Brodyn walked up to him, taking him by the bad shoulder, making him wince. Leaning in, his king and best friend murmured, "If ye cannae even handle a man grabbing yer arm, ye arnae ready to fight. If ye keep this up, ye will truly render yer arm worthless by damaging the tissue. Stop being an arse. Ye arnae the first man to heal after a sword wound. Ye could have died in battle. Be grateful yer alive and have a chance to heal."

"I'd rather have died than be an invalid," Goodwin said through clenched teeth.

Brodyn sighed. "I was injured after the last battle. Ye dinnae think I felt the same way? But I pushed through and recovered. So will ye. What I didnae do was push everyone away with my anger. Emilie is working hard to become a part of this village, and she's working even harder to plan the wedding feast that yer due to share in two days with the village. Cannae ye stop shouting about yer arm and focus on the woman yer about to marry before ye push her away for good? She may be staying here either way, but ye arnae the only man with eyes for her."

"What?" Goodwin growled and looked around at the shirtless men sparring as if each one was now his enemy. "Who has eyes for her?"

"Have ye seen her? Aside from my wife and, as I'm told, my sister, she is the bonniest woman in the village. But ye staked yer claim on her before everyone, dinnae ye recall? Now yer yelling at her in front of everyone. Make no mistake that other men are trying to console her and much more. Watch yerself."

"Mayhap Emilie is better off with any one of them. She has no use for a husband who cannae lift a sword if danger comes knocking. She'd still be married to Arwyn and likely carrying his bairn had I not the strength to protect her."

Brodyn furrowed his brow. "Are ye the only warrior in this village now? I swore we arrived at Arwyn's camp with hundreds of men, each capable of running the man through. Ye simply received the honor. Honor comes with a price. Ye were injured. But the enemy is dead, and any one of us would have stepped in, just as ye stepped in when I was injured. Dinnae start believing ye are the only man in this village who can protect us. Caitriona told me that, in her time, there is a saying. 'It takes a village.' It means it takes a group of people working together to achieve goals. If one man takes the world upon his shoulders, he will fail. If we all lift together, we succeed. Ye arnae alone, Goodwin, but if ye keep up this behavior, ye may find yerself alone soon enough."

Brodyn walked away, leaving Goodwin feeling foolish and well-scolded. He knew he behaved childishly. He hadn't had a tantrum since he was a wee lad still in nappies. Now, at seven and twenty, he'd behaved worse than a bairn. Mayhap Brodyn was right, and he needed to cool his temper with a dip in the loch. He was to marry Emilie in two days, and he wanted that honor more than anything. But, he'd run her off with his foul mood, and now he had to suck up his pride and woo his bride.

Looking at himself, he realized the dust he'd kicked up caked his sweaty skin, and he looked like a wild beast from the forest. He behaved like one, too. Slowly exhaling, Goodwin walked away from the sounds of his fellow warriors sparring and decided to do what his king recommended. He'd cleanse his mind and body at the loch, get ahold of himself, then seek out Emilie. He had a gift for his future wife that he planned to give her at the altar, but something told him he had better give it to her now to show his steadfast commitment and devotion before the lass decided she could do better than an injured, belligerent man who lived in a wee hut and had nothing to offer her now that he couldn't raise his sword.

"DID YOU TELL him?" Cait, Murielle, and Samantha, the blacksmith's ever-smiling wife, all looked at Emilie curiously as they mindlessly milked cows.

"Nope." Emilie continued to focus on her own milk bucket, cursing herself for being so behind the other women, whose pails threatened to overflow as hers was barely half full. "How could I when he was throwing a fit and blaming me for his injury?"

"He didnae!" Samantha gasped, no longer smiling as her hand stilled on the cow's udder.

"He doesnae mean it," Murielle insisted. "He's never felt so unmanned. He's devoted his entire life to swinging that sword and protecting his loved ones."

"And now, it's my fault that he's lost that ability. At least he seems to think so. Perhaps this is all one big mistake." Emilie huffed and blew her loose blond hair away from her face. How did these women tie kerchiefs in their hair that actually stayed in place without bobby pins? Hers seemed to continuously slip back on her head, and more hair slipped out every time she pulled it forward.

"Did he say as much?" Cait asked, tilting her head as she leaned forward to grab Emilie's bucket, placing it beneath the cow she milked now that her bucket was full.

"Yes. He stopped himself from finishing the sentiment. But clearly, he's thinking it."

"What an ass," Cait scoffed. "You know it's not your fault."

"Honestly, I don't know that," Emilie said with a sigh.

"Em, you literally went back to Arwyn to keep Goodwin alive."

"Yes, but I distracted him right before Arwyn attacked. Had I not, he would have deflected. His injury may as well be caused by me."

"Dinnae blame yerself, lass," Samantha said. "He kenned the risks of combat. Men start conflicts that end with injury or death. He was fortunate. He's also fortunate to have ye, lass. He isnae the only man in this village who'd try to stake a claim on ye."

"So, I've been told, yet I see no men even look at me."

Because yer marrying Goodwin, and he is verra well respected, lass! He's the king's champion, and yer the queen's sister. No man would dare attempt to take ye from Goodwin but mark me. If he loses ye, men will line up for a chance."

"I've no desire for another man. If Goodwin decides he doesn't want to marry me because I caused his injury, that's his decision and his mistake. As for me, I'm not prepared to turn my back on him. I love him. I know he's struggling. We don't walk away from those we love during hard times. However, I cannot force him to do the same. If he wants space from me, he's got it."

"Then, ye willnae be telling him about the bairn?" Murielle asked with concern creasing the corner of her eyes.

"I was going to tell him today before he yelled at me and told me to leave him alone. I will not have him marry me out of obligation. If he chooses to marry me in two days, it won't be because I carry his child. If he decides not to marry me, I will still tell him, but I will refuse marriage if he suggests it."

"Emilie, Goodwin loves ye," Murielle insisted.

"I know he does, Murielle, but love isn't always enough. If he resents me, or I him, we cannot marry." She shook her head, pushing back the tears. "I just don't understand where this is all coming from. We spent weeks together while he recovered. We laughed, shared stories, bonded… we were so happy. But as soon as he was cleared to pick up a sword, he turned to ice. He even ignores me and rolls away from me in bed. It's like he expected to pick up a sword immediately and be back to full health, and when that didn't happen, it was my fault."

She swallowed hard, feeling her cursed nausea roiling again. She'd been sick a few times throughout the weeks, but because it wasn't in the mornings and every day, it took her a while to realize her cycle never came, and she was definitely pregnant. However, the day she discovered this was the same day he first tried to spar with Brodyn. Emilie met Goodwin in the longhouse that night, excited to tell him the news, but he'd barely looked her in the eye and retired home before she'd finished her dinner. The nights had been similar since, but it wasn't until today that Goodwin openly showed his disdain for her.

"Cait, I'm not feeling well, and the smells in this byre aren't helping. Even the smell of milk is starting to make my stomach turn."

"Go, go. Get out of here and go lay down. We are nearly done here. Soon it will be time for the evening meal in the longhouse."

"Yeah, I think I'm going to skip it tonight. I can't face Goodwin and his open dislike for me right now. Is it all right if I stay at your home tonight? I haven't felt very welcome at Goodwin's this week."

Murielle, Samantha, and Cait all looked at her with a mix of pity and anger. "I'll make him cry, just watch," Murielle said with a scowl.

That made Emilie crack a smile. Of course, she didn't want Murielle to do any such thing, but she knew her friend would try if she asked.

"Of course, Em. Whichever chamber you want is yours."

"Thank you." Gripping her stomach, Emilie hurried out of the byre, the smell of milk, hay, and dung making her near ready to toss what little lunch she'd had. Though she was desperate to lay down, she needed to head to the well first and grab fresh water to wash with later.

Hastening through the village with a bucket in hand, she spotted Sarah, that she-wolf who'd tried to ruin their lives. Brodyn hadn't been able to do much more with her than keep her under close guard and put her on hard labor duties. He couldn't send her away because she'd likely only bring more trouble upon them. If it had been a man, Brodyn would likely have brought the hounds of hell down on him, but Brodyn figured being stuck in her village, facing everyone's wrath while she dug holes and cleaned the byres—any menial task he could think to give her— was a better punishment.

Two nights ago, Goodwin had laid into her until she cried, and Emilie almost felt sorry for the lass. Now, spotting Emilie walking toward the well, Sarah stopped digging a hole long enough to glare, but Emilie wouldn't bother to give the woman the satisfaction and continued walking past her.

"I saw him yelling at ye. He hates ye now. 'Tis only a matter of time before he gives up on ye!" the lass hollered at Emilie as she walked away. Emilie kept her eyes locked on her destination and pretended not to hear her.

Humiliation made her throat sting with repressed emotion. How many people in the village also heard Goodwin yelling at her, blaming her for his injury? How would she face him at the altar in two days and act like everything was all right? Nothing was all right. Maybe she should stop preparations for the wedding. At this point, she wasn't confident that Goodwin still wanted to marry her, and she'd rather call it off or postpone it than marry a man who'd resent her the rest of her life.

Remembering all the laughter and love they'd shared since she arrived here nearly two months ago, her heart sank at how quickly things had changed. Maybe they'd both rushed into marriage. In 2023, everyone would think they were insane. But in these times, quick courtships were the norm. Many never courted at all, having arranged marriages. She reminded herself that she and Goodwin had already faced more trials in their short time than most couples face in a lifetime. And yet, it appeared Goodwin had fallen out of love just as quickly as he'd fallen into it.

When Emilie reached the well, footsteps crunched behind her, making her look over her shoulder, half hoping Goodwin had come to apologize. Instead, she found herself facing Sarah, who'd apparently not taken Emilie's silence as a sign to leave her alone.

"Why are you following me?" Emilie shouted, having had enough of this vile woman and her venomous tongue. "What the hell do you want with me?"

"I want ye out of our lives so things can return to how they were!" Sarah snarled as she took another step toward Emilie.

"So, you can go back to meaning nothing to Goodwin? Nothing has changed in that regard. Leave us alone! We are getting married in two days, and I'm pregnant with his child," Emilie whispered, not only to keep from being overheard but to soften the blow. She didn't want to hurt Sarah or make her jealous. She simply wanted the woman to get the hint and move on. Already, she had become less than a servant due to her behavior. How much lower could Sarah sink?

"Ye whore!" Sarah shouted, charging toward Emilie with malice in her gaze. The well stood directly behind Emilie, and as Sarah ran toward her with wild hatred burning in her eyes, Emilie knew she had better move before the crazy bitch tried to push her down the well. Her heart cracked against her ribs as Sarah drew closer. She was too weak and nauseous to fight Sarah off, nor had she any interest in an altercation with this meddlesome lass.

When Sarah reached out with her claws drawn toward Emilie's face, Emilie panicked and stepped to the side, barely missing the impact.

It happened so fast that Emilie's desperate attempt to grab Sarah's skirts proved futile. A guttural scream released from Emilie's throat as she dropped the bucket and lunged forward to catch Sarah, landing on the dirt ground with a thud as Sarah fell headfirst into the well.

Another scream of terror tore from Emilie as she heard Sarah scream before a faint splash echoed. Scrambling to her feet, Emilie looked down into the well, facing only darkness. "Sarah!" she cried. Turning around, Emilie ran toward the village's bustling center and screamed for help.

Eyes widened as people ran forward, but when Emilie saw Lawrence's hulking form jogging toward her, she filled the distance, clinging to his arm when she reached him. "Sarah! She fell down the well!"

When the villagers heard it was Sarah who needed help, many of them shrugged and turned away, clearly having no interest in saving the woman who tried to harm their heir. Emilie couldn't exactly blame them, but she couldn't stand by and do nothing. Ronan showed up as well, and together they looked down into its bleak darkness and called the lass's name several times without a response.

"We need a ladder!" she cried. "We have to get her out of there!"

Lawrence frowned at Emilie, placing a hand on her shoulder. "The lass is gone. She isnae responding, and she wouldnae be able to tread water in that small space for long."

"No... we have to try!" Panic dug its claws into her gut, making nausea roil for entirely different reasons than before she headed toward the well.

"How did this happen?"

"She saw me leave the byre and began shouting insults at me.

When I ignored her, she stopped her work to follow me. I... I tried to reason with her and asked her to leave me alone. I told her... something about me and Goodwin that I thought would make her understand that it was time to move on. Instead..." Emilie lowered her voice and wrapped her arms around herself as her body began to quake. Murielle came around a corner and bolted toward her, wrapping a supportive arm around Emilie's waist to keep her upright. "Instead, she charged toward me with her hands primed to attack. All I could think to do was move out of the way. But when I did, she couldn't stop and fell inside. I tried to catch her. I did! But, it all happened so fast."

"Oh, Em!" Murielle wrapped her arms around Emilie. "Come. The men will retrieve Sarah's body. Ye shouldnae be here for that. Ye need rest. I'll escort ye back to the house and let Brodyn and Goodwin ken what happened."

She wanted to beg Murielle not to tell Goodwin. He was angry with her, and she didn't need his sympathy right now. He would come to her when he was ready, not because he caught word that Sarah had attacked her. But, she knew there was no sense in keeping this from Goodwin. Too many people had seen and heard the commotion. He'd hear about it soon enough.

Silently, Emilie allowed Murielle to walk her back to the house as villagers busied themselves, not at all feeling the loss of Sarah. But Emilie knew that the memory of Sarah falling over the edge, and the sound of her scream, would haunt her for the rest of her life. True, the woman was evil and died trying to push Emilie down the well first, but it didn't make any of this rest easy on her soul.

Reaching the front entrance, Emilie pushed through with a sob, finally able to let her pain show. "Thank you, Murielle. I'm fine on my own from here. I just... I just need to be alone!" She ran past Murielle and Anya without a word, desperate to find some privacy and a chamber pot.

Running up the stairs, Emilie entered the first door on the left and ran to the emptied—thank God—chamber pot, leaned over, and lost her stomach. Feeling slightly better, Emilie plopped on the bed and pulled the covers over herself, enveloped in darkness as she curled into a ball, feeling all the pain and anguish rip from her lungs as she cried until she could barely breathe. As usual, crying made her eyes sore, puffy, and tired, so Emilie closed them and hid away from the world, hoping nobody would bother her until morning.

HOURS HAD PASSED since his poor treatment of Emilie, and the guilt had only increased with every passing moment as he calmed himself down and began to think rationally again. Goodwin prided himself on being a grounded, level-headed man who always respected women. Yet this sennight, he'd been a monster to Emilie and everyone around him. Even logical men were prone to bouts of emotion at times, and for Goodwin, he'd made up for lost time, taking years of cool-headed thoughts and washing them away with a sennight-long temper tantrum.

Escaping into the woods helped clear his mind and reminded Goodwin that he was alive and fortunate for it. And, it was solely Emilie's actions that had saved him. She literally ran toward the enemy to save him, and he'd rewarded her by turning his back on her every night as he sulked. Today, he'd gone too far with his accusations. It festered within his belly. He felt genuinely sick when he walked into the longhouse, his gaze desperately scanning the crowd for her long golden locks. Platters of roasted hen surrounded by vegetables were passed around the hall as cheese, bread, and fresh fruits rested on plates. Spirits were high, as always, after a long day of labor, but Goodwin felt as if a gray cloud hung over his head when he saw no sign of Emilie near the head table. Caitriona and Brodyn sat with Lucas taking turns on their laps, and Murielle chatted with Samuel, apparently latching on to his every word. If Goodwin didn't know any better, he'd think Murielle was enraptured by the foreign man. Mayhap she was, but she'd better not get attached, for more kings were scheduled to arrive soon to court her. Brodyn would tighten security and take extreme measures to barricade all escape tunnels, but he still had a duty to host foreign kings and find his sister a husband.

For the first time in his life, Goodwin felt like an outsider among his own people. Eyes slid over him warily, as if everyone in the longhouse worried he might start throwing stones and stomping his feet. He deserved those looks after publicly berating Emilie. He'd walk down the aisle with her in two days' time, and he hoped to resolve the mess he'd made before then.

Her gift rested inside a pouch tied to his belt, and he clutched it, confirming it still remained at his side. But the woman he longed to give it to was not at his side. Nor was she in this building.

Pushing through the crowd, Goodwin forced a smile at everyone who hesitated when he walked past, trying to portray his usual attitude, but the knots inside his stomach wouldn't release until he found Emilie.

Reaching Cait and Brodyn, Goodwin leaned over the table. "Have ye seen Emilie?"

"Why? Ye wish to yell at her some more?"

Turning his head to the side, he looked at Murielle and frowned. "Nay. I wish to speak with her."

"She isnae here."

"I can see that. Where is she?"

Murielle shrugged and turned away from him, and he realized how much damage he'd actually caused. He owed everyone an apology for his behavior, but not until he first apologized to the woman he loved.

"She is at our house," Cait said softly, with no judgment in her tone or gaze. Leave it to his queen to be diplomatic. "You've not been in the village until now?"

He shook his head, sensing her question ran deeper than

simply questioning where he'd been. Queen Cait pursed her lips and looked at Brodyn before speaking. "Emilie experienced some trauma today. She is physically unharmed but badly shaken."

"What happened?" Goodwin growled, clenching his fists until his nails dug into his flesh. "Did Sarah harass her?"

"Yes, she tried to push Emilie down the well, but Emilie moved, and Sarah fell instead," Queen Cait told him as she bowed her head and closed her eyes, clearly struggling with this loss even if Sarah had caused her own demise. "Her body has been recovered, and she will be laid to rest. Emilie, however, has shut herself away."

Emilie had nearly been killed, and he'd been too busy sulking in the woods to notice. If she'd died while he was away... he yanked at his hair, beside himself with regrets.

Panic overcame him, and he turned to push through the crowd again, desperate to reach Emilie.

"Unless ye intend to make things right with the lass, I'd ask ye to leave her alone." Brodyn's warning made Goodwin turn back with a frown. His king wasn't quite as diplomatic as his wife. Goodwin knew he'd been an ass, but had he messed up so badly? It seemed they all knew something he didn't, something that made his behavior toward her even worse. What it was, he couldn't say, but this went beyond an argument between a man and his woman. It seemed even more personal than the incident with Sarah.

He nodded again, having no desire to discuss this with anyone else. Leaving the longhouse, Goodwin sprinted up the hill and tore through Brodyn's home, spinning in a circle only to discover the main room empty.

"Emilie?" he called but received no response. He checked the chambers on the first floor but came up empty before running up the stairs to check Murielle's chamber. Her bed was nicely made and a small fire burned in the hearth, making the room warm for its mistress when she returned. But there was no sign of Emilie. Shutting the door to keep the heat inside the room, lest he face more of Murielle's disapproval, Goodwin began throwing doors open at random as panic overwhelmed him. Had she been taken again? Would he fear for Emilie every time she was not easily found?

After every chamber on the right proved empty, Goodwin yelled her name again and burst through the first door on the left. A screech from the bed caught his attention, and Emilie's head peeked out from beneath the thick blue coverlet.

"Emilie?" he ran to her side and sat on the bed. "What's happened? Are ye injured?"

She shook her head and burrowed beneath the covers again, turning away from him. "What is it, Goodwin?" she whispered.

"Ye werenae at the evening meal, and I became worried. I suppose part of me will always worry when I cannae find ye."

"Well, now you've found me."

He'd found her, but he couldn't see her beneath the blanket she used as a shield. He tugged it down, earning a hearty growl of annoyance from Emilie, who wore only a thin, white undertunic. Had she intended to sleep away from their bed tonight? He supposed he hadn't exactly earned the privilege of sharing a bed with her, but it still stung that she'd planned on staying elsewhere without telling him.

"What do you want?" she huffed. "You told me I was hovering over you, so I decided to give you space. Now you come in here and invade my space?"

"Em..." He slowly reached a hand out to run his fingers through her messy hair, ruffled from the sheets. "I wanted to apologize for how I've behaved, especially today. I need ye to ken I dinnae blame ye for anything. But, I just heard about Sarah. Are ye all right, my love?"

"I was in shock for the first couple of hours. The moment she fell through the well is permanently engraved in my mind, but she attacked me and meant to push me down the well. I would never have been safe as long as she remained in the village, nor would any of us. I'm sad it happened but also relieved. That may make me a bad person, but I feel safer now. As for you," Emilie shoved a finger in his face. "You say you don't blame me for your injury, but you *did* blame me only hours ago."

"I did, aye. And I've hated myself every second since. Ye saved my life. Ye put yerself at risk for me, then ye stayed by my side as I recovered, and I rewarded ye with cruelty. I dinnae deserve ye."

"Is that why you're here, then? To call off the wedding because you don't think you deserve me? I certainly didn't deserve the way you treated me."

"Nay, ye didnae. And nay, I am not here to call off the wedding. Christ Almighty, Emilie. I'm in love with ye. Dinnae ye ken that?"

"I thought I did, but after this week..." her voice faded, and sadness clouded her eyes as she looked away from him. "You couldn't stand to even look at me."

Goodwin lifted her gaze to him with a finger beneath her chin. Her sorrowful yellow-green eyes made his stomach clench and his heart twist as pure disgust for himself ate at his soul.

"I am a bastard, and I dinnae deserve ye or yer forgiveness, but I've never felt so low. My only skill in this world is fighting to protect those I love. Without that skill, I feel like less of a man. I felt undeserving of ye. How can I protect ye the rest of my life if I cannae wield a sword? Christ, I couldnae even protect ye from Sarah!"

"Goodwin." Emilie placed a hand on his knee, and he felt a small amount of tension leave his body. "Your injury is fresh and still healing. You simply cannot expect your shoulder to move as it did before. That's just not how life works. You require time to train and recover. But even if you never fight again, that is not what makes you a man. Do you think the men who tend the farms while you're off fighting are less of men than you?"

Goodwin frowned and shook his head. "Of course not."

"Do you think they cannot protect their family just because they aren't expert swordsmen?" Again, he shook his head. "Being a man is more than wielding a sword, Goodwin. You should absolutely not give up on training and regaining your strength, and you're allowed to be angry, but you cannot push everyone away. I gave up everything to be here—my career, home, and life. I've never blamed anything on you or made you feel responsible for my circumstances, and I'm devastated that you believe I'm to blame for your injury. If that's how you feel, we should cancel the wedding until this is sorted."

Goodwin blinked several times as he absorbed Emilie's words. She was right on all accounts. She'd lost everything. So, what if he'd lost his strength? He could work to regain it, but Emilie could never have her old life back. And, though she'd decided to stay here, the decision to ever return was taken from her when she was assumed dead in 2023. Still, she always supported him, loved him, and accepted her circumstances gracefully—something he couldn't claim to have done.

"Ye are right about all of it, love, except the wedding. Please dinnae call it off." He took her hand in his and pleaded with his eyes. "I love ye. I've been an angry fool. I dishonored ye in front of the village, and I regret that my emotions overcame me, and I lashed out at ye. Before ye arrived at Pinnata Castra, I felt empty and lost inside. I began to wonder if there was more to a man than the ability to wield a sword. I have discovered there is so much more for me now than fighting battles, but only if I have ye by my side."

Goodwin gripped her hand, desperate for her forgiveness. "I will do anything to make this right, Emilie. Anything. I have something I wish to give ye, a gift to show my true love and desire to make ye my wife. I meant to give this to ye on our wedding day, but I think I should give it to ye now."

He released her hand for a moment to open the small leather pouch tied to his belt, reaching inside as Emilie silently watched with curiosity. When he felt the circular band, he pulled it out and held it before her.

Placing her hand on her chest, Emilie gasped as she looked

down at the ring. "Is that... *amber?*"

He nodded. "Aye. This was once a silver brooch, the only trinket I had left of my birth mother. I had the smith melt it down into a ring, so I could honor my wife with something that belonged to my family. It was her mother's before her and so on for three generations. Now, if it pleases ye as it pleases me, it will continue in our family for many more generations, passing down to our eldest child, and I pray, his child after that. As for the amber, I recall ye telling me about the amber ye had from yer mother, and how it reminded ye of my eyes, so I hunted a wee piece of amber down to have placed in the ring. I ken it isnae a precious gem, and I am but a humble warrior with little else to offer, but everything I have and everything I am is yers if ye will accept this ring and agree to be my wife."

He felt the bed begin to shake as she suddenly burst into tears, nodding her head before wrapping her arms around his neck and burrowing into him.

"Yes! Of course, I will still marry you. This is the most beautiful ring I've ever seen!"

"I wouldnae go that far, lass," he said with a chuckle, feeling his heart fill to nearly bursting as he held her against him.

"I mean it." She pulled away and wiped her tears, smiling at him. "I couldn't ask for anything more precious."

"I feel the same way," he whispered, looking her in the eye as he took her hand in his, carefully slipping the ring on her finger, relieved that it was a perfect fit.

"I'm so verra sorry I was cruel to ye, my love. I will spend the rest of my days proving my love for ye. Ye are the angel who saved me from a life of loneliness. I dinnae ken how to begin proving my gratitude or love, but I vow I will never stop trying. Moreover, I wasnae there for ye today when Sarah attacked. I truly believed the lass had learned her lesson. I'm only sorry ye had to experience her death."

"You are not to blame for her behavior, Goodwin. You will not always be around to protect me every second. But, it's over now, and I just want to move on with our lives and forget this horrible incident," Emilie said, leaning in to kiss him gently. "You've saved me from loneliness, too. I had no family before I arrived here. You opened your home and heart to me, you gave me love, you gave me life. And, I look forward to starting a family with you."

"We will get started on it right away," Goodwin said. "I cannae wait to see ye expand with my child."

Emilie's features sobered, and Goodwin worried he'd said something to upset her.

"We've already gotten started, it seems."

"What is it ye are saying?" Goodwin's stomach flipped, and he wanted to jump off the bed and dance like a madman, but first, he needed to contain his excitement until she verified what he hoped was true. "Are ye... with child?"

She nodded, and a beautiful smile slid across her face. "I am. I'm certain of it. I believe I'm about five weeks—or sennights as you'd say—along. I think it must have happened the very first time we made love in the cabin."

Goodwin jumped off the bed, pulling Emilie into his arms. "I'm going to be a father!" he shouted, twirling her around. She laughed and clung to him before he gently placed her back onto her feet. "Och, I ought to be gentler."

"It's fine, Goodwin. I'm pregnant, not made of glass."

Emotion clogged his throat, making words hard to form, but he did his best to speak his heart's truth. "Ye've made me the happiest man in the land, Emilie. I love ye, and I will be the best damned husband to ye and father to our one dozen children."

"Four," she murmured, leaning in to kiss him.

"Five," he replied, guiding her toward the bed where he gently laid her down as he hovered above her, feeling very little pain in his bad shoulder. At least he could still hold himself aloft, for it meant he could look down and gaze at the angel who'd soon become his wife and the mother of his children.

"I wish to make love to ye right now." Rolling over to lay

beside her, Goodwin gathered her undertunic, exposing her legs. Slowly, he trailed a finger up her thigh, desperate to feel her warm heat. Her hand gripped his, stopping his progress, and he frowned.

"I want that more than anything, but I haven't felt well today." When concern laced his features, she gave him a reassuring smile and squeezed his hand. "Nothing to be concerned about. It's a good thing. It means our bairn is growing. It also means I might vomit at any moment, and you should leave."

She gripped her belly, and he shook his head. "I'm not leaving ye alone. I cannae do much to help ye during this time, but I can at least hold yer hair."

Emilie looked at him with a wry smile. "That may be the most romantic thing I've ever heard."

Then, Emilie scrambled off the bed to grab the chamber pot, and Goodwin slid to the floor beside her, holding her hair, determined to be there for her every step of the way.

CHAPTER FIFTEEN

"**W**ELCOME HOME, EMILIA Jean Mac Dougal," Goodwin said with a wide smile as he carried her over the altar.

"Be careful of your shoulder, Goodwin," she scolded, but he refused to put her down as he continued toward the back of the house, gently placing her on their bed.

"I'm perfectly capable of carrying my new wife over the threshold. In fact, I'm perfectly capable of any and all physical activities involving my wife." Goodwin waggled his brows as he tore off his tunic and threw it onto the floor, just missing the hearth fire. It would not bode well if their home burned down on their first day of marriage.

"You were also perfectly capable of making a fool of yerself before the entire village at our wedding feast." Emilie tried to sound stern, but she couldn't hide her bemused smile when she remembered her husband climbing atop the longhouse's head table to proclaim his love for his new wife and beg her forgiveness for publicly insulting her honor. Instead, he embarrassed her publicly with his over-the-top show of love, but she knew it was part of Goodwin's journey toward forgiving himself for his actions. As for Emilie, she'd forgiven him the moment he apologized. Life was too short to hold onto anger.

"Nay, I made a fool of myself the day I shouted at ye in the lists. This was nothing." With a glimmer in his eye, Goodwin sauntered toward the bed, crawling over her as he aligned his lips to hers. "Ye look breathtaking in yer wedding tunic, but I'd prefer to see ye bared to me, if yer feeling well enough."

She felt beyond well enough. They'd fooled around a fair amount while he recovered and even made love a couple of times toward the end of his bed rest, but it felt like an eternity since she'd felt him against her. Looking down at her gown, she remembered the first time she saw it in the chest of tunics from Cait. Emilie hadn't understood why it was in there, but now she knew. Her best friend had been so convinced that Emile would marry Goodwin, she'd commissioned the dress almost immediately upon Emilie's arrival at Pinnata Castra. It was funny how the rest of the world so readily saw that which she could not. But, she was here now, in their home, in their bed, with her husband as their child grew within her womb... and never had Emilie felt more at peace. She had the rest of her life ahead of her, and it would be a beautiful life because they had one another.

Reaching around her back, Emilie tugged at the ties securing the bodice to her bosom, slipping her shoulders out of the top and pushing it down until her breasts were free. Goodwin kissed her throat as his warm fingers trailed down her breast, pinching one nipple and then the other before his lips followed in their wake, nuzzling and sucking each one in turn.

When she responded by jerking her hips, Goodwin took that moment to yank her tunic down her legs, gently tossing it aside. "My wife is the most beautiful creature to ever walk this earth," he whispered, blazing a hot trail of kisses down to her belly, where he paused. "And she will only get more beautiful as our child grows."

Emilie sighed with love for him. He'd dispelled every assumption she'd ever had about ancient men being aggressive, unrefined, or sexist. Even compared to modern men, Goodwin had an inherent respect for women. She felt safe, cherished, and finally at home for the first time in her life.

Rolling over, Emilie pulled Goodwin down to trace the muscles on his abdomen with one finger. "And my husband is the sexiest man who's ever lived," she purred before kissing his nipples and moving lower until her fingers reached his trouser ties. "I never stood a chance against your charms."

"I'm a hella sexy dude," Goodwin replied with upturned lips.

Emilie looked up at him and clapped. "Look at you. You're ready for your California vacation."

"I dinnae ken about this thing ye call *vacation*, but I will go anywhere with ye, no matter how far. But right now, with my naked wife hovering above me, I wish to be nowhere but here."

"Nor I," she whispered as she tugged the string, loosening his trousers. Goodwin lifted his hips and yanked them down. His erection sprang free, and Emilie wasted no time gliding down him to connect their bodies. She arched as they moved together slowly, savoring every stroke. He cupped her breasts as she looked down at him through heavy-lidded eyes, filled by him completely. His breathing hitched through parted lips as he looked up at her, his cheeks flushed and his eyes glassy.

"I love ye, Emilie," he cried as he neared completion. Emilie shuddered, panting as waves of pleasure shot through her core. Her hands glided up his muscled chest, memorizing the feel of his soft flesh and hard muscle as she bent down to connect her lips to his.

"I love you, too," she whispered as her breasts pressed against his chest. Together, they rode the waves of ecstasy as they seemed to explode into a million pieces, then lay still in one another's arms.

Goodwin rolled over and enveloped Emilie in his strength, placing his large palm over her flat belly. No words were necessary. In the silence of their home, nothing mattered but their wildly beating hearts, their frantic breathing, and the promise of life growing between them.

Her life may have ended in 2023, but in the year 686, it was just beginning.

EPILOGUE

Ten months later

R UMMAGING THROUGH THE chest at the end of the bed, Goodwin came across a leather satchel he recognized as the one holding Emilie's belongings from her previous life. Their daughter, Anya, cried and shivered after having a wee bath. They'd named her for the woman who'd saved his life with her healing skills only months before she'd slipped peacefully into the Otherworld to join her beloved husband Edwin.

"Did you find a blanket, Goodwin? She's quaking," Emilie whispered as she cradled Anya against her bare chest, trying to calm her daughter so she'd latch onto her breast and feed.

Grabbing his tunic from the top of the pile, he ran over and gently wrapped his daughter in the warm, soft fabric. The hearth fire raged, but it seemed the wee lass was always cold no matter how warm the room was or how many layers she wore. "There ye go, love."

Wee Anya's wails settled into light fussing just before Emilie squished her leaking nipple into the bairn's mouth. Goodwin smiled while watching his wife feed their perfectly precious, healthy daughter. He'd never tire of these moments, even if they'd barely slept—or made love—since she'd been born two months earlier. Labor had been easy enough, but Emilie had shouted and lamented about not having access to something called *an epidural* to numb the pain. Despite her shouts and screaming at Goodwin that she would never have any more children, Emilie soon forgot the pain and became the most wonderful mother Goodwin had ever known.

Beside him, Emilie sighed with relief. "Thank God. My breasts are so engorged. No matter how much she eats, I feel like a cow in the byre ready to be milked."

"My offer stands. Ye ken I'm always willing to offer ye relief." He raised his brows and gave a cheeky smile, but Emilie just rolled her eyes at him.

"So, you've reminded me about three hundred times."

He decided it wise to change the subject. His beautiful wife was tired and cranky, and not in the mood to be teased. "I hope ye dinnae mind, but I found yer satchel from the year 2023 and rummaged through it. I found this odd piece of...well, it's hard as wood, but I believe it's parchment. Anyway, it's got yer likeness on it."

He held up the item in question, along with the object she called a *cell phone*, which contained likenesses of people from her time.

"Oh! That's my driver's license! Can I see?" He handed it to her, and she smiled widely as she peered down at it. "It expired last month on my birthday. I cannot tell you how nice it is not to go to a DMV to renew it."

Goodwin shrugged, used to hearing words he didn't understand.

"Can I see my phone? It's likely nearly out of battery. I've kept it off so I can look at the photos now and again, but soon, they will all be memories." She took the rectangular object in her hand and pushed some buttons. The glass front lit up, and Goodwin, wary as always of the item, backed up a step. It didn't matter how many times she explained it was something called *technology*. To Goodwin, it was terrifying, and he always felt uneasy when he saw the images of the people it contained, fearing their souls were trapped within the rectangular object.

Emilie laughed at him when he backed away. Meanwhile, wee Anya continued to suckle her breast while Emilie used her free hand to swipe the screen. "Hey, Goodwin?"

"Aye?" he looked up at her just as a light flashed, filling the room for a split second before disappearing. He blinked at the balls of light hovering in his vision. "What have ye done, Emilie? Dinnae tell me ye trapped my soul in that thing!"

She shook her head and pursed her lips together. Holding up the phone, she laughed at the image of him stuck on the screen. "Look," she told him.

He looked to see the image on the surface of the device. The eyes of the man there were wide, and his dark hair hung loosely around his shoulders. His muscles gleamed in the light; on his right shoulder, a ragged scar showed white against his skin.

"Is that how I appear to ye?" he asked, taking another step back. She nodded and smiled.

"Have ye trapped my soul?"

Emilie laughed until tears streamed down her face. "Would I do anything that would trap your soul?" she asked incredulously.

"Well, I dinnae ken! I see my likeness staring back at me, and I feel a sudden need to run to the priest and pray for forgiveness."

"You are a ridiculous man. Here..." she pushed a button, and the image disappeared. "Now, you're free as a bird."

"I dinnae like that odd box. It belongs at the bottom of the loch!"

Emilie shrugged and tossed it to him. "I don't need it anymore. Burn it. Drown it. It doesn't matter."

He let it fall to the floor and stared at it with wide-eyed terror. Using the tip of his boot, he kicked it closer to the fire, but before he could successfully engulf it into flames, his boot touched the screen, and another flash blinded him before his image appeared once more on the glassy surface, this time with him looking like a wild-eyed fool.

He yelped and cursed that damned object she called a cell phone. "I'm off," he declared and left the room before he lost anymore of his dignity—though he feared it was too late. Emilie's infectious laughter chased after him.

"Cursed technology," he mumbled as he walked toward the training field, determined to feel like a man as he swung his sword at things that didn't steal his soul. He may never understand the world Emilie came from, but he knew his world was better for her in it. She'd given him love, a beautiful child, and a reason to live. Even his sword arm was better than ever after her months of encouragement as he trained.

Her soul-stealing cellphone, however, he could do without.

ABOUT THE AUTHOR

Mia is a full-time mother of two rowdy boys, residing in the SF Bay Area. As a child, she often wrote stories about fantastic places or magical things, always preferring to live in a world where the line between reality and fantasy didn't exist.

In High school, she entered writing contests and had some stories published in small newspapers or school magazines. As life continued, so did her love of writing. So one day, she decided to end her cake decorating business, pull out her laptop and fulfill her dream of writing and publishing novels. And she did.

When Mia isn't writing books or chasing her sweaty children around a park, she loves to drink coffee by the gallon, get lost in a good book, hike with her family and drink really big margaritas with her friends! Her happy place is the Renaissance Faire, where you can find her at the joust, rooting for the shirtless highlander in a kilt.

Website: www.miapride.com
FB: facebook.com/miaprideauthor
Amazon: amazon.com/Mia-Pride/e/B01M6VEWGX
Instagram: instagram.com/mia_pride_author
Twitter: twitter.com/mia_pride
BookBub: https://www.bookbub.com/profile/mia-pride